BURNING B

C000131859

Anne Krist
ROMANCE

Nomad Authors Publishing

Burning Bridges
by Anne Krist

Copyright © 2020 by Anne Krist
Cover design by Francis Drake

Nomad Authors Publishing
https://www.nomadauthors.com
ISBN 978-1-7333537-5-5

First published in 2008 as Burning Bridges (Siren-Bookstrand)

DEDICATION

First and foremost, I'd like to dedicate this book to the brave men of the Riverine Force, who fought in the deltas and rivers of Vietnam. If you thought your tasks were thankless, I'm sorry. Belatedly, I'm thanking you now. I'd especially like to remember the sailor whose story I borrowed upon for one of my letters home.

Thanks to my best writing pals, Leigh Wyndfield, who first sat up and noticed this book, Jasmine Haynes, Cheryl Norman, Terri Schaefer, Jan Selbourne, and Pat Wolf. Geoffrey, your proofreading skills are wonderful, but your cyber-hugs helped see me through. Where would I be without all of you?

To my mom, who always said I could do *any*thing, even things I didn't want to do. Maybe especially things I didn't want to do. Last, to my one and only sweetheart, Jack, who has always been there to help me prove Mom right.

Contents

Chapter 1

Beaufort, South Carolina – November 2005

The brown mailing envelope lounged against the back door, appearing deceptively like a friend passing the time. Sara Richards snatched it up with one hand while fitting the key in the lock with the other. A quick glance showed the addressee to be Mary Ellen Noland, her mother. Tape held the flap end closed and her mother's scrawl crossed the other end. "Call me when you've read this."

Strange. She hung up her keys and dropped her purse on the table, examining the return address. Department of the Navy. Her father had been dead over ten years. What would the Navy be sending her mother now?

She loosened the tape and pulled out a letter then spilled a second envelope onto the table. The smaller pouch was addressed to her, Sara, from the U.S. Postal Service and had been forwarded to the Navy. Frowning, she skimmed the letter: *Recently recovered bags of mail...a storage shed in Virginia Beach...enclosed FPO letters sent to Sara Noland...forwarded from Joint Expeditionary Base Little Creek-Fort Story to the Department of Navy...sent in care of Mrs. Mary Ellen Noland for Sara Noland...*

Boneless, she dropped into a chair and stared at the USPS envelope. 1970. So long ago and yet like yesterday. Only one person would have written her from overseas, and he hadn't sent any letters. In fact, he'd disappeared, forgetting she lived and leaving her to face the disastrous months following their separation alone.

Then he'd died.

No, these letters couldn't be from Paul Steinert.

But who else?

Sara's Siamese, Pi R Squared, rubbed his head against her ankle and pled for food, but she ignored him. With surprisingly steady hands, she opened the postal service pouch. Someone—her mother?—had slit the end of this also, and then taped it closed. Three smaller envelopes fell out. She'd seen his handwriting only once but recognized it immediately. Her hand flew to her mouth. Blood roared in her ears, blocking Squared's plaintive meow.

An image filled her mind. Not how he looked the first time she'd seen him, but after they'd been meeting for several weeks. The wind off the ocean ruffled his short blond hair and love filled his eyes, eyes bluer than an autumn sky. That was Paul as she dreamed him after he left and later, when she damned him for forgetting her. When she heard he'd been killed in action and all during those interminable months when she longed for one last chance to hold him, she pictured him there, on the beach at Sandbridge.

For the first time in years, the pain of his death crashed over her. Her grief now was nothing compared to the agony when she'd first heard, when she'd wanted to die, too. Worn down over the years, his memory was a dull ache, familiar, expected, almost like a photo she could pull out on demand and examine.

She picked up one of the small envelopes. On a back corner, he'd noted it as number twenty-nine. Checking the other two, she saw a twenty-eight and thirty. He'd written thirty letters? How could that be? She hadn't received even one. Thirty letters couldn't have been lost due to a foul up in the mail.

Mechanically, she dumped a packet of dry food in Squared's dish and then called her mother.

"I thought it would be you. Have you read the letters?"

"No. What happened, do you know?" Scattered on the table, the three packets drew her gaze and she stared as though trying to read their meaning through the sealed paper.

"Only what the Department of Navy letter said. Some bags of mail were lost. I suppose if I weren't still receiving part of Dad's retirement, they wouldn't have found me."

Sara closed her eyes and leaned against the wall. "I mean, do you know what happened to the rest of the letters?"

"What?" There was no mistaking the naked fear in her mother's voice.

"The envelopes are numbered. I have twenty-eight through thirty. What do you think happened to the others?" Tension radiated through her shoulders and neck. Her mother was about to say something she didn't want to hear, she knew it.

Burning Bridges

"Sara, you have to understand, Dad and I only wanted what was best for you. You were a child, a high school senior with a wonderful future in front of you. You'd been accepted at William and Mary. The last thing you needed was to get mixed up with a sailor who would love you and leave you. Which, I might add, is exactly what he did."

Sara could barely suck air into her lungs. Her fingers whitened with the hold she had on the phone cord. "What did you do, Mother?"

"More than anything, we didn't want you hurt." Moments passed. "Your father made the decision, but I was in favor of it, I want you to know that. He's not here, so if you're going to get mad, I suppose it will have to be at me." She ended with a sigh. "After—that man—left Virginia Beach, we determined it would be best for you to make a clean break. We never had any doubt that he was wrong for you. So, we intercepted the letters."

The blood drained from Sara's face and she pulled over a chair. If she didn't sit she'd fall. "You did what? How could you do that?" Her voice broke.

"You put your letters in the mailbox and I took them out after you left for school. And his…"

All too well, Sara remembered days of rushing into the house to sort through the stack of mail on the hall table, never finding a letter from Paul. Each day with no news added a stone to her wall of doubt that he loved her and depleted her store of faith that he'd stand by her.

Sara moaned. "Do you know what you did with your meddling?"

"Sara, you were seventeen, a child. Do you know what that means? He could have gone to jail. Your father was in favor of going to his commanding officer—even to the police. It was fortunate for your friend that his ship left."

Sara envisioned her mother sitting alone in her living room. About this time each afternoon, a gin and tonic sat on the table beside her. She'd wear a skirt and blouse and her hair and make-up would be flawless. Sara also didn't doubt that her mother's posture was rigid and that her thumb rubbed the tips of her index and middle fingers. Those were indications her mother's emotions—anger, frustration, fear, whatever— were threatening to override her normal control. Today she deserved every terrible, panicky feeling she was experiencing.

Mary Ellen sighed. "Try to see it from our point of view. You were a good girl with a good future. He destroyed all of that in a matter of weeks. You were our responsibility and we protected you the best way we knew how."

"Protected me!"

"Yes, *protected* you. We loved you more than anything on earth." She quieted, as though considering the next bit. "He died in service to his country. That was at least an honorable thing."

A sob broke from Sara.

Her mother softened her tone. "I have no doubt he might have been a good man, but not for you, and not at that time. I don't regret ending the relationship, whatever else happened."

"I can't believe you did this. I don't even know what to say to you." A headache inched its way forward to throb behind her eyes. She used her free hand to block the light coming through the kitchen windows. "The horrid things I thought about him, the certainty I had that he'd forgotten me…all wrong. I mailed the first letters from school. I wish I'd kept on doing that and asked him to write me at Cindy's house. Who knows what might have happened?"

"Sara, it's been so long. I thought you'd be able to understand after all this time, but maybe I was wrong. Put the whole episode with that man behind you, darling. Just throw those letters out. What difference could they possibly make now?"

"I don't know."

"Darling? We shouldn't talk about this over the phone. I can be there in a few minutes and then—"

Sara's eyes shot open. "No! I may never forgive you for this, Mother. In fact, I'm hanging up before I say something I probably shouldn't."

"Sara, let me—"

Sara pressed the end icon and dropped her phone onto the table. Vaulting from the chair, she paced around the kitchen table. Squared stopped eating and turned to watch, his Siamese-blue eyes following her path. In agitation, she picked up the letter from the Navy, glanced unseeing at the words then tossed it back. Stomping to the sink, she poured a glass of water, then drank it all without taking a breath. Finally, she turned and stared at Paul's envelopes.

"It's true," she told Squared. "There's nothing these letters can do for me now. Paul is dead, no matter what these say."

She brushed her fingers over Paul's bold script, then stuffed everything into the larger Navy envelope. Hiding the whole package in her "all-purpose" drawer at least removed them from sight, but she knew now nothing would erase them from her mind. With a resigned sigh, she went to change her clothes.

As if sensing her discomfort, Squared followed her to the bedroom, stretching out on her bed and cleaning himself. Sara removed her work clothes and slipped into stay-at-home sweatpants and tee shirt. She lay on the bed, covering her eyes with her arm. Squared moved closer, curling against her hip.

"It's all my fault," Sara explained, stroking his back. "I should have trusted him, found some other way to contact him. He understood that I was too young to handle our relationship, yet he trusted *me*. And I let him down, boy."

In the dim light of the late afternoon, she drifted into a light sleep. From one of her favorite memories, she dreamt Paul as she first saw him, a Viking god highlighted by the afternoon sun in the parking lot of the Alan B. Shepherd Convention Center.

* * * *

Virginia Beach, Virginia – January 1970

"Of all days to debate about whether to wear the short skirt or the shorter one," Sara wailed to her best friend, Cindy. "We'll be lucky if we aren't late."

The blue Volkswagen Beetle sped down the highway. Or as fast as it could speed, with the tiny engine pushing from the rear, and Sara having to shift gears so often because of traffic and lights. She huffed in frustration.

"Oh, we have plenty of time. I had to make sure I looked just right. You never know who we'll see," Cindy replied with her usual assurance.

"I hope you're right."

"You always worry, Sara, and things always turn out okay. Just keep your mind on driving and we'll be fine." Cindy clasped her hands and shrieked with excitement. "I can't believe our parents bought us tickets to see Michael Wales!"

That brought a real smile to Sara's face. "I know! Our parents are the best."

She flicked a knob on the radio as she veered into the parking lot, silencing Neil Diamond's "Holly Holy."

"See? I told you. You worry too much. We're here with a good ten minutes to spare." Cindy flipped her straight blonde hair over her shoulder. She turned the rearview mirror toward her and applied a fresh coating of lip gloss.

"We're only 'here' if I can find a place to park." Sara maneuvered her little car up one aisle and down another, until finally, "Good! There's one." Before she could get to the space, a sleek, red Corvette swung in.

"Oh, no! That was our space," Cindy cried.

Two men unfolded themselves from the little sports car, the driver with olive skin and hair as dark as the passenger's was golden. The men started toward the building. Suddenly, the passenger looked at Sara and then back at the space.

The low-hanging sun framed him, a fair giant with short hair and the physique of a warrior. For a brief moment, Sara pictured him with sword and shield at the helm of a Norse sailing vessel. Her heart fluttered and her breath caught. Then she brought herself under control.

The girls watched as he talked to the dark-haired man and gestured to them. The driver looked around and then shook his head before continuing toward the building. The blond shrugged apologetically at Sara and followed his friend.

"Shoot! I thought maybe he would have a heart." Sara eased off the clutch and started forward again.

"They were *cute*." Cindy swerved in her seat to watch the men as they picked their way through the parked cars. "I wonder what the chances are of seeing them–"

A piercing whistle cut through Cindy's words. "Stop, Sara! The blond guy is waving at us."

Burning Bridges

Sara turned to look behind them. The blond man was indeed waving, gesturing for her to come toward him. "What does he want?" she muttered. Deciding to ignore him, she drove on, turning to the right.

He whistled again.

"He wants you to pull around there. He's still waving."

"Oh, all right," Sara grumbled. "But make sure your door is locked, Cindy. And don't roll your window down."

Cindy laughed. "You sound like my mother. What do you think is going to happen right here in the parking lot?"

Sara managed a U-turn and drove to where the man stood. Rolling her window down an inch, she said loudly, "What is it?"

He bent down to peer through the glass at her, a lopsided grin on his face. Good Lord, he *was* cute. Muscled shoulders and arms, angular, strong features, hair a rich blond, and dark, sapphire-blue eyes.

"Oh, my heavens," she heard Cindy say under her breath.

For once, Sara understood her friend's meaning. His grin made her stomach do flip-flops and her palms sweat.

"I don't bite," he said around a chuckle, motioning to the almost closed window. "I just wanted to tell you, there's a place right over there. I think you can squeeze your Bug into it." He turned and pointed at a half space at the end of the aisle, a couple of cars away.

Flashing him a look of gratitude, she put the little car in gear and pulled into the spot. The tall, handsome stranger followed.

When Sara turned off the engine, the guy opened the door for Cindy and held out his hand to assist her. Out of nowhere, a sharp pang of jealousy struck Sara. Its intensity and suddenness disturbed her. After all, she didn't know this man; what difference did it make if he and Cindy hit it off?

By the time she collected her purse, stepped out and made sure the doors were locked, Cindy and the mystery man were like old friends. Again she felt the Green Monster strike, and gave a mental shake to rid herself of its clutches.

"Sara," Cindy said, smiling dreamily at the tall man, "this is Paul Steinert. Wasn't he just *wonderful*, finding us this space?" She tittered.

It was all Sara could manage, not to gape. Cindy always flirted but tittering was something new.

"Paul, this is my best friend, Sara Noland."

Paul smiled and held out his hand. "Hello, Sara. I'm sorry about the other space. This one is closer to the door, though."

She locked gazes with him and her tongue twisted in her mouth. Surges of heat flew through her body. If his smile had that effect, what would his touch do to her? *Something wonderful.*

No, something forbidden.

Sara glanced at his hand but wrapped her own around her pocketbook. "It's nice to meet you, Mr. Steinert." *Ugh, I sound so stiff. I wish I knew how to act like Cindy.*

In fact, she didn't know how to react to this man at all. "Thanks very much for your help in finding our space, but we'd better get inside. Come *on*, Cindy."

"You're right." Paul drew his hand back and held his arm out to Cindy, who slipped her hand through it with a huge smile. "My friend is meeting me inside, so I'll just walk you two in." He extended his other arm to Sara, but she struck off toward the building.

"Your friend doesn't like me," she heard him say in a lowered voice to Cindy.

"Oh, she's fine. She's just more cautious than I am." Cindy tittered again.

Sara strode ahead, fuming, and waited for them in the lobby. *Just like Cindy to latch onto a guy. This is supposed to be our day to have fun together.*

Shame followed the thought. Cindy was just being Cindy, fun-loving and free instead of guarded and serious like…well like her. Until today, she'd never envied her friend's easy way with boys. *But Paul is no boy. He's definitely a man.*

Maybe that made the difference in her reaction to their easy camaraderie.

Once inside, Paul introduced them to his friend, Mitch Hamilton, who said hello and then stuck his hands in his pockets. He absently watched people as they pressed by, but his eyes kept coming back to Cindy. Sara didn't mind *his* attention to her friend.

"You'll have to forgive Mitch's lack of enthusiasm for Michael Wales," Paul explained. "He's more into the Stones."

"Sorry," Mitch said, with a radiant smile.

Dark and swarthy, he would have been the epitome of dreamy to most girls, but to Sara his olive-toned skin and black eyes held no appeal. Though his smile was brilliant, it seemed practiced. Not like Paul's, as natural as sunshine. And just as warm.

Mitch smiled again, this time at Cindy. "I don't suppose you'd like to trade tickets with Paul and sit with me, would you?"

Cindy raised a hopeful brow at Sara. "No, thank you," Sara answered for her.

Mitch winked at Cindy and gave a one-shouldered shrug. "Well then, Paul, we'd better get to our seats if we're gonna listen to this guy. Maybe we'll see you afterward."

"Cindy, let's go." Sara looked at her ticket to determine which door to access.

"*Will* we see you later?" Paul still had Cindy's hand on his arm, but he looked at Sara when he spoke.

"No, I don't think so. Thanks again for helping me find the parking space. We'd probably still be out there if you hadn't."

"Don't worry about it."

Sara tugged Cindy toward the door leading to their seats.

"Bye, Paul! Bye, Mitch," Cindy called over her shoulder.

The lights dimmed and soft music began as the girls took their seats. "Just made it," Sara whispered.

"They were cute. And nice," Cindy whispered back.

"They were okay, but we're here for the concert, so forget them."

Cindy laughed quietly. "You wouldn't say that if you knew what Paul asked while you were walking ahead of us and couldn't hear. I'll give you a hint. It was about you."

Sara turned an astonished look at her friend, who now faced forward wearing a smug smile. The spotlight came on and a disembodied voice announced Michael Wales. She fixed her gaze on the stage, but all at once it didn't matter who stood on it. She was grateful the applause was so loud, for otherwise Cindy certainly would have heard the hammering of her heart.

No one had ever had this effect on her. Was it because he was older? They hadn't even touched but somehow, when she'd first seen him, she knew. Fate had led her to this place and time for the sole purpose of meeting Paul Steinert. The world changed that day. Nothing would look the same, or smell, or taste the same again.

If. *If* she saw him. *If* she pushed her reservations and caution aside.

But she wouldn't. He was a man. She was still in high school. They had nothing in common. Only trouble could come from any further meetings. Besides, despite her friend's comment, he'd shown obvious interest in Cindy, not her.

The hour and a half couldn't have passed any slower. Most of the concert was a blur of lights, a strumming guitar and a soft baritone. It was both amusing and disappointing that after weeks of anticipation, all Sara focused on was blond hair and dark, blue eyes.

Finally, she allowed herself to be pushed and nudged into the lobby.

"Oh, wasn't it just the best thing *ever*?" Cindy gushed. "And now we get dinner out, too." She sighed with appreciation. "I can't wait to tell everyone at school tomorrow."

14

Sara glimpsed the gridlock in the parking lot. "We might as well wait for a couple more minutes."

"Okay, I'm going to the bathroom." Cindy craned her neck to locate the ladies' room.

"I'll wait over there by the window."

Moving out of the way, Sara let her mind wander as she watched people leave the building and cars jockey for position. A few minutes later, she saw the Corvette maneuver around the line and pull away. That was it, then. He was gone. *Good.* So why did it feel like a punch to her stomach?

Nothing good would come from seeing Paul again. The first encounter was an accident and could be brushed away; a second would be from desire.

Desire. The very word sent a rush of heat through her. Heat like she'd known from Paul's smile, a crook of the lips that everyone did but no one did like him. How could she feel this for someone she didn't know? One glance from him and her heart raced. Rational thought evaporated. She wished for less knowledge of math and more cleavage. No, it wouldn't do to spend time with a man who filled her with surging warmth.

"A penny for your thoughts."

Startled, Sara spun around. "Paul!" She looked at him and then back at the parking lot. "I thought… But I saw the Corvette leave. Where's your friend?"

"He's gone. With *your* friend, as a matter of fact."

"What?" This time Sara pushed past him to scan the rapidly emptying lobby for any sign of Cindy. There was none. "What are you talking about? She's just gone to the restroom."

"She was coming out of the ladies' room when we saw her," he explained. "She said you're going to dinner and invited us to join you. When Mitch offered to drive her in the 'Vette, Cindy said I could come with you." He smiled, keeping his distance and his hands in his back pockets. "You don't mind, do you? Like I said earlier, I don't bite."

15

"I *do* mind." Sara paced angrily. "How could she do this? For heaven's sake, she just jumps into a car with a perfect stranger?" She stopped to glare at Paul as though through him she could make Cindy feel her irritation.

"With all due respect, I've known Mitch for weeks. He might be a stranger but he's not perfect. I, on the other hand…"

His smile widened, making the situation worse as far as Sara was concerned. Hadn't she just come to the conclusion that he was poison to be with? And mostly because his damn smile made her *want* to be with him? She'd kill Cindy, no two ways about it.

"Sorry," he said, his expression sobering. "Just trying to lighten the mood."

"It didn't work." She bowed her head. "Look. I'm sure you're a very nice man, and your friend seems nice, too. But as Cindy said, I'm cautious, and I'm not comfortable with this situation at all. Not to mention the fact that my dad will kill me if he finds out." She looked up at him. "And trust me, my dad always finds out. This will do nothing but get me in trouble. And it's not even my fault." The last came out as a whine, but she couldn't help it.

"I'm sorry. I didn't realize this would be such a problem." He thought for a moment. "Tell you what. You head over to the restaurant. I'll catch a cab and then Mitch and I will shove off. Okay? It'll be all right." He reached out and squeezed her shoulder.

It was nothing, a throw-away gesture. The kind of thing a guy would do to his kid sister. But his touch sent shock waves through Sara's body.

Her eyes widened and she gasped. In a daze, she saw his eyes darken, revealing an emotion that hadn't been there a moment ago. She couldn't put a name to what showed in his features, but instinctively she knew it wasn't something one would see in a brother. His hand still rested on her shoulder, branding her with the outline of his fingers and the circle of his palm.

She stepped back and his hand fell to his side. Neither spoke for a second or two. Then, "Thanks, Paul. I appreciate your understanding." Fumbling with her purse, she turned and practically ran for the door and then for the car. When she reached it, she looked back. He stood watching her.

16

Burning Bridges

She climbed in and started the engine, letting its consistent hum work to calm her. Shivering, she turned the heater on full blast. Cold permeated her body—all except her shoulder where Paul left his searing imprint. Dropping her head on the steering wheel, Sara silently implored the little engine to flood the car with warm air so she would stop shaking.

Finally, hot air blasted from the heater vents. Still she trembled. It was then she knew she shivered not from the cool air, but from the heat of his touch.

And she wanted his touch again. His touch and more. The concert, which for weeks had been at the center of her thoughts, devolved to an interval of white noise sandwiched between Meeting Paul and Being With Paul.

She'd never wanted anything so much in her life, nor had she ever risked so much. If her parents found out, she'd be grounded until they sent her off to William and Mary in the fall. She knew in her heart he was worth the gamble.

The parking lot had emptied. She swung the car around to the door and strained across the gearshift to see if Paul was still there. Her heart sank. He was nowhere. Not inside the door or at the window where she'd left him.

Sara heaved a sigh. Her head fell against the headrest and she closed her eyes, wondering if she was more relieved or disappointed. Then she jumped at a tap on the passenger window.

Opening her eyes, she saw Paul looking at her expectantly. She reached over to unlock the door.

"Hi." It was too simple, but all she could manage. Her heart was in her throat and her pulse raced. She was both scared to death and exhilarated.

"Hi." He settled in the seat and turned to face her. "I was about to call a cab when I saw you out here. Were you waiting for me?"

"Yes. Yes, Paul, I've been waiting for you." The words hung there, the double meaning clear to both of them.

"Good." He rested his hand on hers atop the gearshift. Once again, his warmth flowed through her, as though she were a cold, distant planet, and Paul, rays of solar energy bringing her to life.

"I'm sorry you might get into trouble for something that isn't your fault," he said quietly.

"Ah, but now it *is* my fault." Her wry smile sparked a half smile from him. "But I couldn't really let you take a cab, could I? After all, you're just passing through and what kind of impression of my city would my bad manners leave in your mind?"

"How do you know I'm passing through?" He squeezed her hand and rubbed her knuckles with the pad of his thumb.

"Military, right?"

Paul scrubbed his free hand through his short hair. "What gave me away?" He cocked his head, watching her chuckle, then added, "I don't come out and say it because let's face it, the military isn't too popular these days. I'm Navy. Is my being in the service a problem for you?"

"It will be for my dad. He's in the Navy, too, which will make this worse in his eyes." She sighed at his raised brows. "He loves the Navy but not sailors. Not for his daughter."

"I hate to admit it, but I understand why he'd be unhappy."

"It gets worse." She watched his face. "I'm seventeen."

The movement of his thumb stopped and his hand tensed. Then the tension drained away. "I admit, I did think you were older, but I like you, Sara. I felt it immediately. Maybe even before we spoke, while you were thinking about how you'd missed getting that parking space." He looked thoughtful, his brow wrinkled slightly. "I'm not all that much older than you. I'm twenty."

"Twenty isn't very old. But my age…"

"Yeah. Your being underage does strike fear in my heart."

"Might as well call a spade a spade. I'm jail bait." Sara held her breath, afraid he would climb right back out of the car.

Instead, he smiled. "I'm not looking to get physical. I just want to be friends. Can we do that?"

She breathed again. "Yes, I think so."

"Good, because you're right. I'm a long way from home and will be going a hell of a lot farther in a few weeks. I *need* a friend." Another smile.

Would her heart ever beat normally in the face of Paul Steinert's smiles? She doubted it.

"I just have two questions. First, when will you be eighteen?" His grin was impish and she laughed.

"This summer."

"Okay, we just have to get through the next few weeks. By the time I get back you'll be legal and maybe I can take you out without fear of being arrested."

"I'd like that. What's the second question?"

"Can we adjust the heater? It's hotter than blazes in here!"

Laughter bubbled up from deep inside her. "Yes! It's plenty hot, now."

* * * *

Beaufort, South Carolina – November 2005

The insistent ringing of the telephone disrupted Sara's memory. Or had she been asleep? With a squall of protest from Squared, she sat and picked up the receiver.

"Hello?"

"Sara?" Jennette Williamson, Sara's assistant, sounded hesitant. "Uh, you sound kind of strange. Are you okay?"

"Yes, fine. I laid down and fell asleep, I guess. What's up?"

"Well, I was about to close when the mailman delivered a certified letter. Do you want me to leave it on your desk, or open it?"

Sara's forehead bunched in worry. She owned a small art gallery catering primarily to local businesses and regular clients. There were few reasons anyone would need to send her a formal letter. "Who's it from?"

"Beaufort Management." The owner of the building that housed her gallery.

"I wonder what they want. Go ahead and open it."

"Hold on just a minute." She heard paper tearing and Jennette picking up the phone again. "'Dear Ms. Richards. We regret to inform you that Beaufort Management has sold the property at 321 King Street. The new owners have indicated their intention of demolishing the building—'

"What? It says that, Jennette? They're going to demolish the building?"

"Oh, Sara. It *does*."

"Maybe you'd better finish reading." A sick feeling settled in Sara's stomach.

"'Therefore, please accept this as formal notification that Beauty by Beaufort, a gallery owned by you located at 321A King Street must be vacated no later than ninety days from receipt of this notice. Sincerely…' Sara, the *gallery*! What's going to happen?"

Sara sat on the edge of her bed, her head in a fog. Evicted! Her aunt had founded the art gallery in that building almost fifty years ago. What would she do? Where could she go with the business that was not only her livelihood but her legacy? She'd promised, as her aunt lay dying, that she'd take good care of the gallery and of her aunt's long-time clients and artists. What would happen now to the people who depended on her to keep that promise?

"I don't know, Jennette." She rubbed her temple. "I'll think of something. Just leave the letter on my desk and lock up now. Will I see you tomorrow?"

"Yes, in the afternoon. Sara? I'm really sorry."

Sara gave a rueful laugh. "Me, too. Have a good evening."

After hanging up, she made her way into the kitchen where she put the kettle on for tea.

Burning Bridges

What an afternoon this had been. First, like a firestorm from the past, Paul's letters brought back sweet memories of innocence and simpler times, but the notice from her landlord had well and truly catapulted her into the present. She'd have preferred to spend a few more minutes basking in the warmth of Paul's smile.

Her gaze strayed to the drawer where she'd tried to hide the reminder of his existence. Fate had provided the perfect way to extend her nostalgia and dreams of what might have been. Tomorrow would be soon enough to decide what to do next about the gallery. She needed to read Paul's words now, with his memory fresh in her mind.

She opened the drawer and withdrew the envelopes.

Chapter 2

Sara stared at the letters arranged before her in numerical order. The moment in time she and Paul shared was long ago, yet her dream had conjured his presence as though she'd just seen him. In her mind, his blue eyes darkened with passion before his lips captured hers, and he moaned his appreciation when their tongues met. She tasted his sweetness and knew the steel of his arms as he held her. How many nights had she put herself through hell reliving those memories? *Too damn many.*

After the concert, they'd met clandestinely on weekends, mostly at Sandbridge, where they could walk and talk undisturbed. With each meeting, stirrings built deep in Sara that pushed her to want more, but Paul insisted they restrain themselves because of her age.

Then the weekend before he shipped out, she'd planned a surprise and her life changed forever.

The kettle screeched, bringing her back to the present. Sara prepared a cup of tea and then picked up the envelope marked *twenty-eight*. At one time, she would have given her right arm to hold this letter. Now, curiosity and the desire for a brief escape drove her more than the passion of youth. Blind love had faded when she'd had no word to bolster her during the long weeks after the ship left.

First had come the waiting. No letters arrived, even though she wrote him daily. There were no phone calls, no notes, no anything, for days that dragged into weeks then crept into months.

Anticipation morphed into anxiety. She worried he was sick or hurt and unable to write.

One day she admitted that Paul must be afraid to write for some reason, and she feared what he would say if she *did* receive a letter. That their time together had been a mistake, that she was too young to be in love. That he really loved someone else and Sara had been only a stand-in while he was in Virginia. Perversely, she began to sigh with relief when she arrived home and found no word.

Now, knowing why she hadn't received mail, what would she feel if she opened this letter and her old fears proved to be true?

"Nothing," she murmured. "Paul's dead. He can't hurt me anymore." At the very least, his letters might allow her to put his ghost to rest. For that reason alone, she had to read them.

She slid her thumb under the flap and ripped the envelope open. A single sheet held his hurried scrawl.

May 16, Somewhere up the Mekong Delta

Dearest Sara,

Here I am in the middle of another boring day on this LST--Large Slow Target--missing you and wishing I was there to walk the beach at Sandbridge instead of here, making my way up this stupid river.

I can hear you telling me that what we're doing is important, and I know it, honey. The guys up river need us. I guess I'm just in a pissing kind of mood. So many days are the same. Lots of boredom for a little action.

I hope I don't sound like I'm whining when I say that things would be so much easier if I heard from you. The mail comes in bunches, and I wait for some word from you at every mail call, but so far, only two letters have arrived. Honey, if you've changed your mind about us, please tell me. It would be better than waiting and hoping, but never knowing.

I hope everything is okay for you, sweetheart. That school is going well. Graduation must be coming up pretty soon. I got a little present for you, but I don't know if I should send it. Let me know when you write, okay?

I relive being in the back of that station wagon every day, Sara, and I'll never forget our night as Mr. and Mrs. I can't wait to make it happen for real. That is, if you haven't changed your mind.

I need to stop now if I'm going to get this in the outgoing mail. I love you, Sara.

Paul

Sara covered her mouth, trying to muffle the sobs she couldn't contain. He'd loved her. After three months with no word from her, he'd still loved her, and never knew that she loved him.

May 16. He'd died a few weeks later, thinking that she hadn't cared enough even to write and *tell* him that she didn't care. Her tears flowed unchecked, along with the recollection he mentioned. She'd picked him up at Little Creek Naval Base that Saturday with a surprise picnic for two. A virgin when she woke, she'd gone home Sunday a woman.

Though Paul had pushed her off him their first time, he worried that he hadn't had protection with him. Sara, in the first glow of real passion, hadn't given his words much thought. She hadn't really known what *protection* meant.

She'd found out soon enough.

The sip of tea calmed her. She refolded the paper and slid it into its envelope. Picking up the second, she opened the letter quickly and began reading.

May 22, Patrolling

Hello, my sweet Sara,

I haven't had time to write for a few days. First I complain that it's too boring, and then we have several days of action. I expect soon we'll be back to being bored. I'm sure your dad's told you that it's the Navy way, to hurry up and wait.

The past few days have seen an increase in activity in the areas where we've been. I can't tell you where that is exactly, although by the time you get this letter anything that's going to happen will have happened. We've been stepping up our patrols to try and stay ahead of the VC. Last night I had to board a fishing boat. It was just a small little shit of a boat, but there was a papa, mama, uncle and four kids, all crammed on there, living, as well as fishing. The cop we have with us from Saigon was called to interpret for me while I asked for their papers and searched the boat. Lots of weapons get carried up and down these rivers and it's part of our job to stop them. Anyway, this cop counts seven people and we have seven ID cards but there's an extra rice bowl or something set out, making him suspicious. He asks about the extra bowl but doesn't get the answer he wants, so he pulls his gun and is ready to shoot one of them. I'm scared as shit someone is going to get killed because of a bowl of rice, for Pete's sake. So, I'm yelling at him to wait, trying to tell him that we'll figure it out. The poor people on the boat are all waving their arms and screaming and are more scared than I am, and the cop's screaming, too, at the top of his lungs. I tell you, if there were any VC

25

hiding along the shoreline, they would have been laughing too hard to shoot us. I have to admit, if the cop had shot someone, I don't know what I'd have done. Turns out, the woman's brother, who was VC by the way, had been on board, but swam ashore when we approached.

There were no weapons on the boat and nothing for us to do but let them go on and live their lives. But Jesus, I was scared. You never know what's going to happen. The brother could have been hiding, ready to kill us instead of making his way quietly back to his camp. In this case, I had to wonder who was more dangerous, our cop or their soldier. It's a hell of a war, Sara.

These poor people. The VC come in to take the country. Then we come in. Even though we're here to do the right thing by them, they don't understand anything half the time except that they're sick and tired of war on their land. And it's hard for us to know what to do sometimes. One day, a sweet little girl is kissing your cheek and the next day she stands there while her mother shoots you. I feel for them, Sara. I know we're here to help, but I wish there was some way to make it all end for them.

Anyway, I told you in a previous letter all about the Swift boats that patrol the coastline. Remember Mitch? He and I will be on one of them for a short time to give them some mechanical help. To tell the truth, I'm looking forward to something new. There's no need to change my address. Just send mail here and I'll get it when I come back on board. Just please send mail, Sara. I don't know how much longer I can go without hearing from you. I've read the two letters I have over and over. By now I can recite them in my sleep.

I'll say goodnight now. I hope everything is fine with you. I miss you so much. I wish I could hear your voice, and I wish it would tell me what's wrong.

I love you,

Paul

She threw the pages onto the table, not bothering to stick them back in the envelope. She smoothed the last letter on the table, wiped her eyes and began to read.

May 31, Swift boat duty

Sara,

26

Burning Bridges

As you can see, I'm reassigned right now. Will be here for a bit longer than I'd thought, but then it'll be back to my LST. Having been here, Large Slow Target will really be meaningful. Even with the problems I'm here to fix, this baby moves. And she has to, with the action we get into sometimes. There's been a lot lately. The VC must be up to something, with all they're throwing at us. But we're equal to the task, so don't worry about me. I'll be just fine.

But, sweetheart, that's what I want to ask you about. How are we? I've gotten two letters from you, Sara. Two letters in over three months, and they were both in the first mail call. I can only assume that you've changed your mind and don't know how to tell me. Just say it, whatever it is. I'll deal with it, and I'll try to understand. But this silence I can't understand. I would write Cindy if I knew how to contact her, or even risk trying to reach your dad, that's how worried I am.

I have to say, this is going to be my last letter until I hear from you. I love you. I'll come for you as soon as I get home, if you want me to. But if you don't answer this letter, I'll know not to, and I'll leave you alone. Then you don't have to worry about telling me. I hope to hell I hear from you....

I love you.

Paul

They'd met and fallen in love. It should have been easy, but none of it had been. Their love had started with lies she'd told her parents so she could see him, and then lies they'd told her back. Add to the mix a war that kept her and Paul separated by thousands of miles, and it was no wonder everything had fallen apart. Left alone, they might have made it, but they hadn't been the only players.

Sara dabbed her wet cheeks and blew her nose again. Tears were useless. Pushing up from the table, she dragged herself to the bathroom where she began filling the tub. She popped two Ibuprofen to deaden the headache raging behind her eyes and sank into the water.

Wrapped in a cocoon of liquid warmth and with the lights dimmed, her tension began to abate. Soon, Paul's letters filled her mind and his pain ripped at her heart. The dripping of the faucet beat a tattoo that played in her head as *Paul loved you. Paul loved you. Paul loved you....*

27

And she'd loved Paul. She'd loved him and he'd died thinking she didn't. No matter how much she cried, there would never be enough tears to make up for that.

* * * *

"Mother? We need to talk." In the gallery's kitchenette, Sara dumped coffee into the filter as she spoke into the telephone.

"You're calling me 'mother.' I suppose that means you're still upset."

"Upset is a strange word for how I feel, but, yes. Upset more than mad. I think I'm past mad. It's time now for some questions and answers. Can you meet me here at the gallery for lunch?"

"I'll be there at eleven thirty, all right?"

"I'll slip out and bring sandwiches in."

"Don't bother. I'll stop and pick something up. Are you…are you okay?"

Sara rubbed her eyes, gritty with fatigue. "I didn't sleep much." In fact, she hadn't been able to close her eyes without seeing Paul. Sometimes he stared in accusation; other times his eyes pled for something. Her love? Understanding?

"If it makes you feel any better, neither did I. I'll see you later, then."

"Yes. Goodbye."

After setting the coffee pot to brew, Sara sat at her desk and opened the letter from the management office. In ninety days she had to find another location for the gallery or close shop and find something else to do with her life. That prospect seemed so alien she couldn't begin to imagine where to start.

In one form or another, she'd worked at the gallery since coming to Beaufort after high school graduation. Years before that, her father's sister, Barbara, had started selling the work of local artists, paintings that spotlighted the Beaufort area.

Burning Bridges

Beauty by Beaufort developed a healthy clientele in the South Carolina low country. Gradually, tourists who came to the Beaufort area on a regular basis sought out the small showroom located far from the normal tourist haunts.

Barbara hadn't minded the leisurely business pace. She'd built friendships and lasting relationships with her artists and clients. Sara had itched to make changes after she'd graduated from college and later, as she took over more of the business, but daily life gradually refocused her enthusiasm. Barbara hadn't felt the urgency for change, and when Sara might have implemented new ideas, she couldn't afford the time or energy to follow through properly. Now she had no choice but to do something. Ninety days wasn't much time to make major changes.

Sara opened the old Army surplus file cabinet in the corner of the office and pulled the financial records for the last three years. She knew every dollar that passed through the gallery, but now she hoped to see something new, some funding that might magically appear.

Just as it had for Barbara, the gallery provided a comfortable living, although years had been lean when Sara's daughter was growing up and then again when her aunt was sick. But she'd managed to accumulate several thousand dollars in the past few years. Would it be enough to move to a new location, one better suited to the tourist trade Beaufort continued to attract?

Her thoughts were interrupted by the ring of the landline. "Good morning. Beauty by Beaufort."

"Mom?"

With only one word spoken Sara knew something was wrong. "Good morning, sweetheart. Aren't you at work?"

"No, I took a sick day."

Sara's brow creased with worry. "Paula, what's wrong?"

Her daughter's voice caught. "Mom, I feel so silly but I had to talk to you. I was cleaning up the apartment last night and I found an acceptance letter from Northwestern for Dan."

"Northwestern? That's in…uh, it's in—"

"Chicago."

"But I thought he was going to attend law school at South Carolina, in Columbia." Sara took a breath. "Chicago is a very long way. Did Dan say he wanted to go?"

"I didn't tell him I found the letter, but I know he does."

"Oh, Paula. How do you feel?"

Paula's tone tightened as though she held back tears. "I don't want to go. Mom, he's had the letter for two or three days I think, and he hasn't said a word."

"Maybe he's thought about it and decided to turn them down."

"I don't think so. He talked about it months ago, about how great the Northwestern program is. I got upset that he was looking into a school that far away, and he hasn't brought it up since. But I know he hasn't forgotten."

"So, you're not certain he's *chosen* Northwestern. The law school at Carolina is excellent, too."

"I know, and so does Dan. But lately he's been restless. I think he wants a change." Her voice broke. "I think he wants a change in more than where he attends school."

Sara couldn't contain a soft gasp. "Paula! Has he said anything, done anything?"

"No, but for the past few weeks he's been really quiet. Oh, I don't mean he acts mad or nasty, he just seems…uncomfortable around me. And the fact remains that he didn't tell me about the acceptance from Northwestern. I only found it because it fell out of a book when I was dusting."

"You have to talk to him. Believe me, I know the dangers of not communicating when things don't seem right." The bell over the front door rang and Sara stood to see who was entering. She was surprised to see her mother, but a quick glance at her watch showed that the morning was nearly gone. "Do you want to come home this weekend?"

"No, but thanks." Paula gave a nervous laugh. "I'm half afraid if I leave for any length of time, I'll come home to find him packed and gone. You know, he hasn't proposed. He hasn't even suggested I go with him to Chicago."

Sara lowered her voice. "Honey, I'm so sorry. But Dan loves you. You need to talk to him, let him know how you feel."

Her mother entered the office and set a bag from Bay Street Deli on the desk. "Paula?" she mouthed. Sara nodded. "Let me say hello to her." Her mother held her hand out for the receiver.

"Paula, your grandmother is here and wants to say hi. But call me tonight, will you?"

"Sure. I feel better just telling someone about what's going on. I love you, Mama."

Hot tears stung the backs of Sara's eyes, a reaction she experienced whenever Paula reverted to *Mama*. "I love you, too, pumpkin." She handed the phone to her mother.

"Hello, PB. How's my favorite granddaughter?"

Her mother had never called Paula *Paula*, almost as though saying Paula, with Paul's name as part of the address was too much to accept. So, Paula Bethany had become PB.

Sara unpacked the sandwiches and drinks, half listening as her mother launched into a description of the bazaar her church was planning for the upcoming holidays. It was still early November, and her mother was thinking ahead to Christmas. *What will I be doing by Christmas? Making a move to a new location for the new year or wondering what to do with the rest of my life?*

She stepped to the doorway and looked at the paintings lining the walls. The cozy shop had been her focal point for more years than she cared to count. Everything would be different by the first of the year, here at the gallery and maybe at home, too. Like the leaves being whipped from the trees by the wind, the landscape of her life would look quite different in a few weeks. She only hoped it wouldn't be as barren and cold as she feared right now.

31

Dan had been accepted at Northwestern! She was happy for him, but what if he wanted Paula to go with him? Paula had attended school in Charleston and then been offered a job there. Except for brief vacations and visits to Dan's family in Atlanta, Sara and her only child had never been farther apart than those seventy miles. Charleston was far enough for Paula's independence, yet close enough for quick visits, lunches, plays, overnight gab fests. Sara had devoted her life to her daughter, and now reaped the reward of knowing her child as a friend.

Oh, she was blessed, and she knew it. Blessed and spoiled. How could she bear Paula's move to Illinois if it happened? And what if Dan and Paula decided they liked Chicago and wanted to settle so far away? A sob welled in Sara's throat and threatened to burst. She sucked in a breath.

Right now, those were *ifs* not certainties. She could talk to Dan, remind him how hard law school would be with an additional person to consider. Paula could help him, sure, but she would also demand time he wouldn't have to give. And though Paula could teach there as well as here, the expense of a second person, added to that of graduate school, could be overwhelming. Surely Dan would see the logic of Paula's waiting for him in Charleston. He was a reasonable man.

Hearing her mother's chuckle and response to something Paula said brought Sara to her senses. She had never purposely avoided acting like her mother. In fact, she'd often sought her mother's advice, especially when Paula was a child. But knowing what she did now, having learned in the past twenty-four hours the heartache meddling could cause, Sara knew she wouldn't interfere with Dan's and Paula's decision.

If Paula needed arms to shield and shelter, Sara would always be there. But she would *not* become her mother. Suddenly she fully realized just what that meant.

She loved Paula. She didn't want to control her. Sara had raised her daughter to become independent, an adult who knew her own mind and could take her own actions and responsibilities. She could advise and encourage Paula to think about the situation with Dan and Northwestern, but she would use neither lies nor guile to push her one way or the other. With her own heart involved, it would be hard as hell to be objective, but in that way, Sara would become everything her mother was not.

Burning Bridges

Her mother hung up the phone and settled in one of the chairs facing the desk. Sara sat in her chair behind the desk. When they had their food set out and she had taken a sip of her drink, Sara dropped her bombshell.

"I'm making reservations to fly to Iowa as soon as possible. It's long past due for Paul's parents to know they have a granddaughter."

Chapter 3

The stunned look on her mother's face surprised Sara. "Surely you think they deserve to know?"

Mary Ellen gave a slight shrug and rearranged her sandwich on the wrapping paper. "I don't know why. She's a grown woman. What does she have to do with them after all this time?"

"Well, she's their granddaughter, their flesh and blood, just as much as she is yours."

Her mother looked up sharply. "You can't be serious. She's nothing to them. I was there when she was born. I helped nurse her when she was sick. I sat in the hospital with you when she broke her arm and waited up with you when she had her first date. I attended her school plays and her graduations. PB is my granddaughter in *every* sense of the word, not just in blood. They don't even know she exists."

"And whose fault is that?"

"Whose fault *is* that, Sara? Not mine or your father's. We might have stopped you from furthering your relationship with that man—"

"His name was Paul!"

"—but we didn't stop you from anything else. You were the one who chose not to contact his parents."

Sara hung her head. She remembered the days after high school graduation when she'd been sent here to Beaufort. Whether the move had been to protect her from gossip or because her mother and dad were ashamed of her, she didn't know. At the time, nearing the end of her first trimester, she hadn't cared. In those weeks, her thoughts were eaten away by fear, doubt, regret. And anger at Paul's betrayal, and that she had to face her parents and a pregnancy alone.

Two days after she received her diploma, her dad came home with a set of rings, a chip diamond in a solitaire setting and a plain gold band. Unable or unwilling to meet Sara's eyes, he placed the rings in her palm, then sat beside his wife on the sofa and outlined in terse military fashion the course of action she would take.

By the weekend, she'd leave for Beaufort, near the Marine Corps recruitment center at Parris Island, to live with his sister, he explained. She'd wear the rings and take on her mother's maiden name, Richards. If she added a couple of years to her age and explained she'd been married to a Marine killed in Vietnam, he said, no one would doubt her story. She'd have the support of other Marine wives, if she wanted, but the area gave her story cover, and no one would know her. After the birth, she'd place the baby for adoption and apply to colleges for the next year.

Her dad's campaign briefing complete, he produced the train ticket he'd purchased earlier in the day. When he was finished, her mother stood and said dinner would be ready in fifteen minutes. Sara went to set the table, not questioning that her life had been hijacked. In truth, she'd been relieved someone had taken charge.

Sitting in her office and examining her life, she saw a line with little deviation where there should have been a mosaic. From her parents' original plan, she'd pretty much taken the path of least resistance. Keeping Paula had been her only strike of independence, but what else could she do after hearing of Paul's death? And once she'd held her daughter, no other choice made sense.

"You're right," Sara said at last, looking up. "It was my mistake, and it's my decision to rectify it. I've done Mr. and Mrs. Steinert a great disservice in not telling them immediately about Paula, and I've hurt her, too. Paul talked about his folks, and his brother, and the farm they owned. She has a right to know her heritage and that she has other relatives, and they have a right to know her."

"But—" Mary Ellen threw out her hands, "—why now? You never showed the slightest interest in meeting them before."

"That's because all this time I thought Paul deceived me. If he didn't love me, he certainly wouldn't have told his parents about us. I didn't want to show up on their doorstep and have them regard me and Paula with pity or scorn. Or think that I was after them for money."

Her mother huffed. "You didn't need them or their money. We cared for you. As soon as your father retired we moved down with the sole purpose of helping you with PB. Did you think we *wanted* to come back to Beaufort? I know you love it but growing up here was enough for us both. It was where you were, so we came."

"Yes, you did. If it hadn't been for you and Daddy and Aunt Barbara, I don't know what I would have done." She took a moment to compose her next thoughts. "More than anything else, I guess I was afraid the Steinerts would fight me for custody. I was unmarried with limited resources, and as far as I knew, Paula was their only grandchild. More than anything, that fear stopped me from contacting them."

Strangely, she'd never said the words out loud. Years after Paula's birth, she'd had nightmares of a knock at the door behind which Paul's father, a giant, older version of Paul, would demand she produce "the child." She always woke when he made off with Paula, presumably heading back to his farm.

"Does she look so much like him?" Mary Ellen asked.

Sara raised her brows.

"Sara, I've seen the look that comes into your eyes sometimes when she doesn't know you're watching."

"Even as an infant there was no mistaking whose daughter she was. Same blond hair and blue eyes, square face, strong features, and height. I swear, even her laugh and some of her gestures are Paul's. I suppose that's why I never married. If Paula had looked like me it would have been one thing. But being married to someone else and seeing Paul's face every day… I don't know. It would have seemed like cheating."

Mary Ellen picked up her sandwich and nibbled.

Sara did the same then took a drink of sweet tea before speaking again. "I can't forgive your actions, Mother, but I am trying to be rational about them. What you and Daddy did was horrible, but it happened a long time ago. And Paul would be dead whether we'd continued writing or not, so my circumstances really wouldn't be much different. But I want to hear why you hated Paul so much. You and Daddy hadn't even met him."

Mary Ellen took her time answering. *She looks tired*, Sara thought. *Tired and old.*

"I didn't meet him, but I saw him."

"You did? When?"

"Your father and I went to a basketball game one night, just spur of the moment. We couldn't find you but your friend, Cindy, hemmed and hawed, and said you were around somewhere. Dad shrugged it off, but I had a feeling something wasn't right. I made some excuse and walked around a bit. I saw the two of you leave the gymnasium."

That had to be soon after we met, when we spent hours simply talking. He wouldn't even hold my hand.

"I saw he was a man, and you were still a girl. I didn't tell Dad, of course. I thought he'd only go storming into your room and make matters worse. But I wasn't sure what to do. It was frightening being a parent then. When I was growing up, parents and children knew where they fit in society and what was expected. By 1970, there was upheaval over the war, and protestors, and children gone wild."

She pushed her sandwich away. "You'd always been such a good girl, with nice friends. We saw news reports about hippies and drugs and sex, but you hadn't shown any interest in rebelling. Until then, I'd thanked my lucky stars we were spared the trouble so many of our friends had with their children."

Long, silent seconds stretched between them. "I was afraid if I confronted you, it would push you closer to him, but I was just as afraid not to do anything. I told you numerous times that I knew I could trust you, hoping it would somehow shame you into doing the right thing. I felt like a failure when you came home that Sunday. I knew you'd slept with him and I kept thinking I should have told your dad sooner. He would have put the fear of God into one of you."

"Paul wanted to meet Dad, to be up front with him and introduce himself. I wouldn't let him because I knew you'd stop us from seeing each other." Sara cocked her head, her brows furrowed in puzzlement. "How did you know that we'd been together that weekend?"

"You had that 'look.' Your father missed it entirely, but I guess fathers see what they want to in their little girls. Or maybe he did see, and it frightened him so much he denied it." For a moment, her eyes stared blindly at some scene only she saw.

"When you gave us that story about students choosing sailors overseas to write, it was so farfetched we both knew it was a lie. I told Dad what I suspected and that's when we decided to keep you apart and hope for the best."

"What did you do with the mail?"

Mary Ellen picked up her drink and twirled the ice with the straw. "I threw everything out, hiding them deep in the trash so you wouldn't find them."

Sara's eyes filled with tears, but she fought them back.

"When the first letter came, your father knew what ship he was on and he kept tabs. We hoped when enough time went by, you'd both give up. You did, and then finally he did, too. Eventually, Dad found out why."

"Yes, Paul died. That was pretty convenient."

"Sara Lynn! I won't accept that from you." Mary Ellen's eyes flashed steel.

Sara blew out a breath. "Sorry. I know you wouldn't have wished him harm, regardless."

"None of it would have caused any harm if only he hadn't gotten you pregnant. If I'd talked to you or you'd talked to me. Believe me, Sara, we only wanted to protect you. Your father…"

Mary Ellen ducked her head. "Your father thought you moved heaven and earth. He'd never let you know, but he cried the night we found out about the baby. Cried because he would have slain any dragon for you yet hadn't been able to protect you. You have no idea how he grew up, the poverty, the struggle he had, to make things better for us in the military. He wanted so much for you, and then…"

She raised her head to look proudly at Sara. "More than your life changed because of that man. Your dreams went up in smoke, but so did your father's dreams *for* you. He loved you very much."

Sara's voice was soft when she spoke. "And I loved him. But here's the deal, Mom. Paul loved me, too, and he died thinking I cared so little I wouldn't write a lousy letter saying goodbye. He went three months wondering what happened. And then he *died*. Without ever hearing again how much I loved him."

"I hated him, you know. I hated that he changed your life and that he hurt your father, the finest man I've ever known. And he may be dead, and it all might have happened a long time ago, but my feelings toward him haven't improved." She took another small bite of her sandwich and a sip of tea. "Besides, you were too young to know what love is."

"Maybe. But we'd made a child, and he deserved to know he had someone to fight for. You and Daddy didn't give him that chance."

Sara studied her mother, seeing greater depths than she'd known before. If she'd thought Paula had been in danger of making a terrible mistake at seventeen, how far would she have gone? *Not as far as Mother did.*

Easy to think so from the distance of years, but would she really have been less ruthless? Maybe not.

"Why tell me about the letters now?" The question had surfaced in the early morning hours as she lay awake, thinking. Her mother could have kept the secret forever.

"I don't know exactly." Mary Ellen stood and walked to the doorway, looking out into the gallery. "After your friend's death, there seemed no need to tell you. The older PB got, the less anything of the past mattered." Turning to look at Sara, she continued, "I agreed with your father, that we should do whatever it took to keep the two of you apart, but I always hated the deception, the lies. Then last year, Ava died."

Sara remembered the weeks Mary Ellen had helped nurse Ava Parker, her mother's best friend.

"Those final days we had a lot of time to talk. She'd made peace with everyone; she was at peace with herself. We were the same age, you know, and I thought, it could be me lying there, close to death. I wouldn't want to go to my grave knowing these lies had been between you and me. That you'd had PB and raised her without knowing the truth. Still, I wouldn't have told you if those letters hadn't arrived. Somehow, throwing them out, lying to you again, when there seemed no good reason, was more than I wanted on my conscience."

Mary Ellen went back to her chair and reached across the desk to touch Sara's hand. "Even after all this time, I was nervous. I looked at them for two days, knowing I should do what was right, fearing what would happen between us if I did. In one way, I wish those letters had never reached me. In another, they gave me the push I needed to tell you that I'm sorry. I don't know what else to say at this point. I wish we could do things over."

Sara slowly pulled her hand away, ignoring the look of hurt in her mother's eyes. "There's a lot of blame to go around. When I knew I was pregnant, I should have found some way to reach Paul, but I was afraid, too. I know now how wrong I was. And that's why I have to go to Iowa."

"Huh-uh. I won't allow it. There's no good to come of going there." Mary Ellen sat straight and tall and gave Sara the *I'm the mother* look.

Sara straightened in her chair, too. "You have nothing to say about it. Yesterday I was in shock, finding out what you did. I started today thinking that however bad they were, your actions were taken out of love, a way to protect me. But I think now, you just wanted control. In this decision, you have none."

"You can't just drop in on them."

"I can't very well call, can I? This isn't something that should be explained on the phone, so I have to go in person and now, before I talk myself out of it. I know Paul grew up on a farm near a town called Denison. His parents and younger brother were there when he left. I'll find *some*one who knows about them."

She looked at her mother with determination. "I won't be talked out of this."

Mary Ellen shook her head. "I hope you know what you're doing, Sara. Don't forget, this isn't just about you. What are you going to tell Paula?"

Sara started at her mother's use of Paula's name instead of PB.

"Just that I have some unexpected business out of town. Nothing else right now. Not until I see Mr. and Mrs. Steinert and find out how they feel. There's no need building her hopes or upsetting her until I know more."

She narrowed her eyes and her voice was firm. "And just to be clear, you're not to say or do one thing about this. I won't stand for any interference from you. *None*."

Throwing back her shoulders and raising her head, Mary Ellen met Sara's gaze. "I understand." Then her tone softened. "This will be an awfully big shock for them. And I think you underestimate how hard it will be for you." She fumbled with the wrapping paper of her sandwich. "What should I tell Matthew if he calls? You two are so close, he'll be surprised if I simply say you're out of town and give no explanation."

Sara fixed her mother with a stare. "Don't worry. I'll call him before I leave."

Marine Lieutenant Colonel Matthew Abrams had gone from being one of her best friends to an occasional lover. But the subject of Paula's father was something she'd closed to him.

Mary Ellen huffed out a breath. "Well. I still believe you're stumbling into a situation you have no clue about. If you get hurt in the process, don't blame me."

"I won't, Mom. But *thanks*."

* * * *

"I'm home!" Dan Tanner's clear baritone rang from the living room.

"Out here," Paula returned. She dropped her tanned legs from the railing to the deck and stood to fill an empty wine glass with Merlot, then topped off her glass, too.

He frowned with concern as he came through the French doors and onto the deck. "Are you feeling all right? I called the school to let you know I'd be home a little late and they said you'd taken a sick day."

"It was just a touch of something, I guess. All gone now." She didn't want to fly off the handle and get all emotional like she had with her mom that morning. But waiting for him to broach the subject of his acceptance at Northwestern, when his decision about law school might tear their world apart, was awful.

One thing Paula discovered early on was that Dan was cautious, always trying to ensure the right choice. She followed her inclination, remaining cool instead of screaming in frustration when it seemed like he was dragging his feet. She'd pretended it didn't matter when he waited six months before suggesting they have sex, or that she was fine when it took a year for him to think they should move in together. She wouldn't be able to hold in her feelings on this issue very long, though.

"Okay, good." He looked her up and down. "You look like a lady of leisure, having an afternoon wine break on your deck in shorts and tee shirt. Waiting for the lord of the manor to return, no doubt."

Paula smiled. "I hope you don't expect a curtsy."

"Not at all, my dear." Sweeping his glass up in a grand manner, Dan intoned in a theatrical voice, "Poetic inspiration strikes! A jug of wine, a loaf of bread and thou. I could be happier but I don't know how."

Paula laughed. Dan always made her laugh. His talent in that one area would have been enough to make her love him. It hadn't hurt that rich auburn hair and sparkling brown eyes topped his smiling lips. That he was brilliant, tall enough to make her feel petite, and the sweetest man she'd ever known, made him almost too good to be true.

"Surely you can imagine how to accomplish being happier." As soon as she said the words she regretted them. She'd meant to be seductive, but Dan would think attending Northwestern would add to his happiness.

"Hmm, let's see. Would money? Nah, money can't buy you love, as the Beatles said. How about a new car? No, babying my old clunker adds a challenge to each day." He stroked his chin, appearing to be deep in thought. "I've got it!"

Paula closed her eyes, waiting for the words she dreaded.

"A willing lady. Naked. Long blonde hair and blue eyes." He leaned forward and kissed her cheek.

Her eyes popped open to see Dan regarding her carefully. She let out her breath on a sigh. "Hmm, very specific on the naked lady."

"I'm always specific and *very* particular when it comes to naked ladies." He removed the tie that hung loose around his neck. Draining his glass, he set it down and reached for her. "I also insist that my naked ladies actually take off their clothes. See, they're not really naked until that happens. I teach science. I know these things."

43

His tongue brushed her lips. Her heart kicked into high gear and heat coiled in her belly, the way it always did when Dan touched her. Even with the barest of contact her body readied itself for him.

She pushed her anxiety aside. Maybe her mother was right. Maybe Dan had decided against Chicago.

Her tongue slipped out to issue an invitation, and Dan accepted with a groan, pulling her against him, devouring her lips and grinding his hips into hers. One of his hands snuck under her tee shirt to unhook her bra and the other snaked below the waistband of her jeans to rub her backside.

"Dan," she gasped when she broke for air, "we're outside, you know? Some sailor in the bay with a set of binoculars is about to get an eyeful if we keep on."

He stopped nibbling a path to her ear long enough to say, "I never do anything as wild and crazy as exhibitionist sex. So, if I sit on the chair and you straddle me, do you think that will block enough of his view?" He dragged his hand across her ribs to cup a now-freed breast and groaned again. "Oh, the hell with it. Poor guy probably deserves a thrill." With that, he scraped his hand lower, to the zipper of her jeans.

"Dan!" She laughed and inched away, pulling her shirt down. His eyes, darkened with lust, were also a bit bloodshot, and his Georgia accent was thick, always a giveaway that he'd been drinking. She ran her tongue over her lips, tasting a hint of whiskey under the wine.

Staring at her mouth, he caught the act. "Oh, baby," he moaned, reaching for her again. "Don't do that unless you want to—"

She playfully batted his hand away. "You've been celebrating without me."

He grinned. "Just a little. The department decided that as good scientists, we should experiment to determine the best place for my going away party. Today we picked a bar at random from the phone book. It was Mc-Somethingoranother, over on South. Next week we choose another place and then another and so on and so forth, until the final party. See? I didn't get a buzz on for nothing. It was in the name of science."

Fighting the chunk of ice forming around her heart, she forced a smile. "Science is a wonderful thing. But how about eating something? There's left-over pot roast. I'll throw together biscuits and pull out some of Mama's homemade blackberry preserves that you like so much."

Picking up the wine bottle, he started to refill his glass but reconsidered. "I will not be sidetracked from my original goal." He waggled his brows. "I want dessert before pot roast."

She loved him so, she couldn't help but play along. "Pie? With whipped cream?"

"Paula ala whipped cream." For the third time he reached for her. She backed through the French doors and into the attic sitting room. He stalked her, a lusty gleam in his eyes.

"Okay, okay! Let's have dessert."

"Say it in French and I'll make it worth your while." He leered, steering her toward the stairs and bedroom.

"Oh, really?" She stopped and looked him in the eye. "*Donc, mangeons le dessert!*"

"God, that makes me hotter'n a firecracker." He snatched a kiss. "What'd you say, anyway?"

"*Pas aimes-tu savoir?* Wouldn't you like to know?"

"Hell, yes. Does it mean, 'Will you drag me off to your lair, caveman, and make mad, passionate love to me?'" With a dip of his knees, he slung her over his shoulder.

Paula screamed then dissolved into giggles. "*Laisses-moi le bas, toi païen!*"

She bounced against his back as he took the steps and rushed to the bedroom. "Hell, I'm hurrying as fast as I can."

She couldn't stop laughing. "I said, 'Put me down, you heathen!'"

"Oh. Sounded better before." He dumped her on the bed. With a roar, he dove beside her, wrapped her in his arms and pulled her on top of him. "Besides, I like my translation better. Say something else and I'll kiss you senseless."

"Non."

"Huh-uh! In French."

She slapped his arm. "That *was* French, you language-challenged physicist. Why is it you always think I'm saying 'drag me off and make mad, passionate love to me'?"

His hands slid under her tee shirt. "Because it's what I always want you to be saying." He nipped her lips. "I should learn some French, but I know I wouldn't sound as sexy as you do." He caught another quick kiss. "Everything about you is so damn sexy, Paula. I love you."

"I love you, too."

His gaze pierced hers. His fingers roamed lightly up and down her back. A slight adjustment of his hips brought his erection in direct alignment with her sex.

"A lot?" he asked, his eyes half-lidded and his voice thick.

Oh, Lord. The scent of her desire wafted around them. She wanted him and it couldn't be more obvious how much he wanted her. Her breath caught at the thought of making love with him. Rubbing her breasts over his chest, she smiled.

"Mais oui," she whispered in his ear.

He nuzzled her neck. "Will you still love me in Chicago?"

She stilled. The heat pooling deep in her belly cooled and she pushed off him. Sitting on her heels she let out a breath. "I'd love you wherever you are."

He linked his fingers with hers. "But do you love me enough to *be* wherever I am?" She stayed silent. "I was accepted at Northwestern, Paula."

"I know. I found the acceptance letter when I was straightening up yesterday, but I didn't want to spoil the surprise." *Ha! More like I wanted to delay the dejection.*

She fought to keep her voice steady. "When you brought it up a few months ago, I checked. Northwestern is hard to get into. I'm very proud of you."

A million-watt grin lit his face. "I have to say, I'm kinda proud, too."

"You should be. You're brilliant and any school would be lucky to have you as a student."

"There's nothing wrong with the other schools I applied to. But honey, Northwestern is what I really want."

Keep it cool, girl. Don't let him see you're worried. "Then I want it for you. I'm glad they accepted you."

He kissed her fingers. "I'm so relieved. When I mentioned applying there last spring and you got upset, I thought you'd bow up and not let me go."

As empty as she felt inside, her lips turned up in a smile. *"Not let you go? How could I keep you here, you silly man?" Tell me, please. How can I keep you here?*

"Well, I was afraid you'd say you wouldn't go with me. That's why I didn't talk any more about it. I thought first there was no need worrying you again when I might not get in. Then I hoped if you had time to think about it you'd see what an adventure it could be. I mean, Paula, Chicago! Museums, theatre, *snow*. Honey, it'll be such fun." He let go of her hand and propped his hands behind his head.

She poked him lightly in the chest. "You're going to be too busy to have a lot of fun."

"It'll be hard, I know that. But we're not wild kids. We know what's important. I've planned this for a long time and I've saved, so money won't be too tight." He looked at her and smiled. "Besides, with you, any place would be fun." He looked around the bedroom. "I'll miss this house, but we'll find a nice apartment there and look for another house when I start practicing."

Paula's heart turned over at the thought of leaving their home. After two years of living together in Dan's apartment, they'd decided to earn equity in something. They'd never thought they could afford a place like this in the harbor area of Charleston, but the sellers liked them and the deal had fallen into place. After some work, and in a remarkably short period of time, Paula felt as though they'd always lived here. And always would.

"We have several months to figure out what to do about the house."

"Not so long. I thought you read the acceptance letter. I'm starting in January, not next year. That's why the guys started the farewell partying now. We'll need to move right after the first of the year. The good news is, Jack Morgan, one of the guys I know from grad school at USC, is coming in to take over my classes. He's already said he'd like to look at the house. He might be able to assume the loan."

"Wait!" Paula slid off the bed and paced along the side. "This is too fast. How did you get out of your contract?"

Dan sat up and leaned against the headboard. "I warned the front office I might leave early, so they adjusted the contract, just in case. If I stayed here, I'd sign the addendum for the second half of the year. I know *you* think I'm God's gift—" he flashed another smile, though this one was a bit less confident than his previous offering "—but there was a chance I wouldn't be admitted to Northwestern. Now I'm in a hurry to begin the next part of our lives. Is there a problem?"

"I don't want to go to Chicago, Dan. I haven't changed my mind since we talked before." She stopped and covered her eyes with one hand. "I-I have a job I love, and I'm not qualified to teach in Illinois. I love our house. I love my kitchen and our attic area, and our deck that overlooks the harbor. My mother is here, my grandmother—" *I will not cry. I will not cry.* "You're rushing me."

Dan rose and went to her. He pulled her hand away from her face and tilted her head back. "You love me. I love you. The job will work itself out. As for the house, I love it, too, but it's who's in the house that matters, not the place. I know your mom will miss you, but don't you think she wants you to be happy? I refuse to believe you'll be happy without me, and I sure as hell know I won't be without you. We belong together, Paula."

"I do love you. I know you're going to set Northwestern on its ear, and you'll come out the best lawyer they've ever produced. But you'll have to go without me."

He rubbed his forehead. "How long ago did we meet?"

48

Burning Bridges

"Four years."

"At the video store, remember?"

They'd both reached for the last copy of *Airplane.* After chatting for a few minutes, Dan suggested they watch the movie at his house—she could rent the DVD and he'd spring for the pizza. When Paula laughed and said there was no way she'd go home with him, he proposed a compromise. She rented the DVD. They went next door for pizza and Cokes, then stopped by Dan's car for his laptop and an old blanket before continuing to the park across the street.

The laptop battery ran out before Robert Hayes landed the plane, but Paula's interest had been fully charged.

"How could I forget? You were so pleased coming up with the idea of using your laptop to show the movie. You were just a little smug and completely adorable. I was hooked right then."

He didn't smile as she thought he would. "And you fell in love with me very soon after that."

Amazed, she planted her hands on her hips. "I did not. It took months and months. Maybe a year."

He waved his hand dismissively. "After a few weeks you were mine. And I was yours."

"You didn't show it."

"Neither did you. I kept waiting for you to trust me enough to be more than friends. God, I thought you'd never hint that you'd go to bed with me. Even then you played it cool, always acting like you didn't care one way or the other. Every step of our relationship I've had to initiate the move."

"*What?* You're crazy, Dan. I—"

"I love you, Paula, but this is the next step. I'm leaving the tried and true and going on an adventure. I want to do this. Don't you want to come with me?"

She hung her head and shook it. "But I'm glad you want me to come with you. I was afraid you didn't."

Dan sighed. "You're very much like your mother. I don't know how long I'm supposed to pay for whatever your father did to her." He turned and walked out.

"Wait a minute!" Paula stormed behind him, down to the ground floor and into the kitchen. "You just give me your version of our life together, make some cryptic comment about my parents, and walk away?"

"I've had years to analyze the situation." He bent to examine the contents of the refrigerator then set a covered dish on the counter. "I'll put the roast in the microwave. Were you going to make biscuits?"

She leaned against the counter, arms crossed. "What did you mean about my mom and dad? The man died before I was even born, so I don't know how you can make any informed observation of their relationship."

Facing her, he leaned against the opposite counter. "For some reason, your mom won't let herself go. Like she's afraid to believe someone could really love her. She met Matthew shortly after we met, and she still doesn't trust him. I don't think she really trusts herself."

"Maybe she never stopped loving my father. She's never remarried, never taken off her wedding ring."

"I think Matthew loves her, and he's been a very good friend. A good, *patient* friend. But when she looks at him there's no real openness. She holds back. Sadly, Matthew and I have a lot in common."

Paula had thought for quite a while that her mother must love Matthew, yet nothing in the relationship seemed to move forward. At least with her and Dan, things did move—at a snail's pace maybe, but progress was progress.

"I don't think you know what you're talking about. But putting that aside, what about us?" She held her breath.

His smile was everything she'd hoped for. Like a secret promise of sweet surrender, meant just for her.

"Nothing's changed for now. You know how I feel. I've let you have your way to this point, and God knows, you've driven me crazy a thousand times, wanting what you don't seem ready to give me. But in January I'm heading for Chicago. I'll make you a bet. I'll bet you go with me."

"I don't want to bet. This isn't a game, Dan." She forced back tears. Crying would only make things worse. She needed calmness, and a way to persuade Dan to her way of thinking. "If you go to Illinois it'll break my heart."

He took the two steps to reach her. "Your heart isn't the only one at risk here. Mine is, too. They'll both be safe—" he bent close to her ear "—if you trust me."

She slipped her arms around his waist. "I'm just warning you, if I do die of a broken heart, you'll never have a peaceful moment. I'll haunt you forever."

"Darlin', you've haunted my every thought and dream since I first saw you. That'll never change."

"You silver-tongued devil."

He winked. "I have a great tongue, a talented tongue. A long, wicked tongue. Let's forget dinner. Take me back in the bedroom and recite something in French."

"What shall I recite?"

"I don't care. The constitution or nursery rhymes, you make it all sound sexy. While you recite, my long, talented, *wicked* tongue will explore your body."

"Oh, my. You do have a way of making a lady forget her troubles, Mr. Tanner."

"Ladies and their troubles are my specialty, Ms. Richards."

She slipped out of his arms and strolled toward the back stairs, giving her hips a deliberate sway with each step. "I declare, I believe you generate enough hot air to melt the polar ice caps." She swung around and crooked her finger at him.

"Ah, Ms. Richards," he crooned, following her. "That walk of yours alone could do the trick."

"If you're trying to flatter me into submission, Sir, it's working." With a final flip of her hips, she disappeared up the steps.

Chapter 4

"Hi. My name is Sara and my daughter is the spitting image of your son, Paul, because, well, he's her father." She imagined following up her announcement by handing the Steinerts a pin featuring a big smiley face and the caption "Have a nice day!"

What she would say to Paul's family had occupied Sara's mind during the flight from Charleston to Omaha. Hours later, she still had no idea how to introduce herself to a family that likely hadn't heard of her, much less acclimate them to the idea of their granddaughter. What had seemed like an excellent idea sitting at home in Beaufort—in fact, the only ethical idea, considering her new knowledge—seemed more stupid the closer she came to the Steinert farm.

Since the beginning of the trip, a devil on her shoulder coaxed, "Turn around. Paula has grown up without these people. What they don't know won't hurt them." He'd been drowned out by an angel on the other shoulder who chided that the Steinerts would welcome Paula into their lives and that Sara's news was better late than never.

Yes, the idea *had* seemed really good in Beaufort. Not so much, now. Driving down a dirt road with clouds of dust trailing behind her, the devil sang a loud chorus in her ear and the angel was nowhere to be found. Sara kept going only because of the certainty that the angel—though silent—was correct.

She tried to see through the thick dust billowing behind the rental car. She'd never been to Iowa before, but even this early in the fall she'd expected snow to cause visibility problems, not powdery earth.

The heavy clouds in front of her looked like they were ready to drop something, and when she'd rolled down the window for a moment the air had a clean, sharp bite, she associated with snow. Another reason for nerves. She dreaded the thought of driving back to Omaha in a storm. Although, if the Steinerts proved receptive to her news, maybe they'd invite her to stay with them if the weather turned bad.

Or they'd throw her out, regardless. *They won't throw me out. Not Paul's parents. Not when I bring news of their granddaughter.*

The man at the gas station in Denison had told her that the Steinert farm was about six miles down this road, and already she felt like she'd driven twenty.

A glance to the right showed her the white shingle hanging between two posts proclaiming *Steinert.* Only by slamming on the brakes was she able to make the turn down the long drive that led to a large barn and white two-story house.

She pulled up near a garage connected to the house by a covered walkway and turned off the engine. The house and garage were plain but neatly painted. Golden mums competed for attention with red dahlias and scarlet marigolds at the front of the house and along the side of the garage. Beyond the garage lay the remains of a large vegetable garden, and beyond that, the road turned toward the barn. Everything she saw was clean and well-kept. Ship-shape.

Fields stretched out behind the barn, the rich black earth turned and ready to be planted when spring arrived. Two or three men worked to unload a pickup truck backed up to the open barn door. They came into the open briefly and then disappeared back into the darkness of the building with bags balanced on their shoulders. One of those men could be Paul's father or brother. Her palms turned sweaty although the car was rapidly cooling.

Sara looked down at her clothing. Trying to walk the fine line between appearing feminine yet in command, she'd chosen to wear a rayon business suit. The jacket, dark brown with gold trim, was tailored and cinched at the waist, but the skirt flowed, full and soft, to her calves.

With a deep breath, she decided she'd pass muster. *Ship-shape, muster.* Funny, she hadn't thought of those military terms in years. She *was* nervous.

After checking her hair and makeup in the rearview mirror, she clutched her purse, gathered her courage and exited the car. Immediately, a sharp wind struck, swirling her skirt around her legs. With one hand she pulled her jacket tighter around her.

Too easily, she envisioned Paul here, joking with his dad and brother as they worked. She all but saw his tall form walking the plowed fields, his blond head visible among row after row of tasseled corn. Paula could have grown up happily here, maybe with the pony she'd asked for, Christmas after Christmas when she was small. Perhaps, if things had worked out as they'd planned, she and Paul would have had other children, a boy to carry on his name or another beautiful girl. With Paul by her side, Sara would have grown into a confident woman. She certainly would have staked out a different course for her life.

Another gust of wind snapped her from her daydream. Shivering, she looked toward the barn. A young man stepped out from the darkness of the interior, laughing and calling something back over his shoulder. He took off his jacket and tossed it into the pickup cab before sliding his hands into gloves. He bent over the tailgate. Heaving a sack over his left shoulder as if it weighed nothing, he called out another comment that brought a hoot of laughter from inside the barn, and he strode back in.

Sara fell back against the car, her face drained of blood. For a split second, she feared she'd pass out. At a distance, that young man was Paul, just as she remembered him—same blond hair, same build, same gestures. Same cocky walk. She tried to laugh but failed.

As her mother predicted, this trip was turning out to be hard. Much harder than Sara had anticipated. Already she'd pictured Paul here, and now she was imposing his spirit on the people who did live here. She felt his very presence more strongly than at any time since learning of his death.

The devil on her shoulder won. She couldn't do this, couldn't stay here where memories flooded her senses and all of the dreams she'd shared with Paul mocked her. She turned and opened the car door.

"May I help you with something?" Sara looked toward the house where a woman held open a screen door so she could lean out.

Oh, no! Sara closed the door and stepped to the front of the vehicle. "Yes, I hope you can. I'm here to see—" At another sound from the barn, she turned and halted, thought as well as motion suspended.

A tall man stood behind the pickup, wearing a denim jacket and western style hat. He must have become warm at his work because even in the chill wind he stopped to remove his hat then scraped his sleeve across his forehead, as though wiping away perspiration. At that moment, he looked toward her and stared.

The world stopped turning. The man must be Paul's brother, but her heart gave a leap. Longing filled her. God! If she stayed here another minute she'd go crazy. She had to leave, but her feet refused to move.

He reacted first. Replacing his hat, he turned his head only a fraction to call something into the barn. Tossing gloves into the bed of the truck, he slowly came toward her.

Time compressed into a single moment as she waited for the man to reach her. Waited so she could confirm that his eyes weren't the same blue, his lips didn't turn up in a smile the same way. Then her mind would compute that he wasn't Paul and she'd be able to breathe again.

"Miss?" As though from a distance she heard the woman at the door, but she couldn't respond.

"Paul, do you know who this is?" The woman's question came just as the man reached Sara.

"*Paul?*" Sara reached out her hand, grasping only air. Her knees buckled and she sank into unconsciousness.

* * * *

Sara scrunched her forehead and shut her eyes more tightly, unwilling to open them and find she'd only been dreaming. She smelled furniture polish and roasting meat. A clock chimed the quarter hour. She sighed, nervous and on the verge of tears, knowing she wasn't at home, knowing she hadn't been dreaming. She forced open her eyes and blinked, once, twice. Then focused on him.

Her hand flew to her mouth and she stifled a sob. Paul stood looking down at her, concern shadowing his eyes. If anything, they were bluer than she remembered, and she hadn't thought that was possible.

From her position, lying on a sofa and staring up, he looked like a giant. His shoulders seemed broad as a football field, his arms like posts, and the muscles in them bunched, filling out his flannel shirt, even as he stood casually. His legs, encased in worn jeans, looked hard and strong. The blond hair she always pictured ruffled by the beach wind, had lightened, though he still kept it short. Lines bracketed his eyes. He'd aged, yes, but there was no denying, Paul Steinert stood before her.

"Are you all right?"

His voice washed over her, taking her breath away. Her eyes closed again as she tried to stem the threatening tears and calm the pounding of her heart. Her hands trembled and she licked dry lips. When she opened her eyes again she

56

gasped at his nearness. He'd dropped to one knee, putting his face mere inches from hers. "Would you like water?"

"Yes, please." How had she gotten out the words, when her lungs seemed unable to take in air?

He reached to the low table behind him and brought a glass to her lips. She sipped, keeping her eyes on him.

"*Are* you all right?" The woman who had called to her from the doorway stood at Sara's feet. Her left hand rested on the sofa back and light from a table lamp reflected off her gold wedding band, making it shine like a beacon.

"Yes, I'm okay. Thanks." She struggled to sit up, but Paul pushed her back.

"There's no hurry. Just lie still." He stood and handed the glass to the woman. "Thanks, Becca. Will you give us a few minutes?"

With a slight frown directed at Sara, the woman took the glass and moved toward an arched entryway that led into a dining room. The young man Sara had seen at the barn leaned against the archway. "Who is she, Mom? Is she okay?" he asked quietly as he followed the woman out.

"She's a friend of your..." The two moved out of earshot.

The resemblance between the younger man and Paul was so remarkable it seemed obvious they were father and son. Which meant the woman was Paul's... She couldn't get the word *wife* past the wall hastily erected around him in her mind.

Paul was alive! She silently thanked God for the miracle that had allowed him to defy death and make it home. But her joy at that discovery was immediately tempered. She took in a deep, painful breath. He'd returned to the States, yes, but hadn't returned to her, hadn't sought her out or checked to see if she still remembered, still waited. Okay, he hadn't received her letters but still, wouldn't he have tried to find out why? If he loved her as he'd proclaimed, he should have come for her. Her parents had been wrong to intercede between them, but it seemed their instincts about his unsuitability had been perfect.

Paul moved the coffee table out of the way so he could place a straight-back chair beside her. He examined her, moving his gaze from forehead to chin, resting for a moment on her lips. "I caught you before you hit hard, but I'm afraid your clothes are pretty dirty."

"That's okay. I'm sorry for the trouble. I-I never faint."

They lapsed into silence. Lemony furniture polish tickled her nose. In the background a door opened and closed. After an ear-splitting whistle, a man called, "Here, boy!" and a dog barked as he raced past the window. Then, kitchen sounds of dishes, pans, and drawers opening and closing were all that interrupted the quiet.

"If you don't normally faint, what's wrong? Do you want me to call a doctor?"

"No! Good heavens, no. It's been kind of a long day, and I haven't had much to eat. I… It was seeing you again, I guess." The miracle of it still hadn't sunk in. Despite his abandonment, she ached to touch his arm, to run her fingers through his hair, to kiss him and hold him. Her Southern upbringing meant they were all things she wouldn't do.

And then there was the fact of his wife.

He huffed a laugh. "I wasn't expecting to see you either." Then *he* raked his hair.

The years fell away. Her eyes followed the movement hungrily. She couldn't get enough, wanting nothing more than to drink in the sight of him and savor the fact that he was alive and sitting less than two feet away.

"I guess I don't understand what you're doing here, Sara. It's been a long time."

She barely heard him. Her mind was swimming, but she had to think. She'd come prepared to talk with his parents. Her story was rehearsed and ready to dispense in a logical sequence. To find Paul here completely unnerved her. He displayed a mature confidence and bearing only hinted at when she'd met him. Sara wouldn't have thought it possible, but he was even more breathtaking than the man of her memories.

Licking her lips, she bided for time.

He spoke again. "You seemed shocked at seeing me, but imagine my surprise at finding you standing in my yard. After all, I didn't think you even remembered me." He paused as though waiting for her to fill the silence. When she didn't, he sighed and leaned back in the chair, crossing his legs. "What *are* you doing here?"

"I came to see your parents."

"My parents? Why?" His voice was neutral, reasonable.

"To-to talk to them. To introduce myself." He raised a brow obviously doubting her. This wasn't going well. How could she tell him about Paula when he was like this, so polite, so distant? He might be married and happily settled in his life, but she couldn't stand to think their love had been all one-sided. He'd claimed a corner of her heart when she was seventeen, and she'd never evicted him. Didn't he have any feelings for her at all?

"Things have changed in my life recently, and I thought maybe...maybe they'd be interested in meeting me."

No hint of openness showed on his face. His eyes narrowed, setting off internal warning bells. She stared, unable to form the words that would tell Paul he was the father of a grown daughter. A beautiful woman who shared his features but not this aloofness. Sara rubbed her temples, knowing that no amount of massage would stop the oncoming headache.

"My father died fifteen years ago, and my mother soon after him. So, you're a good many years too late." Uncrossing his legs, he edged forward on the seat, ready to stand. "Truthfully, their passing aside, I'd say you're a few decades too late." Lightness laced his voice that wasn't reflected in his eyes. "If you're feeling better, you probably should head back to wherever you're staying. I think it'll start snowing soon, and the roads may be hell to drive on for a while." He stood and replaced the chair against the wall.

Sara had no option but to follow his lead. Swinging her legs to the floor, she sat and took stock of her condition. Lightheaded, but not from fainting. Short of breath, but not from the fall. Trembling, unsteady, ready to fight a stream of tears, but not at the thought of a snowstorm.

"Okay?" There was no real interest in Paul's voice, just the casual questioning tone he might use with an acquaintance. He really had put all they'd meant to each other behind him. She'd come to start a relationship with his parents. Instead, she found a man who had already burned all bridges to the past.

She stood. "Yes." Determined to maintain a modicum of composure, she smoothed her skirt, tugged on her jacket and held her head high.

For the first time, she saw where he'd carried her. The bright and comfortable living room normally would entice a guest to linger, visiting over a cup of coffee. But not her, not now or ever. This pleasant room belonged to a Paul she didn't know, and to his wife and son. She couldn't imagine Paula here, trying to penetrate her father's indifference or perhaps hostility. Sara's mother was right. Things of the past were better left there.

Sara walked toward the arched opening. Paul followed. Without touching, he herded her toward the kitchen.

The woman he called Becca turned from the sink where she was scrubbing vegetables. Wiping her hands on her apron, she came forward. "Are you all right? Is there anything else I can get you? Some food, maybe?" Concern filled her voice.

"I'm fine, thanks. I'm sorry to have been so much trouble."

"Nonsense. I'm just glad you're feeling better." She looked expectantly at Paul.

"Becca, this is an old friend, Sara Richards."

In shock, Sara stared at Paul. How had he known her married name? Shifting into protective mode, she decided it didn't matter how. Her purpose had changed. She wouldn't bring Paula into a family where her father would resent her.

"I met her just before I went to Nam. Sara, this is Becca. Becca Steinert."

The women shook hands. "Nice to meet you, Sara. So you came by to see Paul?"

"She came to see Mom and Dad. Didn't realize they weren't here anymore." Looking at Sara he added, "It's too bad you have to go so soon. It might have been nice to catch up on old times." His eyes betrayed the lie. "But that storm is coming in fast." He moved to the door.

60

"Where are you from Sara?" Becca seemed as eager to chat as Paul was to prevent it.

"I live in South Carolina. A little town called Beaufort, on the coast."

"Oh, that sounds lovely. And *warm*," Becca said with a chuckle. "South Carolina…" She pondered for a second and looked at Paul. "Isn't that where your—"

"Becca, not now. Sara needs to get ahead of the weather."

Paul opened the wooden, inside door. Sara shivered from the immediate chill that resulted.

"Paul is right about a storm coming in," Becca added. "Where are you staying? Or are you heading right back?"

Sara glanced at Paul, who stood as rigid as a rock, and wore an expression every bit as friendly. "To tell the truth, I'd hoped I might be visiting for more than one afternoon. But just in case, I booked a room at The Best Western in Omaha. I'd planned to go home day after tomorrow."

Becca also shifted her gaze to Paul and back. "Well, it was nice meeting you."

"Thanks."

Silently, Paul ushered her to the car and opened her door. She slid behind the wheel and started the engine. He closed the door and took a step back.

She lowered the window. "I'm sorry if I made trouble for you and Becca."

"Becca's a good woman—faithful, loyal, honest, and she understands love. There's no way *you* could make trouble for us." There was no indifference now. The outside temperature couldn't match Paul Steinert for bone-chilling, brittle frigidity.

Even so, she fought leaving. "How did you know to call me Sara Richards instead of Noland?"

He crossed his arms, spreading his feet and glowering at her. He looked like a Germanic god. An angry one.

"Did you think I wouldn't track you down when I came home? I found your friend Cindy in Williamsburg, where I thought you'd be, too. After being lectured about how I'd just wasted a year of my life killing women and babies, she finally told me that you'd gone to South Carolina for a visit after graduation, that you'd had a whirlwind romance and were pregnant before the fall semester started. She said the guy proposed so the kid would have a name." He nodded to her hand resting on the steering wheel. "I see you still wear your wedding ring, so I assume you're still half of a pair."

Her eyes fill with tears, and she hated it. Hated looking weak in front of him. He *had* come for her. *Oh, God, give me strength to tell him.*

"This—" she twisted the ring, "—is hard to explain." Despite her best efforts, a tear rolled down her cheek.

"Not so hard. You met him, slept with him and got caught, all within a few months of promising to wait for me. Simple, really. I guess once you give it away it's not so hard to do it again. At least he did the right thing by marrying you."

She gasped at the cruelty in his words. If she'd been outside the car she'd have slapped him for the insult and for belittling the feelings they'd had. He didn't *deserve* a daughter like Paula, who was fine and good, and who'd come from what Sara always thought was a union of love.

Paul leaned down and wiped the tear, then looked at the spot of wetness marking his thumb. "Funny, the last time I did that we were saying goodbye, too."

For a few moments they said nothing, just stared at each other. "You've changed, Paul. You're cold."

He snorted, then closed his eyes and stretched his head back. "You get used to this weather after awhile."

He had to have known she didn't mean the weather.

Bending down, he stuck his face within inches of hers. "I'm here to tell you, Sara, you can get used to *anything*. Even more than you ever thought you could. More than anyone should ever have to." He took a deep breath and dropped his

62

head, then faced her again. The anger seemed drained out of him. "Can you find your way back to Omaha?"

"Yes." It was a whisper. He couldn't have heard it over the engine, but he seemed to understand anyway.

Slapping the door frame, he stood back. "Goodbye, Sara."

She backed up to have room to turn. A look at the house showed Becca framed by the window, watching her. With long strides, Paul had already started back to the barn, dismissing Sara as though she meant nothing. That certainly explained how he could act as he had. He'd put her in a box and hidden her away. Today she'd forced him to remember she existed and discovered that he chose not to. He'd married, had a family and moved on. No old loves need apply.

The long driveway blurred through her tears. For all of her adult life, she'd lived without Paul. Accepting his death had been agonizing, but she'd managed. How hard could it be now to know he was alive but wanted nothing to do with her?

Impossible.

* * * *

Paul surveyed the scenery on either side of the highway. The storm had swept through just as he'd predicted, bringing a few inches of snow with it. People seemed to think that during the winter months farmers loafed around the house. But if you had stock, responsibility didn't let up just because the weather turned cold and nasty. In fact, the work only became harder in the frigid wind, sleet and snow that swept across the plains. So why was he taking off the day after the first real snowfall to chase after Sara? He had no good answer to that question.

When he'd come out of the barn the day before, the woman standing beside the car had seemed familiar. Her stance, the tilt of her chin, the color of her hair all stirred memories he'd thought long dead. He'd needed to go closer, to assure himself the woman standing in his yard wasn't the same who had shown him heaven only to turn around and damn him to hell.

Like a Siren seduced sailors, her still figure had drawn him. With each step, his heart beat faster and his throat constricted. Then there was no doubt that the woman staring at him was none other than Sara Noland—no, Sara *Richards*.

63

She'd married instead of waiting for him—the woman who had haunted his days and tormented his nights for years. The intensity of his feelings, the hurt, the feeling of abandonment came back like someone'd slugged him in the gut. It was a wonder he'd maintained any kind of composure, and in fact her presence had required more strength than he remembered having. The sense of relief when she drove off had overwhelmed him.

But after only an hour more of unloading feed, he'd called it a day, spending the rest of the afternoon restlessly puttering around his little cottage behind the main house. A sleepless night bled into a haggard day where he was unfocused, causing his brother, Mark, to shoot him several worried looks.

After lunch, Mark suggested Paul take a break for the afternoon. Maybe ride on into Denison "...or even Omaha," and see if there was some diversion he'd find interesting. Paul snorted at his brother's lack of subtlety, but played along with the suggestion.

He started the trip in no hurry. One moment he convinced himself he wasn't going to town to see Sara; the next he planned how to make their meeting look accidental.

For years, he'd literally hated her. Later, hatred dulled to detachment. But he'd never forgotten her. After all this time she still frequently haunted his night dreams, although he'd trained himself never to allow her into his daydreams. Now that had gone right out the window. *Why the hell has she come here, messing with my life and my mind?*

Carrying her inside the house yesterday had taken him back to when he was twenty years old, full of idealism and anxious to believe in love. Young and alive.

Young and stupid, more like it.

Still, the feeling had been heady. Holding Sara in his arms had been an elixir, making bad dreams fade and years of ennui on the farm seem nonexistent. He didn't understand it, but he longed to feel it again.

Maybe she really had come to introduce herself to his parents. Maybe her arrival was without agenda. But even if done innocently, her visit had opened old wounds. With that feeling of youthful euphoria had also come the pain of failure. He wanted to know—make that *needed* to know—what had happened all those years ago. Nothing less than that would have made him tear off impulsively after the woman who had almost destroyed his sanity.

When he glanced up and saw a plane headed east, he realized she might have changed her flight after being virtually thrown off the farm. Unable to fool himself any longer as to why he was driving into town, he broke the speed limit until he reached the outskirts of Omaha. Taking a chance that she wouldn't venture into the city for the night, he took the airport exit and found the hotel easily.

Striding into the lobby, Paul still had no idea how he would handle the meeting. The woman behind the counter gave him a warm smile. Smiling back, he removed his hat and unbuttoned his sheepskin jacket.

"May I help you?"

"Yes. Sara Richards, please."

She busied herself with guest records for a moment before looking up again. "It's cold out, isn't it? But that jacket looks like it would keep whoever it's wrapped around snug as a bug. Do you ever share?" The smile was accompanied by a wink.

Paul leaned on his elbow on the counter. "It *is* cold, and the jacket *is* warm. But I'm afraid I never learned to share. It was my mama's biggest failure."

"Oh..."

"Mrs. Richards? Will you see if she's in?"

"Oh! Oh, yes." She looked at a room charge slip. "I remember her now. I saw her go into the restaurant just a few minutes ago."

She's still here. "Thanks."

She smiled again but Paul paid no attention, his mind on one thing only as he entered the restaurant. A quick glance revealed Sara sitting alone at a table on the opposite side of the room. The hostess approached but he waved her off, showing himself to the table.

Sara looked up before he could say anything, seeming to sense he was there. Her expression wary, her eyes held questions. And no wonder.

But he had questions of his own and he wanted answers. Answers, and to experience again that lightness of youth she'd made him feel yesterday.

He hoped like hell he hadn't made another huge mistake over Sara Noland Richards.

Chapter 5

"Paul. This is a surprise."

The guarded look didn't leave her face. That's all right. He felt plenty wired, himself.

"I imagine it is. For me, too, if you want the truth. May I sit down?"

"Of course."

He removed his jacket and laid it over the back of one of the other chairs, then placed his hat on top.

"That's a handsome coat." Her softened consonants and slow speech inspired memories of hot, humid nights when his ship was docked in Charleston a few days before heading for hell. Just hearing her voice raised the temperature in the room a good five degrees.

"Thanks. Looks warm, too, I've just been informed." At her puzzled look he gave a lopsided smile. "Never mind."

The waitress came by and Paul ordered coffee. Except for a man sitting several tables away they had the dining room to themselves.

He eyed the empty place in front of her. "Have you ordered?"

"Yes. A sandwich. It's early but I didn't have anything else to do. I thought I might get out and see some of the city, but I'm afraid my winter coat won't stand up to your weather."

"I'm sure it doesn't get this cold in South Carolina."

"No, it doesn't."

His coffee and Sara's sandwich arrived together. In the silence, he took a moment to study her. Her hair fell in soft waves and curled under her chin, shorter than he remembered but still a rich brown, like her eyes. Laugh lines showed beside her mouth and eyes, as though she enjoyed life. Many women her age had thickened around the hips and waist, but she seemed as trim as when they were young. If anything, maturity had made her even more beautiful. But he'd learned long ago that beauty was indeed, only skin deep.

After a moment, Sara asked, "Would you like to split this? It's ham and cheese." As soon as she spoke, she looked up in alarm. It had been a ham and cheese sandwich she'd offered him on the "picnic" in the back of the station wagon just before he'd taken her virginity. He'd thought there would be no turning back in their relationship after that. How wrong he'd been.

He tried to keep his voice calm. "No, I don't think so, thanks." When he didn't say more, she seemed to relax. Did she honestly think he wouldn't remember?

Before taking a bite she said, "You didn't drive down here to make small talk, did you?"

"Maybe." He watched her take a small bite, saw the delicate movement of her jaw as she chewed and the tip of the napkin she raised to her mouth to touch the corner of her lips. She wrapped them around a straw to sip lemon water next, and just as in his youth, a longing to taste those lips surged through him. He fisted his hands and pressed them against his legs, fighting to control what his body naturally wanted.

Then he reminded himself of what she'd put him through, and that checked his desire. "I wanted to make sure you arrived back here safely."

"Yes, that was quite a storm yesterday," she said softly.

There was double meaning to her words again. Intentional? He was sure of it.

She took another sip through that damn straw, the action sending his pulse into overdrive.

"You weren't too anxious to chat with me yesterday. Why are you here, Paul?"

"A variety of reasons. Mainly, I thought I behaved a little foolishly, letting my emotions dictate my actions. I try never to do that anymore. Every time I have, it's caused trouble."

68

She put her sandwich down and sat back, giving him a cool look. "I'm so sorry to have been the cause of your backsliding into bad habits," she said stiffly. "Maybe you'd better go before I inadvertently do something else horrible."

"Don't be so sensitive. I said it was *my* flaw."

"You implied I brought it out."

"I didn't, either." He held up his hand to stop whatever she opened her mouth to say next. His brows knitted. He blew out a breath.

She looked down to her lap where she'd placed her hands. "I'm sorry. I'm nervous. I thought I knew exactly where I stood yesterday, and now I'm not sure." She looked back at him. Her eyes, liquid pools of rich, chocolate brown with tiny flecks of gold around the rim, looked as though they would overflow at any minute. "Where do I stand, Paul?"

She'd torn his heart to shreds but if he said that straight out he'd sound weak, not to mention the wounds such a blunt admission would tear open. Wounds he'd worked hard to cauterize so they'd heal.

And who knew how she'd react? The last thing he wanted was for her to cry and rush out without his getting what he came for: answers first, a light brush with feelings of the past, second. But without the power she'd exerted over him when he was a kid—she'd never have that again. No woman would.

"It was the shock of seeing you there," he mumbled.

"What? I couldn't hear you."

He cleared his throat. "I said, it was the shock of seeing you there. Looking so much like the girl I remembered. If I'd had time to prepare, I wouldn't have been such an ass."

She took a deep breath and looked somewhat calmer.

"Don't get me wrong, I still wouldn't have wanted you there, Sara. Seeing you stirred up a lot of bad memories."

Pain skittered through her eyes, but it was true, damn it, and better that she knew. His life wasn't what he might have wished, but he was settled. Then here she came, digging up emotions that were better left buried.

"Did you tell Becca you were coming to see me today?"

He gave her a steady look, more confident than he felt inside. "Yes. She encouraged it. Thought I'd feel better if I faced you."

"She's a very understanding...wife."

He watched her face. The denial and heartache he'd seen in her eyes yesterday was hidden today. He'd let her think Becca was his wife. He'd wanted to hurt her, to show that she wasn't the only one who'd found happiness with someone else. But today he'd woken with the conviction that their short relationship had been filled with too many lies.

"Becca isn't my wife. She's my sister-in-law."

"But, you led me to believe—"

"I *let* you believe, yes. I said she was Becca Steinert, and she is."

Sara cocked her head. "Why did you mislead me?"

"Because of that, I suppose." He nodded to her wedding band. "And because like I said earlier, I was being an ass."

"So, that young man, he's-he's...."

"My nephew, Luke."

"Oh, Lord!" She fell back in her chair, shook her head and stared at a point somewhere behind him. When she faced him, there was something more than caution in her expression. She seemed decided on something. "I thought he was your son. You look so much alike."

"I'm sure he thought of me as a second father when he was growing up. Either Mark or I was always around when he got into trouble. I don't have any children, thank God. It's the last kind of responsibility I'd want to be saddled with." He gazed directly into her eyes. "In fact, that was the only good thing about

70

not getting mail from you. I knew you'd have written pretty damn fast if we'd had an accident."

Sara looked as though he'd slapped her. For sure he'd shocked her. Part of him wanted to. Yes, and hurt her, too. There was no percentage in revealing how he really felt. That if they'd married, a child with her would have completed him. *Instead,* he thought bitterly, *she'd wasted no time completing some other guy.*

Easy, he warned himself. *That train of thought won't get you anywhere.*

Paul took a deep breath. "Luke is a good kid, and all the son I could wish for. None of the accountability and all of the fun." He shrugged. "I've loved him without reservation, but he's one of the few people I can say that about. I learned early on that loving someone can come back to bite you."

Her face paled. She reached forward, took the straw from the water, and tipped the glass back for a long drink. When she finished and dabbed at her mouth with the napkin she looked a little better. "It's not always bad, investing so much love it hurts. Sometimes things work out just fine."

He pointed a look at her ring again. "Is that the way it is with you and your husband?"

She twisted the ring self-consciously, glancing at it then back to him. "He was the husband of my heart, but he died. In Vietnam, ironically. He never saw his beautiful daughter, but I like to think he would have loved her as much as he said he loved me. I guess I could be wrong. Maybe he wouldn't have."

What was with her? Did she have a thing for guys going off to war? The poor bastard could have been there the same time I was.

Suddenly, he wished he hadn't come. He was wrong—talking to her wasn't making anything better. What in hell had he hoped to accomplish? He'd fought for years to recover from the damage Sara had caused, and he'd succeeded.

Pretty much.

Most of the time, the ache was like a bruise he couldn't help but poke. He noticed it and then went on. But being this close to Sara was like hitting his funny bone. He gritted his teeth, incapacitated until the piercing pain died away.

"If you think he would have loved her, then I'm sorry he never got the chance. Although being over there, thinking every day you might die and knowing your child was being born here would have been hard as hell. Thank God I didn't have that distraction weighing me down. At least he died knowing you loved him. I mean, I assume you wrote *him*...." He caught his breath at the bitterness he heard in his own words.

Tears rolled down Sara's cheeks, but she faced him squarely.

"Where was he assigned?" He softened his tone, but the grief he'd hidden over the years came roaring back, no longer dull but sharp as a bayonet between the ribs.

"I don't want to talk about this."

He nodded. "Okay. I can understand not wanting to talk about the war, or even about that time. So, what did you come to Iowa to talk about, Sara? Tell me the truth."

"I told you why I came, Paul. I'm not lying."

A challenge jumped to the tip of his tongue and then died before being born into words. Given free rein, he would have mentioned that in his experience, lying had been part of her persona. First to her parents and then to him.

Quietly, she rubbed the edge of her plate. Her hand shook slightly.

"I find it hard to believe you came all this way, after all these years, just to introduce yourself to my folks. As what? The girl their son used to love? Why now? And how did you think you'd get by with it? Didn't you think I'd set them straight?"

She pushed the half eaten sandwich away.

"Aren't you going to eat?"

"I'm not hungry anymore."

He took a taste of coffee, she took a swallow of water. No onlooker would have discerned the turmoil raging between them. The waitress approached to refresh their drinks.

Finally, Sara sighed deeply, and looked into Paul's eyes. "I wish I had something stronger than this water."

"That can be arranged if you really want it."

"No, it won't make this any easier. I might as well just tell you. A few days ago, my mother brought me an envelope. Inside were three letters. They were the last three letters you wrote me."

Paul listened, not quite comprehending. "Letters *I* sent? You just *now* got them?"

"There was some mix-up with the mail, but yes, they were from May 1970. In the last one you said you wouldn't write anymore if you didn't hear from me. And of course you didn't, because I never received the letter." After a beat, she added, "That's why I came here. I knew then that you loved me after all, no matter what I'd thought, and I wanted to meet your family. Even after all this time, I knew they'd want to know about..." Her gaze flew to his.

The pulse point in her neck throbbed and the rapid rise and fall of her chest showed her quickened breath. *An attack of nerves?*

"About..." he prompted, when she didn't continue.

"About...me. I thought they might want to know that their son had been in love. And that he was loved in return."

Something cracked inside, like a block of ice subjected to sudden high heat. The fissure was tiny, but in the glacial region of his heart, any movement was significant.

Paul stiffened his defenses. The letter snafu didn't really explain anything. For long years he'd suffered from the emptiness and disappointments of the war and Sara. He couldn't afford to let his guard down at the first excuse she offered.

"I have the letters with me. Would you like to see them?"

He huffed. "I wrote them, Sara. I think I know what they say." She wasted the crestfallen look she sent his way. He was in control again.

Although they simply tumbled from his lips, the words had played in his mind and heart for more years than he cared to acknowledge. "I know well what I wrote in the last letter, and if what you're saying is true, that explains why you didn't answer *that one*. What about all the letters before that? What about the changes in your life, the man you married, the child you bore? Didn't you think you owed me an explanation?"

Tears threatened to overflow her eyes yet again.

Damn! Tears won't change a thing after the hell she's put me through.

With steely resolve, he picked up his coffee cup. He'd finally asked the question that had plagued him. She owed him an answer—a decent, reasonable answer. He doubted anything she could say would make a difference, but he wanted her to *try* before he got up and walked out.

Like the steel magnolias he'd heard about, she seemed to gather herself and take command of her emotions. "I was told you were dead."

Her response wasn't decent or reasonable, but it was a surprise, and for that he couldn't help but smile. "Who told you that?"

"My father." Turning her head to look out the window instead of at him, she sat quietly. In profile, she appeared sad, perhaps a bit wistful. When she looked back at him, her face was shuttered. Her right hand went back to her left, worrying the little solitaire diamond. "This is the complicated part. My parents figured out about you."

Hell! He wished she'd stop playing with that damn ring. "Did they?"

"As soon as I told them I was writing to a sailor, they knew you were someone special."

"But you didn't write, did you? There were just a couple of notes at the beginning, and then nothing, while I—" He stopped, closing his eyes for a brief moment.

"I did write, Paul." She leaned forward to emphasize the words, staring at him directly. Her voice dropped, her eyes widened. If he hadn't known her so well, he might have believed her.

"I *did*. For weeks. I wrote dozens of letters." She heaved a sigh. "But because my parents didn't want me involved with anyone, they…the letters were never mailed. Mom picked mine up before the mailman arrived and stole yours before I came home. I never received a word from you the whole time you were gone. I imagined… Well, take what you thought about me and multiply it by a hundred. I had no one to talk to. Cindy wasn't any help, and besides, she didn't know how far we'd gone." Her voice dropped even lower. "I didn't tell anyone about us."

She sounded sincere. She certainly *was* upset, no question there. Her hands couldn't seem to stay still. She linked her fingers and unlinked them, twisted her ring, rubbed her knuckles. At the least, she was nervous. At the worst, she was hiding something.

Paul motioned the waitress over and asked for a couple of whiskeys. She disappeared and he leaned back in the chair, silently studying Sara.

When the drinks came, he pushed one toward her. "Here. It'll make you feel better." He waited until she picked up the heavy glass and drank. She coughed, scrunched her eyes and made a face. The second sip appeared to go down easier.

"How did you send the first letters, the only ones I received?"

Sara looked less shaken now, fingering the glass. The late afternoon sun glinted off the amber liquid and the gold of her ring. The damn ring that, forget letters and parents, still represented her betrayal. All hers.

"I mailed them from school. Wrote them after class and left them in the out tray in the office. Then I wrote from home. I didn't know anything out of the ordinary was happening, except I didn't hear from you." She spoke in a monotone, as though all of her energy had been drained. "Going to South Carolina after graduation was my father's idea. It seemed right at the time. And then things happened so fast—"

"I'm *sure*." Did she really think using the excuse of being carried away by events, being swept off her feet by some other man would mean shit to him?

She stopped for a deep breath, giving her head a shake. "Anyway, I didn't know about any of the rest until a few days ago when my mother told me what she'd done."

75

"You should have found a way to contact me, Sara. Once you went weeks and didn't hear from me, you should have found a way. And you would have, if you'd loved me." Where Sara had taken tentative sips of the whiskey, Paul lifted his glass and nearly drained it.

The gold flecks in her eyes burned when she snapped her head up. "And the same can be said for *you*, Paul. I could only have meant so much to you, despite your fine words of undying love and how you'd come back for me. There were people at Little Creek, friends of yours, who could have contacted me, but you didn't ask. When you got home you found Cindy, but you couldn't find me? You didn't even try, did you?" Sitting straighter in the chair, her voice rose correspondingly. "*Did* you?"

"No, I didn't. After the concert, that first night, I should have stayed away from you, but I couldn't. That was my failing, not yours. I knew all along that you might change your mind. You were young, but all you had to do was be up front with me. One lousy Dear John letter would have done the trick. It would been hard to deal with, but not as hard as all those months of wondering."

He shook his head, knowing she couldn't begin to understand what he'd been through. "I sure as hell didn't want to compound my humiliation by making myself a bigger fool than I already was. Add the fact that you were underage, and you might figure out yourself why I didn't involve anyone else."

Paul tossed back the last of his whiskey and stood. "Okay, so your parents screwed with the mail. I left in March. When you didn't hear from me by April, you should have known something was wrong. You knew Mitch's name, Sara. You knew the ship, and obviously you knew how you could find my parents. If you'd wanted to, you could have reached me. Unlike me, you had nothing to lose by contacting people to help you. Instead, you found someone else to get in bed with. And pretty damn fast, the poor son of a bitch."

Fitting his hat low on his brow, he picked up his jacket and laid it over his arm. "As it was, your father was almost right. If I hadn't left the Swift boat that morning, I would have been killed when it was attacked that afternoon. A twist of fate, really, when you consider I would have been willing to trade places with any of the guys on board. I already felt half dead, thanks to you."

He took a deep breath. Damn! He'd given her too much, admitting the control she'd had over him. "Luckily, I got over that feeling, and I got over you. Once I made up my mind, it didn't take as long as I'd thought."

76

Burning Bridges

Throwing some bills on the table, he took one more look at her, seeing the girl she had been in the woman she now was. She was older, yes, but he still sensed the indefinable quality that had first drawn him to her. God, a part of him still loved her. And he hated that in himself.

Fisting his hand under the coat, he once again quashed the anger and pain he'd kept at bay for so long. "I still wish you hadn't come, but at least now I can stop wondering what happened. Have a safe trip home."

Pride filled him. He'd not only survived the encounter, but prevailed. Now he could obey the command to tuck the dreams and memories into the back of his mind and forget her.

From the lobby, he stole a surreptitious glance. Not only didn't she appear to have moved a muscle, she looked completely lost. With every ounce of will power he could muster, he fought the urge to march back into the dining room, take her in his arms and kiss her until neither of them remembered the heartache.

Until they banished the past forever.

He left the building before giving in. *Thank God.*

* * * *

The drone of the jet's engines lulled Sara. Another thirty-five minutes remained until she had to lock the table tray and bring her seat into the upright position. Then she'd be caught up in the inevitable hectic dash through O'Hare to catch the connecting flight to Charleston.

Using the receipt for the paperback she'd bought in Omaha to mark her place, she closed the book. Might as well; she couldn't recall anything from the last two pages, anyway. Absently, not really tasting the coffee, she drank from the Styrofoam cup before letting her thoughts drift to Paul and the confrontation of the previous afternoon.

She'd come so close to telling him her marriage was a sham, and about Paula. But he'd made clear he didn't want to know anything real about her. He'd made up his mind and developed his fantasies about who she was, and facts be damned.

Surprisingly, she hadn't cried. Not when he left and not later when she'd made her two calls to South Carolina. Paula had been in the middle of something and their conversation was short, but Sara had only called to say hello, anyway. After the upheaval with Paul, she wanted to hear her daughter's voice, to reaffirm that the love she and Paul shared, which seemed almost ugly now, had resulted in something truly beautiful.

Matthew sounded excited when she told him how anxious she was to return home. He confirmed that he'd meet her at the airport then said he had something to discuss with her. He ended by saying he loved her. That last bothered her, and not just because she couldn't respond with the same emotion. Perhaps hearing a man say that he loved her so close to reliving the past with Paul was too much to handle.

Her mother would wonder why Sara didn't call her, but the reason was simple. At the thought of her mother, anger—deep, dark, soul-consuming anger— washed over her. Before, she'd rationalized what her parents had done. Meddling in her life had been wrong and hurtful, but in the long run, nothing would have been changed for her and Paul. He had died, that was the extent of the story, and whether their letters had continued or not, the fact of his death remained. She'd believed that three days ago.

Now, the events of the past had changed everything. She'd been denied a life with Paul. Their daughter had grown up without a father. Every single moment of her adult years, every instant of Paula's life would have been different if not for her parents' interference. Maybe Paul wouldn't have grown into the hardened man he was if their love had been allowed to flourish.

Even if things hadn't worked out fairy tale style, she would have controlled her own destiny, not been moved like a pawn in a game she hadn't been aware she was playing.

She gripped the Styrofoam cup so hard her nails punctured it. Coffee leaked all over the tray table. Like her happiness had drained from their cup of love.

She smiled wryly at the flowery analogy. Using a napkin to soak up the spill was simple. Too bad life's mistakes couldn't be cleaned up as easily. How could she ever forgive her mother? The sad answer was, maybe she never would.

The steady hum of the plane combined with a virtually sleepless night, caused her eyelids to drop but she didn't sleep. Instead, she saw Paul as he stalked across the yard toward her. The grim line of his mouth and the barely controlled violence of his muscles would have frightened her to death if she hadn't already been in the process of fainting.

The fierceness of his look the first day had been matched by his words and attitude the next. At first, she'd been optimistic that he would listen with his heart and not his mind. But nothing about the Paul Steinert she'd seen in the past two days was soft or forgiving. He was someone she didn't know.

Nor did she want to.

They'd faced the past and instead of coming to terms with what had happened, they continued hurting each other. The chances of ever seeing Paul again were non-existent, so she let most of what he said go.

What she couldn't get past, would *never* find it in her heart to forgive, was his comment about not having the distraction of a child. Children were a responsibility he hadn't wanted? Their child, instead of being a symbol of their love, would have been a *burden*? Worse, an accident. Something unintended and unwanted. Sara shivered at the thought of his reaction if she'd written him when she was pregnant. Thank God he never knew!

"I'll never tell him," she vowed in a whisper. "He'll never know. *Never*."

Instead of twisting her ring nervously as she had the day before, she wrapped her right hand over her left, protecting the set of rings and the lies they represented.

No, the lives *they represent.*

She'd raised her daughter as a Richards but had imbued stories of the absent husband and father with all of Paul Steinert's qualities, the qualities she'd fallen in love with, not as he was now. Her daughter had become a fine woman. Not knowing her father hadn't slowed her down or kept her from finding a wonderful man of her own.

Sara herself had lived a full life without Paul. For the past several years, Matthew had helped her through the difficult times and shared laughter in the good ones. Since she was an empty-nester, his soft and loving touch had been welcome on those nights she was too lonely to be without someone to talk to or hold.

Yes, Paul could stay out of their lives, as he had for these many years. They would continue without him just fine.

They *would*, she told herself with conviction. *She* would.

She had to.

Chapter 6

"Sara, did you hear me?" Matthew Abrams had casually delivered his news in the lobby of the IMAX theater in Charleston. Making the announcement in front of hundreds of strangers, as well as Paula and Dan, meant she couldn't express herself. Instead, she had to mind her manners when she really wanted to throw something.

I can't take Matthew's leaving on top of everything else. Sara had been home a little over a week, but she was unsettled and tired. Most nights, her sleep was interrupted by a new variation of her old nightmare.

Instead of Paul's father, the giant at her door was Paul himself. He inspected the grown child he demanded to see, but instead of taking Paula away, he spun on Sara. "You're a liar," the nightmarish Paul screamed in each dream. "I am not the father of this accident."

Sara woke each night at that point, not frightened but angry. That she believed his sentiment would be just what she dreamed, affirmed her decision not to tell him about Paula.

Closing her eyes, she rubbed her temple. The stress of finding a location for the gallery and her trip to Iowa was taking its toll. Now, one of her best friends was leaving. How could she handle everything?

"Mom!" Paula shook her mother's arm.

Sara snapped her head up. She must have appeared as addled as she felt, for Matthew reached down and took her hand. That was a sure sign of worry because no PDA—public displays of affection—was generally his policy. When she looked up, his deep blue eyes showed real concern.

Pulling herself together, she even managed a tiny smile. "Yes, I heard." For someone who didn't like change, she was certainly getting barrels of it. Was the whole universe under a full moon, or something? "Don't get me wrong, Matthew, the promotion to full Colonel and a headquarters assignment is wonderful, but why must you go to California?"

He squeezed her hand. "Have to go where the Corps sends me, Sara. I was lucky to stay here as long as I did."

"When do you leave?" She wished he'd broken the news when they were alone. Then she could have smoothed her hands through his rich hair, as black as night, and held him. His kisses would let her know that even though they'd be separated by the whole country, she wouldn't be alone.

"I report after the first of the year, but I'll make several trips out beforehand. And I might take a week or two of leave over Christmas."

Dan shook Matthew's hand. "Congratulations."

"Thanks."

"Say—" Dan stroked his chin as though thinking, "—isn't Pendleton right on the ocean?"

"Sure is. Beautiful weather in southern California. I'll be deployed overseas a fair amount of the time, but it's sure a nice place to come home to."

"Matthew, you'll be going overseas?" Worry for him invaded Sara's mind. Every evening, news anchors detailed the continuing war in Afghanistan and Iraq, and the Marines had a heavy presence in both places.

After 9/11, she worried Matthew would be sent over, and she'd only begun to know him. How hard would it be to worry about him now, when he meant so much to her? In those dark days, even Dan had wanted to join the Corps and go, but he'd been too old. Selfishly, she was glad Paula had been spared the anguish of sending off a man she had already started to love, but Matthew didn't have the protection of age—he was already in the military and they could send him anywhere they wanted.

"Don't worry about Matthew going overseas, Sara. Worry about him on the beach with those young, bikini-clad, Marine groupies. They're more dangerous than a war in some foreign country."

Matthew lightly punched Dan's shoulder. "Shh! That's a secret. Why do you ask about Pendleton?"

"I've been thinking about places to vacation when I need a break from school next winter. Since Paula swears she's not going to Chicago, maybe I'll take a few days and visit you. By then you should have the lay of the land."

Sara swung her head toward her daughter. Paula distanced herself from Dan, seeming to watch a family enter the lobby. Her movement appeared to be casual, but her stiff back and studied silence gave her away.

"Try to find me a redhead who speaks French, okay?" At that, Paula whirled on Dan. Her face showed anger then disappointment, but she didn't speak. He avoided looking at her.

Again, Matthew squeezed Sara's hand. "I'll do nothing of the kind. Besides, if Paula doesn't go with you, you and I both know where you'll spend every free moment, and it won't be on the west coast."

Dan gave a one shoulder shrug. "I was just kidding."

"Sure you were," Paula said bitingly, her Southern accent strong. "Dan will most certainly be at liberty to spend his free time anywhere he wishes next year."

Glancing over Dan's shoulder she said, "It looks like they're letting people in now." She plucked her ticket from his hand and started toward the theater entrance without waiting for the others. His face red with anger or embarrassment, or both, Dan stared after her.

"Dan." Sara placed her hand on his arm, "Talk to her."

His expression looked bleak. "Don't you think I have?" he muttered. "I've given her time and space, I've told her I love her, I've tried to make the whole move seem like an adventure we could have together. Pleading hasn't moved her and neither have ultimata. In one breath she says she loves me and in the next she says she'll miss me when I go. I'm beginning to think she has some ulterior motive for wanting me gone."

"You can't believe that."

He shook his head, looking miserable. "I don't know what else to believe." After a moment, he walked off to follow Paula.

Sara stood where she was. Matthew didn't head toward the theater, either, just waited for her to make a move. He was powerfully built and had a commanding presence that others seemed to respect, so a buffer of privacy existed as people moved around them.

"I'm worried, Matthew. They've always seemed perfect for each other, and I hate they're arguing over something that should be so simple."

"You think it's simple?" He tugged her around to face him. "What do you think Dan should do?"

"He's got talent and intelligence and he should develop it. If Northwestern is the best place, then that's where he should be."

"What about Paula?"

"If she loves Dan as much as I always thought she did, she should be packed by the time he comes home tomorrow night." Sara smiled at Matthew's raised brows. "Not a very modern view for a woman, is it?"

"Have you told her your opinion?"

"Lord, no. I don't want to arrange her life. Going with Dan has to be what she wants, not what I think is best for her."

The lobby had almost emptied. Matthew guided Sara to the theater entrance and handed their tickets to the usher. "Would you take your own advice?"

"If I were Paula's age and the man I loved asked me to go off on a mad affair, you bet."

He was quiet as they climbed near to the top where Paula and Dan had saved them seats. Sara couldn't believe the two younger people were the same she'd seen together for years. Careful not to touch, they also weren't talking. For two people in love they looked grim. *What can I do to help them?*

Nothing! Stay out of it!

"How about if you were your age?"

Sara turned. One step up, she was able to look him in the eye. "Hmm? What are you talking about?"

"I wanted to talk to you about this when I picked you up at the airport last week, but you came home in a strange mood. I want you to come on a mad affair with me. To California, when I leave at the end of the year."

84

She couldn't have been more surprised. "Listen to you," she said in a lowered voice. "All this time I thought we were *having* a mad affair."

He didn't smile. "I'm serious, Sara."

"Matthew, I don't know—"

He pressed his fingers to her lips. "Just think about it. I love you, and I don't want to leave you here. Your business is being forced to close and you've said yourself you don't think you can't get financing for a new building. Start over out there. With me."

Her stomach churned. She swallowed hard and tried to think of what to say.

His eyes closed for a brief moment. "I hate that you didn't say yes right away. Give the idea some time. Okay?"

"I will." She cupped his cheek with her hand. "I'll probably think of little else." *Then* he smiled.

The lights flickered, warning that the show was about to begin. They took their seats. Without illumination, the theater was pitch black. She couldn't see her hand in front of her face, but Matthew managed to find her lips for a quick kiss. "I've heard this film is really good," he whispered.

The last thing in the world Sara wanted was to sit for an hour and watch a movie about the moon. On one side of her was a man she cared for deeply but who wanted what she wasn't sure she could give. On the other side were two people she dearly loved who were hurting and therefore lashing out at each other. Inside, her mind tumbled in turmoil, worries about the gallery mixed with the nightmares featuring Paul.

She didn't need to see a film about the Earth's satellite. Lunacy, loon, lunatic. All words related to the moon's effect on people. Tonight, for her, the moon was full, and she felt like the madwoman.

* * * *

Paula couldn't wait to get her mother alone. As soon as dinner ended, she suggested that they excuse themselves, and when the door swung closed on the ladies' room, she was ready. "Mom, what's up with Matthew tonight? I've never seen him so touchy-feely."

Sara blushed. Her mother actually *blushed*. What was going on here? Dan must be right about Matthew loving her mother and maybe this blush meant the feeling was reciprocated.

Dan. Paula tightened her mouth and tried to put thoughts of him aside, concentrating instead on her mom. "I mean, he held your hand before, during and after the film. And he kissed you while we waited for our table. In *public*."

Sara used her fingers to fluff her hair. A stall came open and she stepped in, without commenting. When she exited the stall and they both stood at the counter, Paula pressed her point. "If I didn't know better, I'd say Matthew asked you to marry him."

"He didn't." Their eyes met in the mirror. "It's the thought of leaving. Men get attached to places sometimes, just as women do, and he's lived here nearly six years. That's a rare situation for a Marine."

Paula waggled her brows. "I don't think it's Parris Island Matthew is attached to."

Sara returned Paula's look with one of her own. "Let's talk about you and Dan."

She felt the smile leave her face. "Let's not and say we did."

"Are you two okay?"

Paula sighed. "No, but I have no doubt things will work out eventually. I'll have to move. I don't think I can afford the mortgage for our house on my own. Dan has a friend who's interested in making an offer."

"Oh, honey. I know you love living there. And it is a perfect location. But—"

Curious, Paula stared at Sara's reflection and waited for her to continue.

"Are you sure you've thought through staying here when Dan goes?"

Paula laughed. "Dan would be surprised to hear you say that, Mom. He thinks we're just alike—stuck in limbo because we're afraid of risk."

Sara's forehead creased. "He thinks that?"

"Let me just clear this up. If Matthew *did* ask you to marry him—leave your business, your home, and me and Nana—would *you*?"

Her mother assumed the classic *I'm-the-mother* posture. Her head rose a fraction, her back straightened and her shoulders dropped back and squared. Paula rolled her eyes mentally. Her mom thought nothing could touch her when she stood like that.

"That's different."

"Right." Paula pursed her lips and applied fresh lipstick. "Speaking of Nana, have you talked to her since you got back from the Midwest? She called the other day and said you haven't phoned her."

"Right now, I don't have anything to say to your grandmother."

Paula's reflection's freshly painted mouth dropped open.

Sara continued before Paula could formulate a response. "And before you ask any more questions, take my advice and leave it alone. I have some issues to deal with before I talk to her. If she should call you again, feel free to tell her that I'll get with her when I'm ready, and she'd do well to stay out of my way until then." She smoothed her dress and picked up her bag, looking every bit the unruffled Southern lady.

But Paula knew. There was a fire-breathing dragon lurking below the cool surface when her mother used that firm tone and words like "take my advice," or "she'd do well." What issues did her mom have that involved her grandmother, too?

She'd let it drop for now, but only because she had enough issues of her own. Paula picked up the denim bag that matched her jacket and slung it over her shoulder.

She and Dan wore their normal jeans and tee shirts to the IMAX and for dinner at Sal's, whereas Matthew and her mother dressed in what Paula considered work clothes. That was dress, or skirt and blouse for her mother, and slacks and sports jacket for Matthew. Even in this Matthew and her mother seemed just right for each other. So, how lost would her mother be when Matthew left?

"Paula?" She turned and faced her mom. Sara hesitated before speaking. "Do you love Dan? I mean really love him?"

"Yes."

"Do you know how often that kind of love comes along? Have you considered what your life will be if you let him go? You're used to being a couple. I'm afraid you don't realize how empty the nights can be, and the days, too, when you're alone."

There was the certainty of experience in those words. Her mother was trying to help, but Paula wasn't a child. She had given their dilemma consideration from every angle. The move wasn't right for her. If Dan couldn't respect that and love her enough to stay true and come home when he was finished with his adventure, well, she'd wasted her time with a rogue.

"Don't worry about me, Mom. I'll visit you and you can come up. We'll see a lot of each other—even more than we're used to—and you, Nana and I will take care of each other, just like when I was in school." Throwing an arm over her mother's shoulders, she opened the door. "By the time Dan comes back, we'll be three crazy, single ladies raising cats together," Paula confided with a laugh.

But her mother's warning left a chill inside. Paula's own words sounded brave and encouraging, but a pall hung over her. The two men she cared for most in the world would both be gone after the first of the year. She'd miss Matthew's calm and confidence, his humor and good advice, and because she'd worry more about her mom with him gone. But Dan… When Dan left, the light would go out in her world.

Or at least she'd thought so, until he made that snide comment about a redhead who spoke French. He'd been trying all week to get under her skin, and with that one sentence he'd not only accomplished his goal, he'd stepped on every nerve. It would serve him right if she never said anything else to him in French.

Burning Bridges

Tears stung her eyes. She wanted to throw something or at least stamp her foot, but of course she could never do those things except in the privacy of home. *I swear, Dan Tanner, if you turn out to be a rogue, I'll...I'll...*

Want to curl up and die.

* * * *

Paul checked the spreadsheet figures once again. "Becca, are you sure the price you gave me for the silage is right?"

"I checked it the last time you asked. What was that? Five minutes or so ago?"

Half his mouth tipped up. "How does Mark keep from pulling his hair out, married to you?"

Becca closed the ledger where she noted all receipts and bills. "He counts to ten when I irritate him and then thinks of the good time we'll have that night in bed. The man literally bows down and worships me after—"

"That's definitely more than I needed to know." He closed the spreadsheet. "Everything looks real good. I mean, *real* good."

"Wonderful!" She shelved the ledger. "That new tractor will be paid off by the first of the year."

"By your stone age calculations, yes," he said. She swatted at his arm, making him smile. "And by my state of the art computations, too."

Becca liked maintaining the accounts by hand, but Paul had jumped into the computer world with both feet, something he shared with his nephew.

"Do you have a few minutes?" she asked, taking her seat across the desk from him again.

He swiveled to face her. "Sure, what's up?"

She faced him squarely, her gray eyes meeting his without flinching. Becca had been a pretty girl, but she was a beautiful woman. She was much younger than he, but when he'd come home from the Navy all the single men in the area

89

talked about Rebecca Heiler's stormy gray eyes, blond hair and flawless complexion. Suggestive talk of her soft curves or trim figure earned a glare, or once, even a punch from Mark, so it came as no surprise when he started dating Becca regularly.

Because she'd also been raised on a farm, Paul had assumed she knew the ins and outs, ups and downs that came with their life. But he'd been amazed at how she'd thrived in their family, the fun and laughter she brought each day, the way she fearlessly took him on and put him in his place when needed. He'd never known a woman who worked as hard and enjoyed it as much. Or a person who gave as much love as Becca did. She was the one woman he trusted implicitly.

So, he was blindsided when she said, "I've been waiting for you to be straight with me about Sara Richards."

The walls went up, and after the initial surprise of her question, he knew he'd show no emotion. Shrugging he asked, "What do you want to know?"

"She's the one, isn't she? It's because of her you broke your engagement with Betty Thurman and have shunned a serious relationship with every woman since."

"Betty Thurman was a long time ago. Thank God I came to my senses before it was too late, or we would have hated each other within a year. Besides, it didn't take her long to find someone else and she's got a passel of grandkids now, so don't try to tell me I made a mistake with her."

"They should be your grandchildren."

He snorted out a laugh. "Forget Betty Thurman. Forget grandkids. When Luke gets married I'll help you and Mark spoil his kids."

"So what did this Sara woman do to you?"

Paul sighed. "I don't suppose you'd take 'none of your business' for an answer?"

She didn't even consider a moment. "No."

Running his hands through his hair, he took time to think. He could tell a lie, and because she was Becca and trusted him as much as he did her, she'd believe him. But he couldn't do that, not to Becca. "I met her in Virginia, before I left for

Nam. She was very young and made a few promises she couldn't keep." One shoulder rose and dropped. "It was no big deal, really. She's just all tied up with the war going on now, and it's brought back memories of those times I don't like to talk about. It's all in the past. So I wasn't happy when she showed up unexpectedly."

She digested what he said and nodded. "I can see that. Mark told me once that you had a time of it, adjusting after the war. Not that we talked behind your back," she added, "but I was concerned for him. He felt guilty for not being able to take care of things himself when your dad got sick."

"That's crazy. How could I stay in the service when I was needed here? Mark has carried more than his share on the farm. He's got nothing to feel guilty about."

She smiled. "Well, that was a long time ago. Like Betty Thurman," she teased. She cast him a shrewd look from the corner of her eye. "You know what I noticed about Sara Richards?"

He sighed disgustedly and shook his head. "I'm sure you're going to tell me."

"She didn't look at *you* like your relationship was no big deal. And I also noticed how pretty she is."

"And did you notice the wedding ring on her finger?"

"Of course. I'm not suggesting you have an affair. But a wedding ring doesn't mean you can't be friends, does it? And she lives in South Carolina, where your ship's reunion is."

"South Carolina is a fairly large state, Becca." He put a patronizing edge to his words.

"It's a hop, skip and jump from Charleston to Beaufort, where she lives, Paul."

Well, shit. She'd thrown his own tone back at him.

"I'm not going to the reunion. I cancelled my trip, so there was no need for you to add up the mileage on the *Rand McNally*." A twinge of guilt struck when he saw her face fall, but his remorse disappeared when her expression went from crestfallen to determined.

"Really? I don't think Mark knows you cancelled."

Great. Now she'd have his brother butting into his private life, too. While it was true that he didn't like remembering the war years, he'd liked the men he served with. Beginning about a decade after the war, every few years he'd receive an invitation for the ship's reunion. In the past, he'd tossed them aside. But this year, his old friend, Mitch Hamilton, served as coordinator. Mitch had added a personal note, saying he hoped Paul would attend, and in a moment of weakness he'd reserved the hotel and flight.

"When did you cancel?"

Paul hadn't realized Becca was talking. "I don't know. Last week, I guess. There's too much to do around here to take off for some party I don't really want to go to, anyway."

"So, you cancelled after Sara said she lived in Beaufort." Before he could protest, Becca stood and leaned over the desk. "You're a big coward, Paul Steinert." She spun on her heel and left him unable to retaliate.

"That was her plan all along. Grab the last word and beat me over the head with it," he muttered, clearing the desk. *Besides, she's wrong. The timing might look suspicious, but I'd decided to cancel my reunion reservations long before Sara came.*

He flipped the light switch in the office, called out goodnight, and left the main house for his own cottage. His empty, cold cottage. Damn it! Before Sara arrived, he'd been settled. Happy, even. Content with the hand life had dealt him.

God, I'm a lousy liar.

* * * *

Two days later, the landline in the barn rang. "It's for you, Uncle Paul." Luke handed him the receiver when Paul came down from the hayloft.

"Paul Steinert."

"You old dog! It's Mitch Hamilton."

"Who you calling an old dog? It's great to hear your voice. How're things going?"

"Fine, just fine. Except I looked through the list of reunion attendees and saw you'd cancelled."

Paul noticed Luke working in one of the stalls near enough to listen. He turned his back only to see Mark pouring a cup of coffee out of the Thermos close by. His talk with Becca a couple of nights ago rang through his head. She said she'd tell Mark about his cancelled trip and now here was Mitch, making a personal phone call. Subtlety wasn't a Steinert trait.

"Yeah, Mitch, I thought I could make it, but then things piled up here. Maybe next time."

"Paul, besides the fact I was looking forward to seeing you again and shooting the shit for a few days, I had a personal reason for hoping you'd make it to this reunion. I have a business proposition I wanted to talk over with you."

"Really? Like what?" Even as he said the words, a small drum of excitement beat a note in his chest.

"I bought a charter fishing company last spring. I checked the boats over well and went through the books with a fine-toothed comb. Everything seemed all right. But I had trouble all summer keeping the engines running right. Had to cancel a few big charters. I wondered if you might be willing to take a look and see what I must have missed."

Disbelief made him laugh. "I'm a farmer. You know? Farmer, fisherman. They might start with the same letter, but…"

"Still the smart ass I remember. That's another reason I'd like you to come to the reunion. We were good friends. You had my back and I had yours. I can trust you. I need you, Paul, pure and simple. How long's it been since you stood on any deck and felt the swells of the ocean under you?"

Too damn long. "You have ocean-going boats in that fleet?"

"Yes. Smaller boats for the river and sound, and two big ones for deep-sea fishing. The water off the Carolina coast is great."

If Paul wished for a job opportunity, anything related to the ocean would do. The dream of seeing the world and feeling the waves beneath his feet was what drove him to join the Navy as soon as he could. As much as he loved his family, coming home to take over the farm when his dad fell ill had been one of the greatest disappointments of his life. Only the love he had for family had gotten him through the change.

His heart raced. The receiver practically cracked with the grip he had on it. He raised his head and saw Mark staring at him. *Go*, Mark mouthed silently.

"It sounds real interesting, but I'm not sure I can reverse the cancellations now, Mitch."

"The hotel still has a room. I'll finagle the rate if you can get a plane ticket. I'll arrange a rental car here if you want one. When you go down to look at the company, everything will be paid for, of course. Why don't you schedule your departure from Charleston for a day or two after the convention ends?"

A swell of excitement caught him off guard. "I think I can work it out. I'll let you know the details as soon as I have them."

He heard a sound of relief from the other end of the line. "Several of the guys have mentioned they were happy to see your name on the attendee list, Paul. It'll be a good time. But I'm even more relieved you'll take a look at my boats. You always were the best mechanic I knew."

"Just so you know, I'm a—"

"Farmer, yeah, yeah. John Deere or Evinrude, an engine's an engine. So, I'll talk to you later."

"Oh, one more thing, Mitch. You said you'd make reservations for when I go to look at the boats. Where is this charter company?"

"In Port Royal, less than two hours from Charleston. The docks and boathouse are on a creek, but real close to where it meets the river. From there it's just a short distance out to the ocean. Greatest damn fishing you've ever seen." Mitch's excitement infected Paul.

"Only saltwater or freshwater, too?"

Burning Bridges

"Both, although we don't do any freshwater work right now. I'd like to, though. Maybe you can give me some ideas after you see the operation. Listen, it's winter out there, right? Snow and all that shit? Consider staying an extra week instead of just a day and we'll test the boats. You know, have a little shakedown cruise and do some fishing, too. Whadya say?"

It was tempting, really tempting. "You think I got nothing to do just because there's a measly foot of snow on the ground?" Paul saw Mark's brows rise. "I don't think I can be gone a week, Mitch."

Mark straightened and fixed him with a laser-like stare. "You should go," he said.

God, he wanted to. When had he become so restless? Stupid question. He could pinpoint the day, the hour. The woman responsible.

"Well, maybe I can work something out with my brother." Mark grinned at him and nodded in satisfaction.

"Great! When you call with your schedule, I'll get you a room in Beaufort. It's only six or seven miles from the dock and the hotels are much nicer than anything in Port Royal."

If Mitch added something more, it was wasted on Paul. They must have said their goodbyes, because the next thing he consciously noticed was the dial tone sounding in his ear.

Of all the shitty deals. They say for everything good there's a price to pay, and he'd spent a good bit of his life weighing the cost of what he wanted against the reward. Mitch's offer would be a welcome diversion, but the price of spending time in the town where Sara lived might be just a little too rich.

95

Chapter 7

Monday afternoon, Sara entered The First Bank of South Carolina. Normally, this filled her with pleasure. An architectural anachronism, the building boasted exterior white columns and interior marble floors. The soaring ceiling, crowned with a painted rotunda, had always meant safety, in the old-fashioned sense of the word.

"Give us your money, and you can rest easy. Bring us your trust, and we'll give you ours," the bank said to her. Usually, that is. Today she heard, "*You* want a loan? Some people are born to be disappointed."

Sitting in a leather chair outside the bank president's office, she tried to will herself confidence, but it was tough going. She'd asked a few close friends in the Beaufort business community about rental availability and prices. Their answers were disappointing. She wanted a space on Bay Street, the area most frequented by tourists and locals, but the space she could afford didn't provide the space she wanted. Prices on the islands were even higher if the property had walk-by potential. If she was going to make a move, she wanted to make a splash at the same time, or what was the point?

Of course, whether she made a splash or simply sunk into obscurity was a great deal in the hands of the man she waited to see. Rob Taylor's wife loved painting, so as patron as well as bank president, he'd taken particular interest in the area galleries, including her aunt's. When Sara assumed more responsibility for Barbara's business, she had gravitated to Rob for advice. His recommendations were invariably conservative, which had served the gallery well until now. But she worried over what he would say about her new ideas.

That worry led to the next, Paula and Dan. In the years they'd been together, she'd never seen them act the way they had Saturday night. She'd called several times on Sunday, but neither had answered.

Of course, not answering their phone didn't mean they weren't home. Perhaps they just didn't want to talk. She understood that feeling. Like a stubborn child, she still hadn't talked to her mother. Every day she returned to the house to find at least one message on her answering machine. The time would come soon when she'd have to face the chore, but it wasn't quite yet.

"Sara, you can go in." Amanda, Rob's secretary smiled at her as she hung up the phone.

"Thanks." She stood and smoothed her dark brown wool skirt. With the muted gold of her sweater set and understated plain gold jewelry, she projected the right image, she thought. Stable, trustworthy. The kind of person to whom the bank would consider making a loan.

She took a deep breath and entered the office.

Tall and distinguished looking, Rob walked around the desk and toward her. Gray streaked his brown hair, and lines from being in the sun and on the water creased the area around his eyes.

He held out his hand and clasped hers warmly. "Sara, you're looking well."

"Thanks, Rob. You, too."

"Sit." He motioned toward a leather wingback chair, taking the adjacent chair after she was seated. "What can I do for you?"

"I received an eviction notice for the gallery, effective the first of the year."

He frowned. "Oh, dear. The gallery's been in that space for a good long time."

"Yes, it has. I've considered closing up shop."

"Really?" His expression showed interest but not dismay, which made Sara even more jumpy. "What would you do?"

Matthew's invitation from Saturday night flashed through her mind. One of the reasons she hadn't given him an answer right away was her desire to save the gallery. She couldn't do both, work at making her business successful and follow Matthew. She loved him as much as she could ever love a man. Not with the open, willing trust she'd given Paul, but as an adult, with all the baggage and therefore caution that entailed. However, moving across country, putting that much of her future in his hands…? She needed to think hard before giving Matthew or anyone that much power again.

"I considered looking for work in one of the Charleston galleries. I even went so far as to contact one or two of the owners I know."

"That seems like a feasible plan. At least in Charleston you'd be closer to Paula."

Would I? Only if she's as wary of Dan as I am of Matthew. "Yes, but Rob, I'd really like to keep the gallery. A short while ago I visited a friend's farm. The place has been in his family for generations, and you can feel their pride in maintaining the legacy. I know the gallery hasn't been in our family very long, but I've decided I don't want to give Barbara's life's work up without a fight. It's my life's work, too, after all, and I'm proud of the low-country perspective we provide. The artists, the paintings—they mean more than just a paycheck."

Rob nodded, steepling his fingers where his hands met over his stomach and tapping his fingertips. "I understand what you're saying, but the realities are this. Rental space per square foot is high in town where you could benefit from tourist traffic. Even those businesses located on Bay Street haven't done as well as expected the last couple of years, what with bad weather and higher fuel prices causing a drop-off in visitors to the city." He paused for a moment. Sara knew all of this but hearing the facts from Rob made them even more grim. "What is it you want to do?"

"I'd like to be on Bay Street. I'd like to expand. I've spoken with my artists, and except for Lynne Andrews, whose husband is sick and requiring more care, they want to keep selling through Beauty by Beaufort. I know there are several art shops in town already, but I have a few ideas that will distinguish me from the others."

"Do you have a proposal?"

Silently, she handed him the sheets outlining her plans and financial information. He studied them before looking up, and she saw the news in his eyes.

"Sara, you've done well with what Barbara left you. Your profits are good for the size shop you have and the limited niche you've carved out, but it isn't enough to rent or buy space like you want. Even for less floor space than you have now, you'd stretch yourself too thin to cover emergencies."

She'd feared this estimation. "I can't give up yet, Rob. Isn't there some way I could get a loan?"

He stood and walked behind his desk then flipped a Rolodex file. "Do you know Nicole Brown? She's got a small coffee shop on Lady's Island and she's also had thoughts of expanding over this way."

"I don't know her. What does my business have to do with a coffee shop?"

Rob pulled the card from the holder and placed it in front of him. "Maybe nothing. But let me do some checking. I'll get back with you as soon as I can." He came to stand beside her. "Don't get your expectations up, though. I really think in this business climate, and with the number of galleries you already have as competitors, you'd be smart to consider that move to Charleston."

Sara rose to her feet. "Thanks for your time, Rob."

"Of course! I'd be hurt if you went somewhere else for advice. I'll tell you a secret. I'm retiring at the end of this year."

"Oh, how wonderful. I know Millie will be happy to see more of you."

"Yes, we're going to travel a bit and spend time with the kids and grandkids out west. Barbara was a good friend, and I consider you one, as well. One of my goals before I leave is to make sure you're on your feet."

Forcing a smile, she said, "I appreciate that. After all Aunt Barbara did for me, I just can't lose her business."

But she had the sick feeling that she might.

* * * *

On a crisp afternoon two days later, Sara drove across the bridge to Lady's Island. She'd wanted to discuss Rob's comments with Matthew, as well as her upcoming meeting with Nicole Brown, but he'd gone into the field the day after the IMAX movie. His unique way of approaching a problem always cut through the clutter and pinpointed the important facts. She missed his input now.

This time though, because of his transfer, Matthew's opinion might be affected by his own desires. Sara needed a clear idea of what her possibilities were before talking to him.

Rob called the day after their meeting and set up a time for her and Nicole to talk. "Then," he'd said, mysteriously, "get back with me." Sara detected a hint of enthusiasm beneath his usual conservative words, and she'd champed at the bit for the chance to hear Nicole Brown's ideas.

After several turns, she pulled into the small parking lot of The Lady's Cup. The building hardly looked large enough to house any business, much less one requiring seating and the serving of food. The outside was neat. Pots of geraniums lined the wall facing the parking area.

Warm, Caribbean colors covered the walls inside, giving the tiny shop a casual ambience. Three round tables lined the front wall, with barely enough room for chairs. A man sat at one table, with a cup of steaming coffee and an open newspaper in front of him.

Two cake platters filled with cookies jammed the serving counter and plastic-wrapped brownies filled the space under them. Four pump containers, each labeled with a flavor of coffee, sat on a back counter. The aroma was heavenly.

An African American woman poked her head through a doorway in the back wall. "Be right with you," she said with a smile. Thirty seconds later, a statuesque woman emerged, wiping her hands on an apron. From a generous bosom, her body shrank to a slender waist then blossomed into curvy hips. Black hair, cut short and with touches of gray, curled against her scalp. She wore a broomstick skirt and colorful cotton blouse as opposed to the usual low-country-casual jeans and top, and no jewelry but a wedding band.

"May I help you?"

"Are you Nicole Brown?" The woman nodded and Sara held out her hand. "I'm Sara Richards. I believe Rob Taylor spoke with you about me?"

The woman's smile involved her whole face. Where before she'd been remarkable, her wide, ingenuous smile transformed her into a real beauty. At that moment, Sara knew she'd found a friend. The realization struck like lightning, stunning her. She'd never made friends quickly, never trusted easily. Holding back was a result of living a lie, no doubt. For years she had to watch what she said, remember not to reveal too much. Now it was a part of her nature—until meeting Nicole Brown.

Nicole grasped Sara's hand. "Oh, yes. I'm happy to meet you," she said in a clipped New York accent.

The man scraped his chair across the floor while getting up. "See you tomorrow, Nicole."

"Okay, Mike." The door closed quietly behind him.

"Would you like something to drink? After making coffee all morning, I'm in the mood for something cold." She moved around the counter and turned the sign on the door to "Closed."

"Nothing for me," Sara replied. She waited a few seconds for Nicole to return, a can of Diet Coke in hand.

"Have a seat," Nicole said. They pulled chairs away from one of the tables. She took another swig from the can and sighed. "That tastes good. You own an art gallery?"

So much for small talk. "Yes, on the other side of town, out past the national cemetery. The building I'm currently in has been sold and I have to leave. Trouble is, I can't afford where I want to relocate."

Nicole nodded. "I know what you mean. I've had this place for a couple of years now, and I'd like to expand, see if I can make it with more than coffee and cookies. I'd have a few tables and limit the offerings to select baked items at first. But eventually I'd like to provide salads and savory goods for people to carry out."

"Sounds like a great idea. There's nothing like it in town now."

"I know. My business has expanded nicely since I opened, but I'm limited in what I can do by my shop size. I recently inherited some money, and my husband said I should go for it." She chuckled. "If only I had enough to 'go for it' with."

Sara smiled. Nicole had seemed abrupt initially, but Sara liked the other woman's open manner. Nicole wasn't pushy and she wasn't rash in her business decisions, or she wouldn't still be in her cubbyhole of a shop. "What did you have in mind?"

"Personally, I'd like to be where the action is for a change. I've researched a few available locations. Some are too large, some too small. They're all high in rent."

"We have far too much in common." Sara thought of the bottom-line figure she had for investment. If she could stay where she was, she'd be doing fine, but to relocate, the amount was far too little. "What are you going to do?"

After raising the can to her lips once more, Nicole leaned forward. "I'm not opposed to buying, but I can't swing it alone. Mr. Taylor suggested we discuss finding a building to share."

"Really?" Sara stared out the window, thinking. She'd asked Rob what a coffee shop had in common with an art gallery, but now she saw the opportunities. She envisioned her art displayed in the restaurant and serving Nicole's coffee to her patrons. The aroma of the coffee and baking would permeate both spaces.

The best part would be having a partner. *And a friend.* "Have you seen a place in town that would suit both of us?"

"As a matter of fact, not many know about it, but the old firehouse is available." Nicole took a piece of paper and a pen from her apron pocket and sketched a rough square. "It's pretty large inside. I'm not sure what you need for your art, but there's lots of wall space, plus enough room to divide the downstairs into separate areas. Upstairs is a kitchen—not huge, but good enough for what I need. Upstairs or down, there's room enough for a display case and several tables. And there's that large driveway in front that we could use, and an actual parking area in back. Seems to me, it would be perfect for two intelligent, beautiful women like us."

Intrigued, Sara tried to stay calm. "How do you know the city is selling the building?"

"My husband used to be a Wall Street elf. You know what that is? A financial forecaster? Anyway, he forecasted well enough for us to retire and now he acts as a consultant for the city. He advised them to sell the building now that the new fire station is built. The plans were announced at the last city manager meeting, but only a few people were present and because business has dropped off a bit the last couple of years, there was no interest." She gave Sara a knowing look. "*But,* I think tourism is going to pick up again this year. If I can convince half my family in New York to come down for a week or so, we can break even."

103

Sara joined Nicole in a smile.

"John—that's my husband—tells me he advised them to wait for a high price but the council's afraid they're going to get stuck with a white elephant. If we slip in and grab a bargain, everyone else can just get over it. This could be our lucky day."

Sara grinned. "Could well be. I hate to rush, but we're already into November and I have to vacate where I am by the first of the year. When can we look at the building?"

"I'll ask John to find out. So, if we can work out the money and the plans, and we like the firehouse, are you interested?" Nicole raised her brows.

"Definitely." Sara took an easy breath. For the first time since receiving her eviction notice and Paul's lost letters, some of her tension lessened. Finally, something was going right.

* * * *

The next day, Sara learned one of the reasons for Nicole's relaxed and sunny personality: her husband, John. At the fire station, he leaned with one shoulder against the wall, arms crossed, and his eyes filled with amusement while he watched the women measure the floor space.

"John, come and help us, please." Nicole tried to balance a clipboard full of papers and a coffee cup while calling off feet and inches to Sara.

"Put down the cup, woman, and you'll do all right." John's deep voice rumbled across the room. He pushed off the wall and walked over to her.

"Sara, have you ever seen such a stubborn man?" But Nicole glowed, smiling at him when he relieved her of the tape measure.

As tall as Nicole was, she could look up into her husband's eyes. John Brown stood at least six feet four and was built like a basketball player. His long-sleeved cotton shirt did nothing to hide his muscular biceps, and he walked with sure, powerful strides. A graying, nappy moustache matched the color and texture of the hair on his head.

"You ladies would have been finished already if you hadn't been talking so much," he said, winking broadly at Sara.

"Uh-huh," Nicole chided. "But there's so much to talk about. Look at all this empty space, and we have to fill it up, don't we, Sara?"

Sara smiled. Not only had she and Nicole kept up a continual conversation since John opened the back door, they'd joked and teased each other. Their laughter echoed off the high ceiling and up the stairwell where the sound bounced off the walls.

She never remembered making friends as easily as she had with Nicole. Sara was quiet, Nicole was brassy; Sara worked better behind the scenes, Nicole relished being out with the customers. Though she and John might have lived in high fashion in New York, Nicole was one of the most down to earth people Sara had ever met.

Sara grinned at John, holding her arms wide. "We have to fill all this. We *must* talk."

They spent the rest of the day discussing where the two shops would fit, how to arrange the kitchen and serving space and how best to display her artwork. A thrill ran up her spine.

She'd always been grateful that Aunt Barbara took her into her home and business, but because she'd been "taken in," she'd never felt free enough to make changes to reflect her own ideas. Now, thinking about the new space and how she could expand her displays and customer base, she felt as giddy as a young girl with an unexpected gift. The day flew.

During a break, John took a sip of Nicole's coffee. "Your shop is called Beauty by Beaufort, Sara?"

"Yes. My aunt had the idea to focus on art of the low-country, and Beaufort, specifically. She had only canvas-work—oils, pastels, watercolor. I'd like to add sculpted pieces. If we can afford this place, there are a few people I'm going to contact for duck decoys and marsh bird carvings, for instance. Everything will still be about our area, though."

John chuckled. "Before Nicole and I started coming down here, we thought the name of the town was Bow-fort. People corrected us pretty quickly when we arrived for our first vacation." He adopted a falsetto and thick Southern accent. "'That's Bue, as in beautiful.'"

Sara laughed. "There is a Bow-fort—in North Carolina. It's spelled the same, but totally mispronounced." John chuckled.

"Hmm," Nicole said, "I wonder if *they* have a gallery called Beauty by Beaufort."

Sara might have been struck by lightning. "I don't know, but that might be a way to expand my offerings. Beaufort, North Carolina is on the coast, too. I might be able to commission artists there to sell here. And who knows, there might be other Beauforts in the country."

"That's the kind of thinking outside the box that'll look good in your proposal and will help get your loan," John said enthusiastically. "Great idea!"

Sara wanted to rush back to the office and start researching the possibilities right away. Questions about floor and wall coverings were answered quickly. When John and Nicole said they thought they'd gathered enough information for the business proposal, Sara practically rushed them to the door.

"The city isn't asking much for the building," John said, standing by their car and looking back at the building. "Frankly, I recommended they start higher, but they're anxious to have it sold and used. Strange, considering it's only a few blocks off Bay Street."

"Better for us," Nicole said in unison with Sara, then they laughed.

John simply smiled and shook his head.

* * * *

I still might lose Aunt Barb's business, but at least now I have a chance. Sara sat in her miniscule office at the gallery and stared at the papers on her desk.

Light coming through the clerestory windows at the back of the shop was fading fast. Sara turned on the desk lamp and shuffled papers. She'd already looked at the requirements for the bank, then she'd read again the details of the loan. Finally—for the hundredth time, it seemed—she examined the pending sale agreement for the old Beaufort firehouse.

106

The city was asking a reasonable price, but still, Sara would need half of her savings to use as down payment. A quarter or more of the rest would go to renovations of the lower floor—assuming the estimates she'd received were accurate. That left her with very little. Having a partner spread the risk, but Nicole was gambling with an inheritance, not her life's savings. Besides, she had a husband to back her if The Lady's Cup did poorly in the city. Sara would be taking a chance with all she had, including the business her aunt had entrusted to her.

When they ended their meeting with Rob earlier in the afternoon, Nicole had taken Sara's hands and stared into her eyes. "I'm excited, girl, are you?"

"Oh, yes. And scared." Sara hated to admit the stone of fear lodged in her stomach.

"Lord, I'm so glad you said that! I am, too. We need to think about this for a day or two and make sure it's what we really want. We haven't signed our lives away yet." Nicole chuckled but her words only increased Sara's nervousness.

Now, in the quiet of her office, she took a deep breath. She could make this work. The move was right.

She hoped.

She wished Matthew was there to confirm what she knew in her heart and to calm the jitters that refused to leave.

"I can do this. Everything will work out."

"Talking to yourself again?" Sara jumped at Jennette's voice. Her assistant stood in the open doorway.

"Oh, for heaven's sake, you scared half a life out of me. And as for talking to myself, I was the most interesting person in the room." She removed her reading glasses and smiled self-deprecatingly. "I was trying to convince myself of something."

"Did you do it?"

"Yes." Sara glanced back at the papers. "Or…maybe not."

"Well, as long as you're sure." Jennette smiled. "You need a break. And I've got the perfect opportunity. There's a customer asking to speak with you. He's been out front talking to me for almost twenty minutes, and when I told him we'd be closing soon, he asked if you were around. Actually, I was beginning to suspect he was here for a reason other than buying artwork, but he does seem interested in that Marilyn Yates piece."

Sara frowned. "He asked for me? Did he give his name?"

"No, but he knows you by name." She lowered her voice. "Let me tell you, this guy is one hunk, and he's nice and funny. If I weren't engaged, I might take a second look at him myself. But... he's definitely asking for the boss lady. Shall I tell him you're gone or that you'll be out?"

Sara sighed. "I'll go out. I'd love to pay Marilyn a nice commission on that painting. Besides, maybe I'll be more convincing to myself tomorrow." She stood, stacking the papers neatly before going around the desk. "Why don't you go on home? We're only open for another few minutes and I'll close up."

"Thanks. Ben is taking me to that new mystery movie tonight, and I have some studying to do beforehand. Exams are in a couple of weeks." Jennette made a face before taking her jacket and purse off the coat tree. The two women walked out of the private area and into the gallery proper.

"Sir?" Jennette addressed the back of a tall man. "Here's the owner, Sara Richards."

Sara's heart went into overdrive and she held her breath. *It can't be.*

Yet when the tall man turned, it was, unbelievably, Paul.

108

Chapter 8

Paul didn't smile, didn't extend his hand or walk forward. He simply stood and stared at her.

Sara couldn't move. She barely heard Jennette say goodnight, hardly noticed the bell over the door tinkle as she left. Like statues, they faced one another, twenty feet, more or less, separating them physically. A lifetime between them emotionally.

The ringing phone broke the spell. Sara glanced over her shoulder at the counter, then back at Paul. "Excuse me." Still there was no acknowledgement of her, except in his eyes. They burned as though he was fevered.

She picked up the receiver. "Beauty by Beaufort. May I help you?"

"You sure can, you beautiful woman. You can say you'll have dinner with me."

"Matthew, you're back!" Without looking up, she felt Paul's eyes on her. She dropped her voice and turned away, as though talking to another man was somehow wrong while Paul was standing there. "I'd love to have dinner with you. Are you at the base now?"

"Yes. Just got in a little while ago. I have to shower and square away a few things yet. Shall I make reservations somewhere?"

"How about Chez Richards? I know the owner and I'm sure I can guarantee a table."

She knew immediately when Paul turned away. Her back, where his gaze had been directed, was cooler.

"It's nice to date a woman with influence."

She laughed. "Well, at this one place, anyway. What time will you be there? Seven?"

"Seven, at the latest. I'll stop and pick up some wine and dessert. Maybe those éclairs you love."

"Oh, a man after my heart. We're only having leftover chicken and rice, so it doesn't matter too much when you arrive. Just do what you need to, and I'll see you when you get there."

"This is one reason why I love you."

"You're so lucky to have me, I know. I'm glad you're home because I have something to talk to you about."

"Yes? I'll be there as soon as I can." His tone was upbeat, hopeful.

"Good. See you later."

She hung up, wondering what Paul thought, hearing her side of the conversation. And she was concerned that Matthew must think she wanted to talk about going to California. She hoped he would understand, but he'd made his feelings clear. That she might hurt him was worrisome.

But not as worrisome as what stood at her back right now.

Crossing the room, she examined the painting that had captured Paul's attention. The scene was of a sailboat on the Beaufort River, viewed from a porch.

"Do you like it?" Marilyn Yates was a favorite artist. Her style was characterized by soft hues accented with bright, bold strokes. This forced the eye to the important section of the canvas, whether it was a quail's nest in the corner or a swooping gull over a gray ocean. Her paintings always evoked restfulness as well as a sense of excitement, no easy task for one canvas.

"Yes. It kind of lulls you into a nap in the hammock and then makes you sit up and pay attention to that boat."

She chuckled.

"I'm not great with art, but I do like this piece."

"But you are great with art—that's exactly what Marilyn intended you to feel."

"Oh. Well, good." Neither moved.

"You made it pretty clear that the last time I saw you, would be the last time I saw you. What's changed?" She stared at the painting as she spoke.

"There was a reunion of our old LST crew up in Charleston."

"You didn't mention the possibility of being in South Carolina when I was in Iowa."

"True."

She remained silent after that response. Could one word spoken with such disinterest even be called a response?

"Mark told me to come."

She was so startled, she finally looked away from the seascape and up at Paul. "Your brother?"

He looked into her eyes. "He told me I needed a vacation. Said that since you'd been there, I was working at such a pace I'd kill him and make Luke old before his time. Becca gave me a map with the road marked from Charleston to Beaufort."

Sara smiled.

"They have the wrong impression of our feelings for each other," he added, frowning at her.

"Giving you a map didn't force you to drive down."

"I know that." He reached out and tucked a strand of hair behind her ear. Her blood changed to fire, carrying heat to her extremities and supercharging her heart rate. Without thinking, she closed her eyes and turned her cheek into his hand, luxuriating in the feel of his touch. It had been so long…

He dropped his hand and stepped back, as though he hadn't meant to touch her, hadn't wanted to. The distaste she saw in his eyes made Sara take a step back, too.

"So, I like your gallery."

"Thanks. I inherited the business but I've worked here for years. I love the low-country art and the people who create it. Unfortunately, I'm being evicted at the end of the year." She turned to take in the narrow, long room. "I'll miss it here."

"What are you going to do?"

She faced him again. "I'm looking at a new location closer to town, if I can swing it." Thinking of Matthew's probable reaction to buying the building and her determination to make the business work, she added, "There's a question about finances, but I'm trying to buy a building."

"Are you in trouble?" Paul's tone changed, became harder. His gaze intensified. He flattened his mouth into a thin line.

She could see the wheels turning in his mind, his thoughts like a train going down a single track, and he didn't appear to like the destination. "What? What are you thinking?"

"Nothing," he murmured, then turned back to the painting. "What are you doing for dinner?" Obviously, he'd forced the words out. As he said them, his body leaned away, putting distance between them when his question suggested getting nearer.

"I have plans, I'm afraid."

He seemed to loom over her, moving his whole body around instead of simply turning his head to see her. The action became more intimidating, more powerful. "Anything you can change? I'll only have tonight free."

A moment ago he'd acted as though he'd prefer a dose of castor oil to being with her. Now he seemed bent on making her go out with him. No wonder she couldn't decide her feelings for him with the mixed signals he kept throwing.

"You still haven't said why you came to Beaufort." His indecision kept her on edge so her tone was harsher than she'd intended.

He shot a wary look her way but relaxed his stance. "Actually, Mitch Hamilton asked me to. You remember him, from the concert?"

The day my life changed forever. I remember every detail. "Yes. He took my parking space."

His face broke into a smile, making her stomach flip cartwheels. "Yeah. But you got a better one."

"So, you came to see Mitch? Becca didn't give you the map hinting you should look me up?" Why did she ask that? It could make no difference why he was here. Most of her wished he hadn't come. Another part—a small, insane part—wished he'd wrap her in his arms and insist they spend the evening together.

He shrugged. "Who knows what's running through her mind? Becca's an incurable romantic. I only know I'm here to see Mitch and to go fishing. I'd forgotten you even lived here."

The challenge in his eyes dared her to contradict him. That he didn't try to hide his lie spoke volumes about his feelings. If not for Mitch, he wouldn't be in Beaufort.

"Are you going to change your plans and have dinner with me?" He asked without the heat of before.

"Becca is a lucky woman to have a husband who loves her so much she still believes in romance. Most of us aren't in that position." There was that look again, that frowning, intense stare. "Perhaps Mitch recommended a good place to eat? If not, since it's Friday night, I'll be glad to call and make sure you get a table at my favorite place."

He hesitated only briefly. "That won't be necessary. I'm sure the people at The Best Western can recommend a good restaurant." Jamming his hands in his pockets and taking another slow turn to view the room, he was quiet for several moments. "Yes, this is a very nice business you've got. You say you inherited? From your husband?"

"No, from my aunt. My father's sister."

"Ah." Finally, he stopped examining the gallery and looked down at her. "Take care, Sara."

"You, too."

The door opened, the bell jangled, he was gone.

She fought the urge to run after him, hating herself for the weakness that desire implied.

Paul's essence lingered, dominating the space as though he still stood beside her. She shuddered thinking of how barren the room would seem when his presence dissipated. Ten minutes remained before closing time, but she gathered the papers from her desk and left, wanting to be gone before that happened.

During the drive home, she berated herself for caring. A kernel of love for him would always be at her core, but there was nothing more for her. He wasn't a man who forgave easily. Why, then, didn't he leave her alone? First he followed her to Omaha, and now here. Each time they spoke churned up emotions better left dead.

Thank God he didn't know about Paula. Hearing he'd spent a few days in Charleston had sent a spear of anxiety through her. If he and Paula had met accidentally, it would have taken only one look for him to know she was someone special. At least now he was here, not Charleston, and—pray God!—he'd be gone soon. In a few days Sara would be able to breathe freely again.

She longed for that moment to arrive.

* * * *

"Sara? Do you know that Martians just landed in your backyard and abducted Pi R Squared?"

"Really?" Sara lifted a forkful of chicken to her mouth, then looked hard at it. Dropping it back on her plate, she jabbed a lettuce leaf from her salad instead.

Matthew sighed, then took a sip of wine. "I don't know where you are tonight, but it's somewhere far away from here."

"Sorry!" She looked into his blue eyes and smiled. Matthew never failed to amaze her with his mellow personality. His even temperament smoothed her moods, a quality she particularly appreciated that evening.

"It's okay. Dinner was delicious." He pushed a green bean around his plate and then looked at her with the hint of a smile. "I hope you're going to tell me I won't have to miss these meals when I leave. Meaning I won't have to miss you."

Sara put down her fork. "Matthew, while you were gone, I had a talk with Rob Taylor at the bank."

He slid his plate aside and sat back, his expression sober. "What did he have to say?"

"He put me in touch with a woman who wants to expand her business, and...well, things have moved pretty fast. I have the papers with me to buy a building downtown."

"*What?*" He shoved the chair back. Jumping up, he walked to the living room and back. His forehead creased in a frown when he looked down at her. "How can you afford to buy a building? The last you told me, you finally had enough money put aside to feel comfortable. That can't be enough to buy property."

"Nicole—that's the woman, Nicole Brown—and I are going to be partners. Her husband knew the old fire station was available and—"

"Fire station! Sara, are you out of your mind? Do you realize what renovations are going to cost, how much upkeep will be in a place like that? And what happens when that Nicole woman's business fails or she decides she wants out and you're stuck with everything? Jesus, I can't believe you did this, without talking it over first. You made a decision this big in a few days?" He narrowed his gaze and his frown deepened. "Or have you been planning this for weeks and just didn't mention it?"

She'd expected him to be somewhat discouraging, but not angry, not like this. His doubts drilled through her confidence, leaving it tattered. Was she crazy to get involved with Nicole and the fire house? Maybe so.

Matthew hadn't stopped moving. She stood and took his arm. "I haven't signed anything yet. That's one reason why I'm happy you're back, so we could talk. I don't think you know what the gallery means to me. How could you, when I didn't fully understand myself until a few weeks ago? It's a future, something for me to create and mold, maybe for Paula to inherit, or her children. It's a part of Beaufort and our family here."

115

"Sara, Paula will most likely go with Dan. Who knows if she'll ever live in South Carolina again, and she's made it clear she doesn't want children. Your mom won't live here much longer, I bet. Each year she leaves earlier for her sister's in Florida and stays later. Are you willing to handle this mess alone, on the *chance* Paula might want to sell paintings someday? Why would you want to start over alone and at your—" His gaze shot to hers.

"At my age? It's okay, you can say it. You're younger, but I'm not exactly on Medicare yet. Lots of successful businesses have been started by people in their fifties, and I'm not starting from nothing, remember."

He closed his eyes and rolled his head back on his neck. "That didn't come out exactly the way I meant it. You're not old, not at all. But if I started something new, I'd not only have a few more years to build it up, I'd have the backup of my retirement pay from the Corps. You won't have that, honey." He looked shrewdly at her. "Unless you started something new with me. I'd be all the backup you needed."

"I owe it to Aunt Barb to try to sustain what she built."

He grasped her shoulders. "You don't owe your aunt anything. Whatever she did, she did for love, not so you'd give up happiness fighting for a business that barely supports you." He pulled her into his arms. "She'd want you to be happy, honey. So do I."

"With you, in California."

"Yes. We're good together. I enjoy watching TV or going antiquing, or just being with you. And I hope our loving makes you feel as happy as it does me. If asking you to leave the place you've lived all these years is selfish, then I am. I want you with me." His lips touched the crown of her head and his cheek rubbed against her hair.

She could let herself go so easily, allowing Matthew to make the decisions for her, drift along where the Marine Corps sent them for the next few years until he retired. Then they'd settle in Washington where his family lived. That's what he'd planned. He had land on one of the islands in Puget Sound just waiting for the house he anticipated building. She pictured the two of them lazing on a different porch a continent away.

She pushed away a few inches to see his eyes. "What happens if I go with you and you change your mind? Or something happens to you? I will have given up everything to go where I have nothing."

He sighed as though exasperated with having to explain the state of things yet again. "God, I wish you had some faith in me. I'm not going to change my mind. We've been seeing each other for almost four years. Doesn't that mean anything?"

She saw the fatigue in his eyes from the past six days in the field. She'd chosen the worst time to talk. Smiling, she lightened the discussion. "Matthew, you're always too polite to remind me, but you're ten years younger than I am. What if one of those Marine groupies Dan talked about catches your eye? They're bound to be a zillion young babes just waiting for a sexy hunk like you to come along."

Her trick worked. He smiled back and the worry lines in his face smoothed. "When you're around, you're all I see. Hell, one of those women could strut around naked and I wouldn't notice a thing if you were there."

"You're such a good friend." His expression darkened again. Before he said anything, she added, "And I think you should go back to the base. You're exhausted. We can talk tomorrow."

He dipped his head for a kiss. "Your bed is closer than the base."

"But I think you need to sleep." She walked him to the door. "Be careful going back."

His hand cupped her cheek. "I will. See you tomorrow."

Pulling keys from his pocket, he walked to the Sebring parked beside her minivan. She waved a last time before shutting the door against the chill in the air. Or was that sharp bite loneliness, a taste of what she could expect in the near future?

With a sigh, she went to clean the kitchen and feed the cat.

Afterward, restless, she poured a cup of coffee and carried it into the living room where she tweaked a flower arrangement and fluffed a pillow. She turned on the television and then clicked it off after channel surfing for a few minutes.

Huffing out a breath of frustration, she picked up a book. Squared jumped into her lap the moment she opened the cover and his demand for attention distracted her. At nine o'clock, the doorbell rang.

"Who could that be," she asked Squared. Dislodged from the warmth of her lap, the cat showed no interest in discovering the answer.

Sara peeked through the peephole and stifled a groan.

She yanked open the door just as Paul raised his hand to the bell again. Exasperation won out over politeness. "Why do you keep doing this? You say you don't want anything to do with me, you demonstrate it in every possible way, and then you show up. Why?"

He took a step back, his eyes wide, his mouth opened in surprise. "I didn't expect wide open arms, but I have to admit, I thought you'd say hello before anything else." Half smiling, he jammed his hands in his pockets. "I don't understand it myself."

"Damn!" she said under her breath.

"I know. It sucks, as Luke says."

"Don't you dare make light of this, of what your being here does to me." God! She sounded like a shrew, but she'd never gain her equilibrium if Paul continued popping into her life.

He sobered immediately. His gaze burned into her and his shoulders tensed as though trying to hold himself in check. "I'm sorry. To tell the truth, I didn't intend to come here."

"How did you find where I live?"

Hesitantly, he smiled again. His gaze roamed her face. That she enjoyed the touch of his eyes unnerved her.

"Phone book, and a nice desk clerk."

"Oh." *A female, no doubt. He could get information out of any woman once he flashed that smile.*

"Are you through with your plans?" His voice was as cautious as his smile.

What? Her mind went blank. "Oh, yes. I cooked dinner for a friend. I was just drinking some coffee and reading before going to—"

The amusement disappeared from his face, replaced with a searing gaze. "Is your friend still here?"

"No, he's gone."

"*He's* gone."

She stood straight and met his stare. "Yes. We had dinner, we enjoyed a nice evening, and now he's back at the post."

"Ah, a Marine." Something in his eyes caused her to take a mental step back.

The furnace clicked on in the house. Paul appeared comfortable in a flannel shirt and an unzipped quilted vest. He'd rolled up the shirtsleeves a couple of turns and unfastened the button at the collar. Even wearing a turtleneck sweater and wool slacks, she shivered in the night breeze.

The same wind ruffled his hair, causing a lock to fall onto his forehead. The inconsequential action went unnoticed by Paul, yet it caused her heart to leap into her throat.

"May I come in?"

She remembered her sense of the gallery after he left. "No, it would be better if you didn't." There was no car in the drive except hers. "How did you get here?"

"I walked. I've been cooped up in a hotel for days trading war stories and lies with guys I served with onboard ship. Stretching my legs felt good."

Sara reached behind the door for her coat and picked up her purse and keys from the entry table. "Come on, I'll take you back to the hotel."

Paul walked silently behind her, then got in the passenger side of the minivan. "This is a far cry from your Beetle."

"Yes, well, times and needs change."

"Not all needs."

She snapped her head around to gauge his meaning but he was buckling his seat belt so she couldn't see his expression.

When he did look up and saw her stare, he grinned. "Like coffee. Can I buy you a cup?"

"No, thanks." She started the car and backed out of the driveway, but without conscious thought found herself taking the long way to the hotel.

"Beaufort is really beautiful. I saw some of it today, trying to find your gallery."

"It's very historic, too. While you were in Charleston you probably saw all the antebellum homes. We have a good number of beautiful homes here, also. And we have the water and great places to eat, but in a smaller, cozier town. You should be here in the spring when the dogwood and azaleas are in bloom. There's no more beautiful place on earth."

Before she realized it, they were approaching the old fire station. She pulled into the drive and parked. "I mentioned before that I was looking into buying a building. This is it." Like Matthew, Paul seemed like a logical man. But he wasn't emotionally tied to one course of action for her, so if he offered an opinion, she hoped it would be more objective.

He snorted a laugh. "A fire station? Interesting." He opened the car door and climbed out. "Can you get inside?"

"Not right now," she said, setting the emergency brake and following him to the big doors fronting the station. "My partner has a coffee shop and food take-out company. We're thinking of keeping both primary businesses on the lower level, and out of season artwork and additional seating upstairs. The kitchen's upstairs, though, which might be a problem."

Holding his hand against the glass in the door to block the lights behind him, Paul peered inside. "Looks like at least three trucks were used here. It's probably

120

pretty well insulated since it has living quarters. Have you gotten estimates on renovation yet?"

Her earlier enthusiasm began to build. "Yes, but only for the main floor. It's a lot of money, but if the estimate's accurate I'll have enough to cover it. Barely, but enough."

"Hmm, just thinking out loud, but if you made the stairs for employees only, you might be able to salvage enough space to make a small dumbwaiter for your friend's food. It can be pulley operated, so it shouldn't be too expensive. And if you were willing to give up a bit of floor space, I'll bet you could have a ramp built to the upper floor. If it's long enough, the rise will be gradual, and that would open the space upstairs. Your art would line the ramp, of course, and there would be storage space under the rise."

"What a great idea. We worried how we'd make the upper level convenient."

He stared inside again then stepped back to look at the exterior. "There might be room for a third business, too. That might help with finances."

She backed up to view the whole façade. "How?"

He pointed to the extension on the roof. "That's where they hung the hoses to let them dry. It should be a pretty decent space in a firehouse of this size. You'd have to floor it, but I'd think there should be plenty of room for an office or small sales outlet."

"I'll certainly bring all of this up to Nicole. I haven't even signed the loan papers yet, I'm so nervous about such a big investment. What if Nicole and I become partners and her business doesn't go well? Or she changes her mind, or wants to sell and go back to New York, and I'm stuck with everything?"

The words came out in a rush, her nervousness outstripping the caution she should have used talking to Paul. He was with her only because he was in a strange town and lonely, not because he cared about her or her future. "Anyway, it's frightening."

Paul leaned against the door, arms and ankles crossed, watching her.

"What?" She took yet another small step back, bumping into the car. He had that look that tense expression that tightened his mouth and made her want to hide.

"Nothing. I guess I expected you to be less hesitant."

It's easy to be enthusiastic when life hasn't turned around to bite you yet. She pulled her coat tighter and held it closed at her neck. "I don't even know why I brought you here."

She heard his sigh over the car engine. "I think I do." Pushing off from the station door he walked to the minivan. "Come on, you're chilled."

They arrived at The Best Western in silence. She pulled into a space facing the street and the river. Paul shifted so his body angled in the seat. The engine rumbled comfortably. Exhaust, white and thick in the cooling air, swirled behind them.

He looked out the windshield to the sidewalk that curved along the riverbank. "Let's walk."

She shook her head. "I should get home."

"Please." Examining her coat, he asked, "Or will it be too cold for you? I have to admit, it feels downright balmy to me, but I guess this is pretty cool for South Carolina."

"No, I'll be fine." *Are you out of your mind?*

She turned off the engine and hid her purse under the seat. When they got out, she locked the doors and pocketed the key. A gust of wind shocked her with its edge. She turned her collar up, buttoned her coat and crossed the street beside Paul, trying not to think of what she was doing.

Companionable and relaxed, they must have appeared to be two friends out for a stroll. Without talking or touching, Sara was infinitely aware of the man beside her. The wind blew in off the water, but the longer they walked the warmer she became.

After several minutes, he stopped and leaned on the safety railing. "I imagined Beaufort on the ocean, with beaches. I never thought about marshland."

"We're on a river. You have to go out to the islands to see the ocean. But the river is tidal, of course, and when the tide's out, it leaves mud, what we call pluff mud."

He smiled at her. "Pluff mud?"

"Story is, 'pluff' is the sound you hear when you step out of your boat, and your keys fall in the mud."

He laughed and she took the opportunity to study him. Tonight he acted more relaxed, easier. Certainly easier with her. But how long would it last? With his mercurial temperament, she shouldn't let down her guard for a minute.

"So, what are the islands here?"

"Oh, we've got islands all over the place." They continued strolling as she talked. "Lady's Island just over there—" she pointed across the river, "—Catt Island, Parris Island—you know what's there, already—it seems the list goes on and on. Fripp is the outermost island in the Beaufort area, but the big resort island, Hilton Head, is over that way." She pointed roughly in a southeasterly direction.

"You know your area." Taking his left hand out of his pocket, he let it hang at his side as he walked.

One breath out of step and their fingers brushed. Just brushed. A light contact that she wouldn't even have noticed if they'd been strangers passing on the street. But they weren't strangers, and Paul's touch sent a surge of electricity up her arm.

Sara didn't dare speak. Didn't dare move toward him. He kept walking as though the touch meant nothing. Maybe he hadn't noticed it. She forced herself to breathe and was proud that when she spoke her voice was natural and calm. "Well, I've lived here a long time."

"Yes, I recall." His voice was low and hard. A change from the easiness of only a moment ago.

"Knowing the area is part of my business. And I love it here. The history, the people, the pace of life—" she stopped and swept her hand out in front of her, "—the marshes and Spanish moss dangling from the live oaks." She snorted a laugh.

123

"Even the awful marsh gas. This was a home of necessity at first, but it's been the home of my heart for a long time."

Turning to look at him, she saw he stared toward the water. "Couldn't you tell me about Iowa? The place you love?"

He said nothing until they reached the end of the walk. The bridge to Lady's Island was swinging open to allow a sailboat to continue downriver and they watched for a few minutes.

"I don't fall in love with places." Then he reversed direction and started back.

When they'd almost reached the public parking area, she touched his sleeve. "Come over here. I want to show you something."

She led him under a covered area dotted with statues, benches and memorials, halting in front of a bronze plaque on a stone pedestal. "This is what I wanted you to see, Paul. I thought of you so very often throughout all those years, but certainly whenever I passed by here."

With a slight frown he stepped up and read aloud in a low voice. "'Dedicated to those who selflessly and willingly served their nation during the Vietnam War. Their hearts were tempered in fire; their souls forged on the anvil of war. No glory of the moment was awarded, yet history will keep and honor them forever.'"

His back rigid, he stood silently. Sara wondered what thoughts ran through his mind, what images he envisioned. She didn't think he was focused on the words any longer.

He cleared his throat. "Did you bring your daughter here, and tell her about her father?"

"I told her all her life about the man he was. She was older when this plaque was dedicated."

Finally, he looked down at her, his eyes full of pain. "Please," he said softly, "I want to go back."

Chapter 9

Sara's heart stopped. *Go back.* If only they could. She'd give anything…

Paul's gaze bore through her. "Let's go back." The plea came out in a broken whisper. His hand came up as though to touch her face, but he stopped inches away. Closing his eyes, he took a shaky breath then let it out slowly.

When his eyes opened the emotion was gone, replaced by the control he'd demonstrated time and again. He jerked his head toward the hotel. "Come on. Let's go back."

The same words, but such a different meaning. Nodding, she started walking. Their steps were measured and slow.

Their fingers brushed again. This time, his hand stretched toward hers, touching, moving against her. Finally, their fingers linked, palm against palm. Silent tears ran down her cheeks. Something had changed. Paul didn't hate her anymore. Although nothing would be different between them, they'd found a bit of peace, a starting point for moving on with less bitterness.

Lost in thought, the hotel appeared more quickly than she expected. Sara glanced at her watch. *Almost midnight. Time for Cinderella to make her exit. But I won't lose a glass slipper. When I leave my prince, it'll be forever.*

As they approached the car, he let go of her hand so she could dig the keys from her coat pocket.

"I still wouldn't mind buying you a cup of coffee." His voice held a smile. "After our stroll I don't think I can sleep."

"It's late. I have to open the gallery tomorrow since Jennette is off, and…" Looking up, she saw the smile hinted at in his voice. "What?"

"Considering we might never meet again you seem in an awful big hurry to get rid of me."

"I just want to end the night on a good note is all, and our walk was nice. When, as you say, this might be the last time we ever see each other, why take a chance on messing up our good moods?"

The streetlight in the parking lot lent a gleam to his eyes. "Just because we have coffee doesn't mean things would get worse. They could get better." He waited, but she kept quiet. "Still, I guess you're right. It is late and I have things to do tomorrow, too."

She held out her hand. "Goodnight, Paul. I'm glad you came by and we didn't let things end as they were in Omaha."

"Me, too. Take care, Sara. And good luck with your business." He shook her hand. How proper. And yet how strange, that this man who had been her first lover and her only real love, shook her hand.

She pursed her lips and nodded once, then got in and started the car. Paul barely moved aside when she pulled away. Out on the street, she drove half a block then stopped at the curb.

Where are you going? Didn't you hear the man? This could be the last time you ever see Paul. Make it count for something.

"There's no way to turn back the clock," she whispered. He'd begged for the chance to go back, and if she were honest, it was what she wanted, too. One night to live a dream that fate had snatched from her.

She gripped the top of the steering wheel and cushioned her head on her hands. In the side mirror she saw Paul waiting right where she'd left him. As though he recognized her turmoil. Like he *knew* she would come back.

He didn't say a word when he got in, just buckled the seatbelt and leaned his head back. There was no traffic, so it took only a few minutes before Sara turned off the engine in her own driveway. For moments, the sounds of the cooling engine supplied the only sound.

"Maybe hot chocolate instead of coffee. To help you sleep." A casual comment, just for something to say. It reflected none of the chaos churning her stomach.

"Maybe so," he responded. He sounded as calm as she. Was he?

Maybe he doesn't feel it. Lord, please make him feel something for me that's good. Please make him—

126

No, she wouldn't go there.

She stood, dizzy and weak-kneed. Heart hammering, she leaned against the car, praying she wouldn't lose control in front of Paul. He stood at the foot of the porch, watching her. Backlit by the porch light, she couldn't see his expression. She took a breath and walked up to unlock the door.

As soon as she stepped inside, Squared made a beeline for her, squalling his displeasure at being left alone for so long. She put her purse on the hall table and dropped her keys in the dish next to it.

"I know you want to be fed, there's no need to scream at me," she chided the cat as she hung up her coat. "I didn't think to mention Squared, Paul. I hope you like cats because if you don't, he's liable to make a point of sitting in your lap."

Paul squatted. Squared immediately rubbed against his leg and permitted scratching behind his ears.

Chuckling, he said, "No problem. I love cats." He stood. "Is the kitchen back this way?" Squared trotted with him toward the back of the house, criss-crossing through Paul's legs, talking all the way to the kitchen.

"What kind of name is Squared?"

Sara quickly put down food for the cat. "My daughter was in geometry when we found him, and she gave him his full name, Pi R Squared. All I remember is it has something to do with circles." She bent to pet the Siamese as he ate. "You're an old fellow now, aren't you, baby?" Ignored by the cat, she asked, "Hot chocolate or tea, or shall I make coffee after all?"

When she looked back, raw need had replaced his smile. Without moving a muscle, he drew her to him, such was his power. When she was close enough to feel soft puffs of air on her hair, he took her hands, holding them at her side.

She held her breath when he bent toward her. For a mere fraction of a second her mouth met his, their breath mingled, and she lost all sense.

He took another kiss, this one longer, more insistent. His fingers tightened around hers. "So sweet," he whispered against her lips. "I need—"

"I know." She broke away, shaken. But in his eyes she saw he was as unsure of their course, as lost and nervous as she. Somehow that gave her confidence. "I won't hurt you."

His eyes softened at that and his mouth hitched into a humorless smile. "I wish I could be sure we won't hurt each other. But right now, I just want you to take me back to before we gave up on each other."

Sara took Paul's hand and led him to the bedroom. He went without protest, acting the follower until she closed the door.

Then he pinned her to the door with his body, holding her hands over her head. His lips moved commandingly over hers, demanding she open to him. It took little persuasion. As his tongue claimed her mouth, she rose to her toes, scraping his body with hers and provoking a grunt of approval.

Hot, open-mouthed kisses trailed along her jaw, her neck, her ear, and finally back to her mouth. Her breath was ragged and short. He seemed not to take a breath, choosing instead to focus all of his energy on conquering her with kisses.

Releasing her hands, he unbuttoned her blouse then reached around to unsnap her bra. Calloused fingers flicked her nipples then cupped her breasts, kneading, massaging as his tongue made love to her mouth.

She dropped her arms and Paul slid her blouse and bra off her shoulders, letting them fall to the floor. She immediately pushed his vest down his arms and tried to unbutton his shirt. He captured her wrists and placed them behind her back.

Feverishly, he took a nipple with his mouth, circling it with his tongue. His hot mouth seared first one breast and then the other.

"Ahhh!" The cry broke from her before she could stop it.

Paul opened his mouth wider, taking more of her breast, suckling her like a ravenous kitten at a teat. His hand covered her free breast, alternately kneading it and rolling the tender nipple between his thumb and forefinger.

"Paul, please. I want to feel you against me."

He broke off then, releasing her and taking half a step back. His hooded eyes were dark with desire, his lips swollen from kissing her. She traced them with her index finger, then leaned up to do the same with her tongue as her fingers unbuttoned his shirt.

When she freed him he embraced her, lifting and crushing her to him. Her sensitive skin measured and catalogued every movement of the taut muscles in his arms and chest, the soft hair rubbing her smooth torso, and the tantalizing effect of his hard, flat nipples pressed against hers. The thumps of his heart reverberated through her.

Sara wrapped her arms around his neck and her legs around his waist.

She pushed thoughts of Matthew and the guilt that accompanied them aside, to be dealt with later. She loved Matthew as her dearest friend, but there was no room for him in her mind tonight.

No one had ever made her feel like Paul, no one. How she'd lived all these years without him she couldn't imagine.

His hand tracing the line of her spine might as well be a torch for the heat he generated. And when his hand reached her buttocks and forced her tightly against the hard evidence of his desire, all of that heat centered in a pool of fire between her thighs.

This was the warmth of springtime for a woman facing autumn. The years fell away and their first time came rushing back. Her tentative touches, his sureness in teaching her blistering passion. His obvious need to make her his, battling with his concern of what was right. The way she'd taken charge to force them where they'd both wanted to go. Spiraling out of control, knowing Paul was there to catch her. It had all been magical.

Paul turned, then edged toward the bed. When he set her on her feet, his lips took hers once more, and his hands roamed her body freely.

Her fingers, which moments before had been skillful in unbuttoning his shirt, now fumbled with the belt and zipper on his jeans. He pushed her hands away, taking care of the task in seconds. Sara freed herself from her slacks, stepping out of them and her shoes all at once. Bending to remove her socks, she stopped, noticing how still Paul had become.

129

"What's wrong?" She stood before him naked, while he remained dressed from the waist down. His jeans hung open and his erection strained against his white briefs, visibly throbbing, seeking an exit and a path to her. She ran her hands up his chest then licked one of his nipples. His breath came in gulps; his heart pounded beneath her hands.

She looked up, puzzled. "Paul?"

His face set, he stared at the bed. She looked, too, trying to see what bothered him. That morning she'd rushed, jerking the spread over the pillows instead of doing the job right. But he couldn't be distressed over a messy bed.

"Sara, tonight, that guy and you didn't…"

"What are you talk—" Realization struck. It wasn't that the bed was messy, it was that it looked used. Almost as though someone had just gotten out of it. Or two someones.

Heat flamed her cheeks. She escaped into the adjacent bathroom, emerging seconds later in a gray sweat suit. Paul had zipped his jeans and was buckling his belt.

"I'll take you back to the hotel."

He looked awful, grim and flushed with high color. Tension screamed from every muscle. Bending to scoop his shirt and vest off the floor, he managed to open the door in the same movement then close it behind him without a sound.

Sara dropped to the edge of the bed to slip into her tennis shoes, trembling so hard she wasn't sure how to stop. Moments ago, she'd stood before him naked, freely offering herself. She hadn't considered how she'd changed since he last saw her. Padding at her waist, gravity-affected breasts and stretch marks hadn't entered her thoughts. For a few minutes, she was young again, a girl enjoying the worshiping lips and hands of her first lover. Now she felt old and used up.

She should never have gone to Iowa. It was easier thinking Paul dead, than riding this runaway train of emotions every time they encountered each other. At this point, she wanted him gone, from her house, from her town. God knows, she wanted to erase him from her mind and heart.

She found him standing in the kitchen. Hands braced on the counter, he stared down into the sink. Squared rubbed against his leg.

"Are you ready?"

He didn't answer.

"Stop that, Squared." It was petty, yes, but she didn't want her cat making up to a man who thought the very worst of her. Sara strode across the kitchen and picked up the Siamese. "The man doesn't trust us, so he doesn't deserve our attention." She took Squared into the living room and put him in his bed near the radiator, then went into the foyer, where Paul waited.

"Sara, let me explain."

"No need. You made it perfectly clear that you thought I would make love with a man in the evening and then bring another home for the night shift. You figured I'd fallen into bed pretty damn fast with you and then again after you, right? And everyone knows a leopard doesn't change its spots." She grabbed her keys and opened the door. "See? I understand very well."

He pushed the door closed. "I'm sorry. I was wrong."

Looking at the hand firmly planted on the door, Sara said nothing.

"Do you hear me? I was wrong to think that about you. I-I was jealous. I heard you on the phone earlier. You made a guy dinner, you sounded so happy that he was back from wherever he's been, the bed wasn't made, and… I let my imagination run away with me. I'm sorry."

"I would never do that to you."

He drew her into his arms and clung to her. His heart beat rapidly under her ear.

"Do you remember our first time? In the back of that station wagon?"

"Of course. You were mad at me then, too, for being determined to give you my virginity before you left."

"I was upset. I wanted to leave you a virgin, not take any chances on an accident."

She stiffened but his soothing hands on her back eased the tension out of her. He didn't know his words affected her as they did, or why.

His heartbeat pounded in her ear as she talked. "I wanted to give myself to you, to prove that I loved you. I thought we'd start with lunch and I offered you a choice of ham and cheese or roast beef sandwiches, remember? You said it didn't matter, that it wouldn't be food you remembered from that day."

The moment came to mind clearly. "When I let you see my breasts, I was so embarrassed, I couldn't look at you. You pulled me onto your lap and I stared out the window so I wouldn't have to meet your eyes. A cardinal on a pine branch stared at us. Wind whipped up a dust cloud and masked us from the rest of the world."

He chuckled. "From the rest of the world? We were so far out in the boondocks we didn't need to worry about hiding." He sucked in a ragged breath. "Your skin was like silk. I couldn't touch you enough. I couldn't believe how lucky I was to have found you. I wondered if you had your way and we made love, how I'd stand leaving you."

They stood silently, rocking gently in each other's arms.

"Then we were naked, and you kissed me. I thought my heart would burst," she said softly. "I was nervous but so afraid you'd forget me when you left."

"I was scared to death that I'd hurt you. Or disappoint you, which is just as bad to a man in love. Then I touched you between your legs and knew that you were willing to give me that wonderful gift. Suddenly, I couldn't stand the thought of anyone else having you. I would have killed anyone who tried."

"The car was so hot. The sun...and you and me..."

"The smell of sex. Oh my God. Nights in Nam I'd lie awake thinking about that day and remembering that station wagon full of your scent... Well, many a time I almost came just with the memory." His laugh was short and harsh. "I truly thought I'd lost those feelings, but I guess I haven't. That's why I lost it in your bedroom. You should have been mine, forever."

She lifted her face to him.

He placed a gentle kiss on her forehead. "I don't want to think about tomorrow. If only for tonight, I need us to be Sara Noland and Seaman First Class Paul Steinert. Can we do that?"

"I'm not young like I used to be. I'm not beautiful or free from—"

His fingers touched her lips. "Shh. I saw you, and you're every bit as beautiful a woman as you were a girl. We'll let our memories take charge and our bodies will follow."

When their lips touched this time, it wasn't with the frenzied passion of before, but with a tenderness she'd last experienced a lifetime ago.

Paul deepened the caress, holding her head steady before sliding his tongue in to touch hers. He stooped and picked her up, turning toward the living room.

Setting her down, he slowly undressed her until she once again stood naked before him. The moon shining through the windows played over him with a watery light as he removed his own clothing. He sank to the floor, taking her with him.

They explored leisurely, touching and caressing and learning once again what brought pleasure. Paul the man was as powerful as the young sailor. His work toned his muscles into ropes of steel and his stomach had remained flat and hard. Hard, like another part of him stretching and pulsing along her thigh. Sara thrilled to the knowledge that he still wanted her. She knew a need that she hadn't experienced even in her dreams.

The clock on the mantle chimed twelve-thirty. Paul raised his head and turned toward the sound. Sara gently pulled him back to her, her lips trying to erase all awareness except for the two of them.

"You're so wet." His hand stroked between her thighs while his tongue rimmed her ear.

"Because I want you."

"I want you, too."

Rolling off her, he dug in the pocket of his jeans. The foil packet flashed in the moonlight. Seconds later, he knelt between her legs.

"I'm not going to ask why you had one of those with you," she said through a smile.

Even half shadowed, the look he gave her sizzled. "I think you know what I was hoping for. Besides, I was a Boy Scout."

"That's no surprise. You do know how to start a fire."

He chuckled, but it faded as he looked into her eyes. Braced on one elbow, he used his other hand to stroke his sex between the folds of her labia. "I'm going to start a fire in you, Sara."

"Already done. I desperately need you to put the fire out."

She moaned as he positioned himself to enter her. Inch by tantalizing inch he pushed, waited for her to stretch and accept him, pushed again. Wanting to be filled by him, the slow dance wore at her patience, but she wouldn't rush anything about this night.

When she took all of him, Paul dropped his head to her shoulder, panting with exertion. Then he nipped the tender skin where her shoulder met her neck and began withdrawing.

She lifted her legs to his waist. Her tongue darted out to lightly lick his lips. He groaned and then gently sucked her tongue as he rocked in and out of her.

Nothing in her memory had prepared her for this meeting of their bodies. They were older, but she couldn't tell from the way they moved together. His thumb flicked her nipple and she melted, just as she had at seventeen. His back and shoulders surged powerfully under her fingers, just as they had that first night. His body coaxed and then demanded hers dance with the passion he choreographed.

Whimpering, she pressed her mouth tighter to his. He thrust harder, faster, deeper. She came with wave after wave of pleasure that stunned her. She trembled with the force of her release. Unable to control her shudders, she knew what it was to be fulfilled, not simply satisfied.

Paul moaned. On arms shaking with strain, he held himself tightly pressed to her until he collapsed, spent. His breath came in harsh gasps.

"Sara." He said it as he would a prayer.

Rolling to the side, he slid his arm under her to pull her close. They lay like that for long minutes, the sound of their breathing filling the air.

"May I stay here with you tonight?"

"Here on the floor?" She wanted him to smile. She wanted him as happy as she was.

He chuckled. "Well, if we must." Squirming as though trying to get comfortable, he added, "I suppose I can deal with the hardness, but I'm not sure I can handle the chain saw."

Sara raised herself to see Squared lying beside Paul's head, his purr loud enough to be heard throughout the house. She laughed. Front paws tucked under him and tail curled protectively around his body, he gave Sara a languid look.

"It's not that often anymore that someone gets down to his level. He's found a friend."

"Squared doesn't mind if I spend the night. How about his mistress?"

She hesitated. His staying was dangerous to her mental health. After the shattering joy of what they'd just done, some part of him would always be here. So, where was the harm now in taking this one night for herself after the years of being alone?

How about if you find you don't want only a night's interlude? Suppose he's every wish you've ever made, every dream you've ever had and—

"I'd love it if you would stay."

He squeezed her to him. "Let's go to bed then."

She nodded against his chest. "Yes, let's."

* * * *

What a night! Paul looked at the clock on the microwave again. Nine-thirty. Mark would be shocked to know he'd slept so late. He grinned. Of course, he hadn't actually *slept* all that time.

Sara was amazing. In her sleep, she'd snuggled to his side, waking him. Then his touch woke her ,and they'd made love as though they'd been together for years instead of finding each other after a lifetime. When he opened his eyes to the morning light, the first thing he saw was Sara, watching him. From his chest, she inched her hand down his torso. By the time she reached his groin, he was erect and more than ready for her. He wouldn't have thought it possible.

"You're pretty damn amazing, old man," he muttered.

The coffee had finished dripping when he heard the shower end. Leaning against the counter wearing nothing but jeans and an unbuttoned shirt, he sipped the hot liquid and allowed his mind to wander, noticing the pedestrian things he'd been too preoccupied to see last night.

The kitchen was compact and utilitarian, with everything in easy reach. A backdoor opened onto a small yard edged with hundreds of flowers still in bloom. The colors and textures of the garden reminded him of Sara. Beauty and depth, order yet with a touch of wildness.

Sara! Last night she'd been just like he remembered. He was right to come here, right to find her. Right to make love to her. In all the years separating them, no one had ever made him feel as she did. That was because she touched his soul, not just his body.

He frowned at such romantic thoughts but knew in his heart it was true. What would happen now, he had no idea. He'd found a passage through time in her arms last night. Going back to Iowa, to his settled, content life, held little appeal, but they'd promised each other only one night.

He'd have to cut his fishing trip with Mitch short. He and Sara needed to talk about what had happened between them. Now that he'd tasted again what his heart had never really forgotten, he wanted more.

Noises came from the other part of the house. He poured her a cup of coffee but before he could move to take it to her, she opened and closed the front door.

Damn, he should have thought of bringing in the paper. At the sound of her footsteps, he turned with a smile.

"If I hadn't thought it would make you late, I'd have come in and washed your back," he said at the same time a woman announced, "Mom, here's your paper, and look what Squared brought in from somewhere."

He held out the cup, staring in shock. The woman seemed stunned, too, and no wonder.

"Oh, my God." Paul broke the silence but not his gaze. She had his hair color and blue eyes, his height and build but Sara's cheekbones and grace. He put down the cup before he dropped it and leaned on the counter for support.

She put the newspaper on the table along with the foil condom wrapper she'd smilingly held up when she entered the kitchen, but clutched the cat to her. "I don't understand this," she whispered. She cleared her throat and started in a stronger tone. "I don't know who you are, but we must be related. I mean, it's like looking in a mirror."

The bedroom door closed, and heels struck the hardwood floor.

"You wonderful man, I smell coffee," Sara stated, coming around the corner into the kitchen. She ground to a halt, and the blood drained from her face. "What are you doing here, Paula?"

"*Paula!*" The word tore from him.

Sara closed her eyes, taking a deep, ragged breath. When she faced him again she stood tall and with shoulders back, meeting his eyes unflinchingly. Like a queen. Or a warrior. Letting him know without words that whatever battle was between them would be fought to the end, but not at this time.

Like hell! They'd settle right now why she hadn't told him he had a daughter. He felt punched in the gut. God, it hurt to breathe. He was a father.

If he'd passed the woman on the street, giving her a quick glance, he might not have noticed the resemblance. But face to face in Sara's kitchen, there was no other explanation. Her stance, the proud tilt of her head, even her bearing were all reminiscent of Sara as a girl. But there was no doubt she was also a Steinert.

A second later, Sara turned her whole attention to the woman—his daughter—and a host of emotions replaced her warrior expression: fear, concern, sorrow. But mostly, love.

"Mom?" Shock was over. Confusion was passing through her eyes, and anger was fast on its heels.

"Paula, please sit down. I have something to tell you, and-and it isn't going to be easy." Her voice caught. "I am so sorry you found out this way, so sorry you had to find out at all."

"Sorry she had to find out at *all*? Sorry I found out, too, I'll bet. Just tell her, Sara. She has a right to know." Aiming his gaze at the woman—Paula—he said, "My name is Paul Steinert, and you're my daughter."

Chapter 10

No one moved or spoke. *Strange how my life can fall apart in such stillness,* Sara thought.

Paul's eyes glittered with fury. Disbelief reflected in Paula's face as she stared at her father.

Sara was the first to take action. Crossing the room, she called Jennette and asked her to open the gallery. Then she fed Squared. Anything to make the day seem ordinary. With the sixth sense animals have for human emotions, Squared had flattened his ears and remained quietly in Paula's arms. But some form of normalcy returned when Sara dumped food in his dish, and he jumped down to hurry across the floor and eat.

"I'm leaving," Paula stated.

"No! Stay." Sara held out her hand. "Please."

Paula turned away. She crossed her arms, but she didn't go.

Sara let her arm drop to her side. "Paul, can we sit at the table and talk?"

A small portion of her mind took note of the fact that she sounded casual, as though the two hostile people standing before her had dropped in for a light breakfast.

She understood how Paul must feel. Shaken, on unfamiliar ground. Yet, he would walk away from this the least scathed. After all, he didn't know Paula. He had no emotional bonds, no responsibility to her, or to Sara for that matter. By simply taking a few steps he could leave here, putting everything behind him.

Paula surely felt the most affected, the most hurt and betrayed. *God, what have I done? It would have been so much better to explain years ago.*

Why hadn't she told Paula the full story? Any shame she'd felt was long past. She'd done what she thought was right, in the best way she could. As an adult, Paula could have handled the truth. Sara had kept alive a lie, much as her mother had with her, thinking the truth would serve no purpose.

It would have served a purpose now.

Sara was comforted by one thought, at least. Paula knew how much she was loved. There'd never been a moment in her life when she could have doubted it, so once truth was separated from fiction, Sara knew Paula would understand. She simply had to.

"Will you button your shirt, at least, so you don't look like you just climbed out of bed with my mother?" Paula's tone clearly showed her repugnance at Paul's presence, but it paled in comparison to the tone she used when her eyes focused on the condom wrapper. "Oh, God. You *did* just climb out of bed." Blindly, she pulled out a chair and dropped into it.

"Excuse me." Paul left the room. Sara poured a cup of coffee for Paula, who sat sullen and silent at the table. When Paul returned, he was fully clothed and looked ready to walk out the door. Sara and Paul stared at each other. Then in tacit agreement, joined Paula.

No one said anything. Paul stared at the table, lifting his eyes only to glance in palpable wonder and curiosity at Paula, who glared into space. Anger twisted her usually open expression into something hard.

Sara fought nausea. How could she deconstruct who she'd been for her adult life? Once she unknotted the thread of lies, would anything be left? Who would she be when she finished?

"Paula, I told you your father was dead, because I thought he was. Before you were born, Grandpa told me that the boat Paul was on had been destroyed and that everyone on it was killed." She paused to take a breath. "We weren't married, so no notification would have come to me."

"But our last name is Richards. Not—" she flipped her hand in Paul's direction, without looking at him, "—whatever his—"

"Steinert," Paul interrupted. "You might not have my name, but you're a Steinert."

Paula ignored him. "What about my father?" She glared at Paul then back at Sara. "The only father I've ever known, the man you told me about, was Paul Richards. Who did you marry?"

140

Looking at Paul, Sara saw the intensity with which he stared back, every muscle tight, waiting for her answer. "No one. I never married anyone." Paula exhaled a deep breath. Sara glimpsed a gleam of satisfaction under the outrage in Paul's eyes. However, it was to her daughter she owed this explanation and she focused on Paula. "Richards is your grandmother's maiden name." She took another deep breath then continued. "Your father and I met my senior year of high school, and we fell in love."

Paul's chair scraped the floor violently as he jumped up from the table. Squared spun away from his dish and fled at the noise. Paul ran his hand through his hair and paced the kitchen.

"Paul, *please* sit down."

"Just get on with it." Rough, harsh. No quarter there.

With a sigh, she looked back at Paula, who watched her father warily. "We thought we loved each other, but we were young, and five or six weeks isn't enough time to build real trust. I didn't receive any letters from him, and thought he'd used me. When he didn't hear from me, he thought I'd changed my mind."

For a moment, she stared into space, unable to proceed. "When you're seventeen, you think you know everything. But you don't." She looked at her daughter again. "When I found I was pregnant, my parents sent me down here to live with Aunt Barbara until you were born." Twisting her wedding ring, she gathered the rest of her courage. The whole story had to be told now. She'd never get another chance to make Paula understand.

What if she hates me after all of this? Oh, God, please, she can't hate me.

"I used Mother's name and told people that my husband was overseas. With the Marine base here, no one questioned it—the situation was all too common. I was supposed to place you for adoption and then go back to Virginia and enroll in college. But then I heard Paul was dead." She forced herself to keep speaking. "You were all I had of him. I loved him, and because of that I wanted you."

Reaching out, she placed her hand over Paula's. "But sweetheart, from the moment I first saw you, it was you I loved and gave my heart to. Never doubt that for a moment, Paula. You've been my life and I've never regretted a minute of it."

141

A derisive grunt came from Paul, who continued to prowl the kitchen. "Get to the decades of lies."

Ignoring him she looked only at Paula. "I changed my name legally to Sara Richards, and held to the story about your father, except that I became a widow instead of a young wife. But what I told you about your father, the essence of him, Paula, was true. I described Paul. As he used to be, anyway."

"In case you haven't noticed, I've been an adult a long time." Paula's voice rose to a strident pitch. "Why maintain the story? Were you ever planning to tell me the truth? Didn't I *deserve* the truth?"

"Yes, you did. I'm sorry. I got so used to wearing these rings, that sometimes I forgot myself that there wasn't a husband behind them." Flexing her fingers, Sara stared at the bands on her left hand. "A short while ago, your grandmother brought me some old letters, and they explained a lot. They made me realize that I needed to see Paul's parents. I thought it was time they knew they had a granddaughter. That's when I discovered your father was alive."

"You mean that business trip? But…that was a month ago. My God! Didn't you think it was important to tell me I had a flesh-and-blood father? It's not exactly a small detail." She drew away.

Sara sensed the withdrawal emotionally more than the actual physical movement. She wanted to cradle Paula in her arms as she had when Paula was small, to kiss the boo-boo and find a way to make the pain disappear. This time, however, she'd been the cause of the hurt and making it go away would take more than a kiss and a smile.

"Yes, Sara—" Paul stopped pacing to look at her, "—there are a couple of people wondering why you didn't say more on that 'business trip.' You said you wanted to introduce yourself to my parents. Huh! I thought you were there to ask them for money. I still think that, but you were going to soften the pot with a granddaughter, too."

"Money? Why would I ask for money?"

"To save your damn gallery. To help finance that building you showed me last night. That's why you took me there, isn't it? Hoping for old time's sake I'd loan you some cash?"

"Wait a minute!" Paula cried. "Save the gallery—what's *that* about?" She snapped her head to her mother, her harsh voice making Sara's eyes widen in surprise. "Is the gallery in trouble?"

"It's a minor problem." She threw a fast glaring look at Paul. "Nothing I can't handle, anyway. And I didn't tell you because you have enough going on right now. I didn't want to add to your worries." Still holding her daughter's hand, she faced Paul forcefully. "First of all, I never would have asked your parents for money. The thought that they might *think* I was after money is one of the reasons I kept silent when Paula was growing up. I admit, I wasn't entirely truthful when we met at your house."

He snorted. "No kidding. Seems to me, hearing about a daughter is more important than hearing about a granddaughter, but you never mentioned her, did you, even the next day when you swore you were telling me the truth about your visit. Do you even know what the truth is, Sara?"

In the seconds that passed, Sara felt she'd lived a lifetime. Or had a lifetime of living destroyed.

Her shoulders slumped with weariness, and she shrank into the chair. If only she could crawl back into bed and pull the covers over her head, the way she had when she was a child, afraid of the room's shadows.

She cast a longing glance at the back door. She could walk out right now. Walk away and not owe explanations to anyone. How wonderful would that be? But in her heart, that freedom wasn't what she most wanted. She wanted Paula to understand that even mothers make mistakes, and for Paul to hold her and confess that he'd always loved her. Loved her still.

She wanted them to say they forgave her.

"Yes, Paul," she said quietly. "I know what truth is. It's deciding to raise a daughter as a single mother, accepting help from relatives you'd hardly known before you found yourself alone and pregnant. It's giving up a future you'd always taken for granted, and nursing measles and flu instead.

"It's holding your breath when she's a few minutes late coming in from a date. And worrying if you were ever going to make a good life for the two of you. It's passing up dates with guys who asked you out because babysitters were expensive.

143

"The truth is nights of crying, knowing that you've made mistakes but hoping what you did right outweighed what you did wrong. My truth is seeing, by the grace of God, that what I did right shines in the eyes of a beautiful woman I've been proud to call my daughter. That's been *my* truth since I was eighteen. What's your truth, Paul?"

His face lost all color and it was a shaking hand he placed on the counter. "I would have helped," he managed, in a strangled voice. "I would have shared all of that with you, gladly, if I'd known."

"Would you? I'm not sure of that. Not sure at all. It's a moot point, since *I thought you were dead.* I had no chance to tell you about our girl."

"That's not fair, and you know it." Strength returned to his voice, and he stood straight, ready to do battle again. "Telling my parents about her would have been the right thing to do, and because you didn't, you took away my chance to be a father. Besides," he said with a sneer, "I was told you'd *married* some guy. What was I supposed to do? Come down here and demand you explain yourself for falling out of love with me? 'Cause that's what I thought had happened."

Sara stood so fast her chair fell over. "That's exactly what you should have done! And why didn't you? Pride!" She tugged on the wedding ring set her father had purchased for her. "Tell me, what was *I* supposed to do, Paul? Let it be known I wasn't married? Should I have given up the only veil of respectability your daughter and I had? Here!" Yanking the rings free, she threw them at him. "There's the husband you were too proud to face. The mere *thought* of those two bands kept you from knowing your child, Paul. Take them! Cold comfort they'll give you on lonely nights. I should know."

"Stop it! Stop it, both of you!" The shout filled the room. Ashen-faced, Paula sat ramrod-straight. Her hands, clasped on the table, trembled and her voice cracked with emotion. "Just stop it."

Horrified, Sara's hands flew to cover her mouth and she rushed the few steps to Paula's side. "Oh, baby, I'm so sorry. I wasn't thinking." She tried to hold Paula but was shrugged off. "I never intended to hurt you, never! If I could have prevented this—" She waved her hand distractedly at the kitchen in general. "I wish I could go back and change things. If I could reverse time, I'd tell you, Paula, I'd try to explain how it was. Please, can't you understand why I did what I did?"

Paula ignored her mother's plea. "You saw *him* in Iowa a month ago?"

"Yes." Sara stepped back, eying her daughter and fearing where this was leading. "That's the first I knew he was alive." Wordlessly, Paul righted the chair and took Sara's arm, guiding her into it. Then he sat down again, himself.

"I repeat my earlier question: when were you planning to tell me any of this? How long were you going to lie to me about my own family and past? Until I had children, or *they* had children? Until you were on your deathbed? 'Oh, by the way, honey, I slept with a man and got pregnant with you. Sorry I neglected to mention it but look him up. He's somewhere in Iowa.' Or maybe you were never going to let me in on the family secret."

Sara's expression must have given her away because Paula gave a shrill laugh. "You weren't, were you? You would never have told me about Paul. Or maybe…" She glanced at him and then at Sara. "Resemblance aside, maybe there's another reason you weren't anxious to talk about him. Are you really sure he's even the guy? I mean, you've been 'seeing' Matthew for years, what's to say—"

Paul's hand slammed on the table, causing both women to jump. "Do *not* talk to your mother that way, do you hear me?"

Bile rose in Sara's throat. She was certain she would be sick.

"Who are you to tell me what to do?"

"I'm. Your. *Father*. For better or worse. You're talking about your mother, a woman who gave up everything, against all advice, to raise you and love you. I might not have known you existed until fifteen minutes ago, but one look in the mirror is all it takes to know the truth of who your father is."

Paula's eyes shot fire, but she said nothing more.

"Your mother was a beautiful girl when we met, and we loved each other. We were caught up in circumstances we had no control over. Had things been even a little different, we would have been married." He arched his brows at the woman sitting across the table from him. "And then we wouldn't be having this discussion with you."

He took a breath and continued. "If you want to know who staged this, ask your grandmother. She and your grandfather kept your mom and me apart and set up the whole charade. If they'd had their way, I never would have known about you. You'd have been adopted and—" His face contorted with emotion. "Ask *her* to explain how they enjoyed playing God with other people's lives." Bitterness colored his words, his gestures. Sara saw his hands curl into fists on the table. And it was all her fault.

"I don't believe you."

Paul studied Paula for a few seconds more, then left the kitchen.

Sara shot from her chair and rushed after him. "Paul, wait!"

"Sara, this is too much to take. I need some time to think." Without a touch or even a glance, he turned. The front door closed after him. For a moment, Sara was engulfed by silence.

"So much for the father figure," Paula stated when Sara came back into the kitchen. Absently, she picked up the condom wrapper. "What about Matthew? Everyone's been assuming…"

"Matthew has nothing to do with this. He got in from field exercises and came for dinner last night. He's asked me to go to California with him."

Paula looked at her mother with a mocking smile. "Well, you certainly had a busy night, didn't you? I guess *Daddy* showed up just in time to provide variety. A man in California and one in Iowa."

Sara's heart ached. Her head ached. Hysteria simmered just below the surface. She didn't have much reserve left.

She pointed a shaking finger at Paula, trying to think before she said something to make the situation worse. "Stop it, and I mean right *now*. Don't dare say another word like that to me."

Closing her eyes, she prayed for strength. "I'm sorry this happened as it did, and that I didn't tell you sooner. I know it's hard to find that everything you believed has been turned upside down. But what's done is done. I'm your mother and I won't take those kinds of accusations from you. *Especially* not from you. I love you more than life itself.

"You're an adult. Even though you might not understand my motives, I always did what I thought was best for you. The fact that you're lashing out as though you've had a miserable life because of me is hurtful. For the first time in your life, Paula Bethany Richards, I'm ashamed of you."

For seconds nothing happened. Then Paula's face crumpled. "I'm sorry!"

Tears streamed down Sara's cheeks. She took Paula's hand and sat beside her. "I'm sorry, too. I didn't know how to tell you. I wanted you to be proud of me, not know that I'd done something I'd cautioned you against. It was easier just to let things go on as they were, but I shouldn't have been such a coward. I should have trusted you."

"How could I have said those things about you? I didn't mean them, Mom, I didn't!"

"Shh, I know that. You were hurt and confused. I'm sorry. I'm so sorry, sweetheart."

As the tears subsided, Sara gave a short laugh. "That's enough sorrys, don't you think? I don't want to be sad, I want to be happy. Now you have the choice of knowing your father and his family. You have an aunt and uncle, and a cousin, who looks very much like you."

Paula wiped her cheeks dry with the heel of her hand. "You know the strange thing? Dan said my father must have done something to hurt you, and that's why you don't trust yourself with men. What happened between you?"

Sara dumped out their cold coffee and poured fresh. "Your grandparents didn't want us together. They made sure to get their way."

"So he was right?" Paula said under her breath. Thinking, she furrowed her brows and sat back. "There's so much to understand. Is this why you still haven't spoken to Nana?"

Sara raised her brows and Paula shrugged. "She calls me every week hoping I'll give her a hint of why you're mad. I asked why she doesn't just go to the gallery and find out what's wrong, but she said it's up to you to go to her."

"That sounds like her. She's my mother and for that I love her, but she's a controlling person. I know she and Dad did what they thought was right. They were strict parents. Others might have, but we didn't embrace the sexual revolution. I was always what we called a good girl." She smiled at the memory.

"When I told them I was going to have a baby they were shocked and hurt, and I was scared and totally lost. It's not like today's world. They did what "good" families did back then, they sent me somewhere to have the baby and then put it up for adoption. If I had done that, I could have gone home, gone to college, and everything would have been back to normal."

She stroked Paula's hair and examined her face. "But things would have been all wrong. The moment I saw you I knew I could never give you up."

"I love you, Mom."

"I love you, too, sweetheart. I knew what she and my dad did before I left for Iowa, but everything changed when I found Paul alive. When I realized then what their meddling cost us, well, I've been afraid of what I'd say if I talked to your grandmother."

"When you came home, why didn't you tell me?"

"Things change with time, Paula. He wasn't the man I remembered. I... Somehow I didn't think he'd welcome knowing about you, and if I didn't tell him, I couldn't very well tell you."

She toyed with her cup. "I've messed up a lot, honey, I know that. I've taken the easy way, letting others decide things for me many times in life. Mostly because it meant security and a safety net for both of us. Paul told me I should have made more of an effort to reach him, especially when I knew I was pregnant, and he was right. But I was so sure he'd deserted me. I was terrified of what my future would be, and I ended up making a decision that affected all three of us. The wrong decision."

Shaking her head, she admitted, "The few times I trusted my own judgment are the times I screwed up the worst. I can never make it up to you, what you lost, but I hope you know I always loved you, above all else."

Paula leaned forward. "Mom, of course I know that. I'm so grateful you didn't give me up!" She stood and hugged Sara. "Look, I'm sure he was a very nice man, or you wouldn't have thought you loved him. And I can see why you didn't seek him out after Vietnam. You thought he was gone forever. He, on the other hand, could have found you, could have fought for you even if he thought you'd married someone else. But he didn't. And now here he is, looking for…what *is* he looking for?" Moving back, she looked at Sara. "A slice of the past or a way to feel good about himself again, regardless of the pain it might cause you? I saw the way you looked at him when he was leaving."

Sara's cheeks infused with heat and Paula gave a satisfied nod. "Maybe this isn't being adult about things, but it's the way I feel. He may be my father, but I don't choose to be his daughter."

Sara watched with sadness as Paula left the room. "I'm sorry," she whispered to the emptiness.

Drained of energy, she nonetheless found the engagement ring and wedding band that had been her badges of honor for so long. "Badges of deception," she muttered.

She held them up to the light. It had to be her imagination, but they seemed slightly mottled. Gold couldn't tarnish, but to her they were suddenly imperfect, cheap, tawdry. Wrong.

She walked to her bedroom and put them in the back of her underwear drawer. Today, officially, she was no longer Sara Richards, widow. This was her first day free from the lies of the past.

If only she could put the truth of her feelings for Paul behind her as easily.

* * * *

"Please be home, Dan," Paula said under her breath. Pushing the final number on the cell phone, she closed the bathroom door. She'd driven like a madwoman that morning to talk to her mother about Dan and what he wanted. And what she wanted but was too afraid to take.

The battle she and Dan waged, the reason she'd rushed to Beaufort, had shredded her emotions before she ever arrived home. Now, she needed to hear his voice, *had* to hear him say he loved her. She swiped the tissue under her nose again. She hadn't cried so much in one day since…since never.

149

"Yeah?"

He still sounds angry. They had caller ID, so he knew exactly to whom he directed his anger.

"Dan?"

One word, yet he must have heard the raw feeling. "Paula? Honey, where are you? Are you all right?" There was no anger now, only concern. And love. Thank God!

Tears struck a path down her cheeks, but she fought to keep her voice steady. "I'm okay. I just needed to hear you." She leaned her head against the wall. "I love you more than anything in the world, Dan."

"I love you, too." He still sounded worried. "Are you at your mom's?"

"Yes. Dan, I think you should ask your friend to come over and look at the house. I don't know if I can get out of my contract, though. If I have to stay until the end year, I'll find a small place, and I'll come to Chicago as soon as the school year is over."

"Paula, you're scaring me. What's wrong, sweetheart?"

"I just learned a lot of things, about my mom and dad, and who I am. I know it's stupid and it doesn't change a thing for me, but I still feel strange. I know now why my mom holds back on so many things. When I was growing up I must have picked up on some of her fears without realizing what was happening."

She gripped the phone tighter and closed her eyes. "I see her hesitance in my holding back from Chicago. I hear her when I tell you I can't go with you. I feel her when I'm afraid to take a step into the unknown. And I let it affect us, my feelings for you. Isn't that the dumbest thing you've ever heard? Because, Dan, I've never doubted you. When you said you loved me the first time, I knew it was true, and—"

"Paula, do you hear this?" Metal jangled in her ear. "That's my keys. I'll be there in an hour, honey. Stay at your mom's and wait for me."

"Dan?" Her whisper came out a rasp. "I have something to tell you."

"What?"

"Je t'aime." She heard his sharp intake of breath.

"Does that mean 'Drag me to your cave and make mad, passionate love to me'?"

"Yes."

He laughed. The sound rumbled along the seventy-plus miles of airwaves, warming her from the inside out.

"You lie. But I appreciate the thought. Paula, there's something I've wanted to say, but the time hasn't been right. I want to tell you now."

His laugh had relaxed her. "What is it?"

"I don't want you to come to Chicago with me. Not the way things are."

She caught the sob in her throat. Their fight this morning had cut him deeper than she'd realized. She'd said she didn't want to give up all she had on the chance they'd still be happy in Illinois. She'd told him she'd wait for him in Charleston—maybe. She'd been a hateful bitch, unable to acknowledge the cold fear she felt. Fear of letting go of one life to step into a new. And now she'd lost him anyway, with her refusal to trust him with her soul instead of only her heart.

"Dan, I'm so sorry about this morning. I wish—"

"Honey, please stop crying. I want you to be my wife."

"What?"

"Marry me, Paula. Living together is ridiculous for two people who love each other as much as we do. I want you to know I'm totally committed to you, and I want you to belong to me in name as well as every other way. It's always been you, only you, ever since we met. In my heart, we're already married."

"We don't need to discuss my answer when you get here because it's yes."

"Je t'adore." Funny, Dan's voice sounded as raspy as hers.

She grinned through her tears. "You devil! You've learned French. And you were so wrong, Tanner, when you said you wouldn't sound sexy speaking French. I've never heard anything so damn sexy in my life."

He laughed. "Well, that's just about the extent of my French, except for a few more words you might like."

She sighed into the phone. "Be very careful driving, Dan, but hurry."

She pressed End on her cell phone but didn't move from the bathroom where she'd gone to talk privately. The house was quiet. Paula took a deep breath and thanked God she'd come to discuss her worries with her mother today. Otherwise, she might never have met her father. She might not have gained the insight into her mother's fears and recognized them as her own. And without that knowledge, she might have made a huge mistake.

Paula bowed her head. Her mother and father had shown her what life could be if she let doubt rule her life. She might have learned behavior inadvertently from her mother's example, but she wasn't her mother. And Dan wasn't her father.

Dan might have insisted he was leaving for the Midwest with or without her, but beneath her insecurities she always believed he'd come for her, coaxing and nudging her to take tiny steps toward a future. Their future. He might make a tactical retreat in their relationship now and then, but he'd never give up the prize of their love, no matter what he thought she'd done. If Paul had been Dan, he would have come to Carolina and stayed until Sara declared her feelings, one way or the other. And then he would have pushed her again.

Squared used his head to bump open the door and sauntered in. "Of course," Paula said to the cat, stroking his back, "Dan and I have known each other for years. Mom and Paul knew each other for a few weeks. Can you imagine how wonderful it is to have a love so strong you hold onto it all those years?"

The reality struck when she gazed into Squared's blue eyes. *Or how awful?*

Chapter 11

Mid-afternoon of that same day, the day he'd seen his own shock of recognition reflected in his daughter's face, Paul stood beside Mitch Hamilton on one of the Hamilton Charter Fishing piers in Port Royal. Paul's arms were crossed and his feet braced, as though balancing on a moving ship. Thanks to Sara, he hadn't felt more off balance in his life.

"What do you think, Paul?" Mitch wore a white polo shirt under a light blue sports jacket. In contrast to Paul, Mitch's stomach bulged over his belt and his black hair, once thick and wavy, showed signs of thinning on top.

Paul took his time answering. Thrown by the events of the morning, he'd almost canceled the meeting, but came because he'd said he would. During the long tour of Mitch's fishing boat company, Paul's interest gradually engaged, despite his internal confusion and turmoil.

They'd examined the fleet of five boats, then Mitch asked for comments on the boathouse, the docks and equipment. The only thing Paul wasn't asked to inspect was the bookkeeping, although Mitch introduced him to the office staff on hand and showed him the booking calendar.

Mitch initially said he wanted Paul to give his opinion on the state of the boat engines—something for which he might be qualified—but he suspected Mitch had pulled a bait and switch. He'd lured Paul in by asking for advice on the boats, but he really wanted something totally different.

"It's a nice set up, Mitch. If they were my boats, I'd spend the time and money to overhaul them before your real season starts. Otherwise, you'll be nickel-and-dimed to death, like it sounds you were last year. I noticed a little dry rot on the *Misty Morning*, so I'd examine the whole fleet real carefully."

Mitch grinned and slapped Paul's shoulder. "See? That's why I wanted you to come down here. When I bought the company last spring, I contracted with the same mechanical outfit the previous owner had. They do good work on bits and pieces, but I think we need someone full time who really knows what they're doing." Mitch jammed his hands in his pockets. "This is a great location, too, huh?"

"Yeah, it is. What did you say this creek is?"

"Battery Creek." Mitch pointed south. "Right up there's where it meets the Beaufort River." Casting a sideways look at Paul, he continued, "A man couldn't find a better place to live than the Carolina or Georgia coast."

Even without Mitch's endorsement, Paul would have agreed that the Beaufort area was pleasant. The wind striking the pier had a nip to it, coming off the water as it did, but the southern sunlight kept the chill from being all-encompassing. He'd heard on the radio that another storm had rolled across the plains, and there he stood, comfortable on the open water in nothing heavier than a windbreaker.

"So, what do you think?"

Paul shifted to look at his old friend. "I think you're an ugly old cuss."

"Yeah, and you're a lying S.O.B., too." The men smiled at each other. "I mean, what do you think about moving down here and taking over operations for me?"

"What?" He'd half thought Mitch would ask him to do some work while he was there. One of the engines could use a quick tune-up now, and he'd considered Mitch might couch the request in terms of, *If this boat ran better, we could use it to go fishing.* But Mitch's proposition took him completely by surprise.

"I want you to come and take over operations. You'd be in charge of all maintenance and repairs, hiring and firing, overseeing the office—the whole works."

"You're out of your fucking mind."

"I don't think so. Look," Mitch said, enthusiasm animating his gestures, "you're the best mechanic we had on the ship. Nobody questioned that. You've run your own business with the farm, and you told me a few days ago that you've even gotten involved in investing."

"That's not the same thing."

Mitch opened his hand and shrugged one shoulder in a gesture of unconcern. "Sure it is. Look, I found this company by accident last year, and I got it for a song. I really want it to do well. Maybe because of the times in Nam we sat around talking about what we missed most. For me, it was fishing off Jones

Beach." He shot Paul a smile and quirked his brows. "After women, of course. Now I've got this great little outfit that's gonna sink if I don't do something."

"You need someone with experience in charter fishing. I know farming because I grew up on a farm. I don't know anything about fishing like this."

"When a certain kind of fish is running can be learned. Leadership and instinct can't. I ended up with almost all new crews after I bought the company. They're good men, but there's no spirit organizing them. You know equipment and engines, and you proved years ago you're a leader. What I need is someone I can trust to pull it all together and get Hamilton Charter on its feet. I can find a dozen guys who know when blues run."

Paul turned to look out at the creek. The tide was out, exposing long stalks of marsh grass. He remembered Sara's explanation of pluff mud and smiled in spite of the knot of anger thoughts of her produced. Too bad the same person who made him smile also enraged him. The fantasy of working on the water again and to feel challenged with something new, enticed him as nothing had in years. And if Mitch's company were somewhere other than Beaufort, he might be tempted.

"I can't, Mitch. In fact, I'm real sorry but I shouldn't even stay for our few days of fishing. I heard on the news coming over here that they got hit at home with a bad storm and my brother will need help."

"Is there anything I can say to make you change your mind? I'll treat you right, you know that."

"Oh, yeah. That's not the problem at all. I just can't leave Mark and my nephew high and dry. You know..." Paul shrugged.

Mitch nodded. "Yeah, I know. But promise you'll come back next spring or summer so we can go out and reel in something big."

"Sure thing."

"Let me buy you lunch at least." The two walked back to their cars. "Did you already reschedule your flight?"

"Yes, I leave Charleston at eight tonight."

"I wish you'd let me have another shot at talking you into giving this a try, Paul, but I understand where you're coming from."

But not what I'm running from.

* * * *

Paul sat across the table from Mitch.

"I haven't eaten here before. It's nice." Mitch swallowed the bite of chicken salad sandwich he was eating.

The local restaurant faced the river and the walkway along its edge. Only the previous evening, he and Sara had walked the very path Paul now viewed. Today, the view was the same, but the world looked different.

"Yes. Nice town, actually. I've seen a little of it since yesterday."

"There's almost always a nice breeze I'm told, but it still gets damn hot in the summer."

"It's a myth that Iowa is always cold," Paul said with a laugh. "In the summer it gets damn hot there, too. But there's no comparison in the winters. Look at this weather, and it's November."

He took a bite and looked up as a group of people came in. His quick intake of breath almost choked him, and he grabbed the glass of tea to wash down the food.

Damn! Why couldn't they have waited twenty more minutes? They took a table on the opposite side of the room. Paula and a man sat with their backs to him; Sara and a man with dark, short hair and an air of confidence sat facing him.

Although he barely touched Sara's arm, the man was definitely proprietary. When she said something and he laughed, as he just had, he looked at her as though they shared an intimacy. Matthew. It couldn't be anyone else. He just *oozed* Marine.

Paul tried to keep his eyes and mind off Sara, but it was hard. A few minutes after the group entered, Mitch turned to follow Paul's glance. In the same moment, Paula pointed something out to the unknown man, displaying her profile.

156

"Shit. No wonder you keep looking back there. Those two women are beautiful." Mitch faced Paul with a leer. "The brunette's pretty, but the blonde—now there's a hot number. If it wasn't for Bonnie…" He shook his hand in the air as though it was on fire.

"You're old enough to be her father," Paul snapped.

Mitch shrugged good naturedly. "Yeah, what's that got to do with anything?"

Paul looked at Paula once more, giving the back of her head a worried frown. Knowing Mitch didn't mean anything by the comment didn't ease his mind. Never again would he look at a woman and not remember that she was some man's daughter.

He shifted his gaze to see Sara staring at him. Making a pointed effort to pick up his sandwich, he concentrated on eating.

"Doesn't matter anyway, because Bonnie'd have my manhood if she saw me look at a babe with lust."

"Bonnie's a good woman, Mitch. You're lucky she was soft enough in the head to take you on."

Mitch laughed, then sighed, as he picked up the last potato chip. "It took me many years and lots of mistakes to find her, that's for sure. And it's true that I was lucky. God only knows where I'd be today if it wasn't for her."

Sober, he leaned forward. "Paul, you should find a good woman and settle down. Trust me. With the right woman you'll never be sorry." He started to pop the chip in his mouth but stopped. "Don't tell Bonnie I said all that. She'd never let me live it down."

Early this morning he'd almost believed he'd found a woman. *The* woman. Again.

Then he'd been blindsided. Forget the times she'd lied in the past, he'd put all of that behind him when he decided to visit her gallery and ask her to dinner. His desire for her was greater than holding onto a pack of untruths that weren't even all Sara's fault.

But a month ago she'd had two chances to tell him about Paula and she'd purposely left him in the dark. He'd missed half of his daughter's life, and Sara would have had him miss the rest.

Even now he saw another lie. She'd said that guy, Matthew, was a friend. The way he looked at her spoke of much more than friendship, yet last night she'd made love with Paul. What kind of woman did that?

Sara was beautiful. At times, she was wonderful. But a liar could never be trusted. Like an onion, each layer of Sara peeled away only to reveal another half-truth.

He fought a lump in his throat. Paula was a grown woman and he'd never known she existed. There should be a thread, a psychic bond of some kind connecting father and child, so that one sensed the other. He'd never felt a thing alerting him to her presence in the world.

Now, by God, I don't want to lose her. Maybe she wouldn't want to know him, but he'd make her. They had a long way to go before they established any kind of relationship, but he had to try, had to make a start, and this was his chance. She lived in Charleston. Beaufort was a lot closer to Charleston than Iowa.

"Mitch, suppose I tell you I've changed my mind about that job?"

A grin creased Mitch's face. "I'd say, good. When do you want to start?" Still holding the smile, his brows furrowed. "What changed your mind?"

"A woman." Paul stretched his hand across the table and they sealed the deal. "I'll start right away. I have to go home, but I'll be back within a week. You're sure of this?"

"Never surer." Mitch kept smiling. "A woman, huh? You work fast."

"Sometimes fate steps in and takes control."

"So true, buddy." He looked toward the door where they'd entered. "I'd better call Bonnie and let her know I'll be home tonight." He threw his napkin on the table, dug out his wallet and picked up the check. "Our first business lunch. Might as well start collecting receipts."

Burning Bridges

"I'll be right with you."

After Mitch left, Paul glanced back at Sara's table. He couldn't help himself. Animated conversation took place among everyone except Sara. She sat quietly, smiling now and then, letting the talk flow around her.

Pushing his plate aside, Paul took a last gulp of tea and stood. After a moment's hesitation, he threw back his shoulders, took a breath and strode to their table.

Matthew stopped mid-sentence to look up at him, then immediately rose to face him. He stood like a lion protecting his pride, warning in that non-verbal way men have, *mine*.

For a moment, electricity crackled between the men. Paul broke contact to look at Sara, then Paula, who sat stony-faced, staring at the wall behind her mother. Finally, he looked at the unknown man next to Paula, who was no longer sitting.

When Paul looked back at Sara, she found her voice. "This is Paul Steinert. Paul, meet Dan Tanner, Paula's friend." Tanner's expression was neutral when they shook hands, then he moved behind Paula and placed his hands on her shoulders.

"And this is my good friend, Matthew Abrams."

With reluctance, Paul shook Matthew's hand. He'd given Sara up in his mind, but he couldn't prevent the twinge of jealousy he felt seeing her with this man. "Abrams? The Marine? Sara told me all about you."

Matthew gave him a cold smile. "Really? Funny, she's never mentioned you once in the years I've known her. At any rate, if she told you about us, then you must know she's thinking of coming to California with me."

Abrams had asked Sara to move away with him? No one else at the table seemed surprised, so this was one more omission, just for him. *Guess she couldn't find time to tell me between bouts of making love last night. Wonder if she's told Abrams about that?*

Paul stared at Sara. "I thought you were going to make an offer on the firehouse you showed me last night. Or is the move a backup plan?" A quick glance at the stony look on Abrams' face told him Sara hadn't shared any information about last night.

"I haven't committed to anything yet," she said stiffly.

Knowing you, that doesn't surprise me. "I see."

"Mom, you shouldn't stay here for my sake." Paula finally came to life and turned to look up with shining eyes at the man behind her. "Dan asked me to marry him today and we'll be living in Chicago." He bent to kiss her and they smiled at each other like two love-struck kids.

"Paula! Why didn't you tell me before?"

Paula's kept her eyes on Dan. "He just asked, when he arrived. He wanted to ask me in French." The two laughed softly at some private joke.

Matthew reached in front of Paul to shake Dan's hand. "I'm happy for you, Dan. And Paula, sweetheart, I know you'll be happy. Dan's one of the good guys."

Who the hell is he to talk to my *daughter like she's* his? The truth slammed into him. Abrams knew his daughter far better than he did, had known her for some time, while he'd only learned of her existence a few hours ago. While this man had enjoyed knowing Paula, he'd been cheated of the same.

His temper simmered while he congratulated Dan and Paula.

Sara smiled, but tears shimmered in her eyes. Abrams laid a hand on her shoulder. A hand she didn't shrug off.

Paul stepped closer to the table, bringing Sara's attention to him. "I wanted to let you know that I'll be talking with you soon about... Paula." He looked at his daughter.

"I'm not a child so please don't go through my mother to talk to me. I don't see that we have much to say to each other, though."

He was encouraged. She wasn't shooting venomous looks his way as she had earlier in the day. "I apologize for going around you. But you're wrong. There's a *lot* for us to talk about. I know it's strange for you to think of me as your..."

Huffing out a breath, he darted a glance away from Paula, then back. "Believe me, it's very new for me, too." With relief, he saw her relax. Not much. Hardly noticeable really, but it was there. "Did I just hear you're moving to Illinois?"

Dan addressed Paul. "I start law school in January at Northwestern. We don't know what can be done with Paula's teaching contract, but—" he glanced down at her, "—we'll be married before the first of the year and hopefully we'll both be leaving right after that."

Without conscious thought, Paul looked across the table to Sara's left hand, resting on the edge of the table. No rings. No more Widow Richards. She was freeing herself from the past, allowing herself to move forward. Forward to California, maybe, when their girl moved off to Chicago.

"Northwestern's a good school, congratulations," he said to Dan.

"Thanks."

Paul forced his gaze back to Paula. "This changes things for me. I'm starting work here in Beaufort." Sara gasped but he ignored her. "It sounds like we won't live near each other for very long, but while we do, I'd like to get to know you, maybe have lunch or dinner a few times."

Paula sought her mother's eyes. "Mom?"

"It's up to you, honey. But he's your family. I think you should take this chance." Her voice was low, pitched for Paula, but Paul heard her. Not only the words, but the appeal she made.

When Paula looked at him directly, he saw some of the same distrust, even anger, she'd displayed that morning. "Let's make sure you're coming back, first." Her tone held challenge.

"Don't doubt it."

She stared a moment longer, then reached for her purse. "Then here's my card. It has work and home numbers on it. I'm not promising anything."

"I understand." He pulled out his wallet and tucked the business card behind a picture of Luke.

161

At that moment, Mitch arrived. Paul introduced everyone, adding only that Paula was Sara's daughter.

"You look very familiar," Mitch said to Sara. "Have we met before?" Without waiting for an answer, he turned the full force of his attention on Paula. Slowly, the friendly smile faded from his face, leaving shock instead.

Sara smiled. "Yes, I believe we did meet briefly. A long time ago."

Mitch looked back at her, frowning, studying her face. Then he snorted a laugh. "I'll be damned! I don't believe it." An awkward silence dropped over the group.

"Well, I'd better head back to Charleston." Paul looked at Paula. "I'll be back in a week or so, and I'll call."

He looked hard at Sara. Was there a message in her steady gaze? He didn't think so. After another handshake with Dan and a curt nod at Matthew, he turned and walked away, not waiting to see if Mitch followed or not.

On the sidewalk, he slumped against the building, taking deep breaths. She would see him. She would get to *know* him and she'd get to *like* him. He'd make sure of that. How, exactly, he didn't have a clue, but he'd find a way. Yesterday at this time, he hadn't known he had a daughter. Today, gaining her acceptance was the most important thing in the world to him. His whole universe had shifted in less than twenty-four hours.

"Are you all right?" Mitch stood beside him, his voice low.

"Yeah, thanks."

"Holy shit, Paul. Holy shit!" Mitch paced to the curb and back again.

Paul huffed out a breath. "I know. I just found out about her this morning. So, no matter what you're offering in pay, I'll take it. The fact is, I need to be here right now."

"Good God. All these years, and you never knew?"

Paul pushed away from the building and they started toward the car. "The irony is, Mitch, she's a big reason I took your offer, to be closer to her. And I just found out that after the first of the year she'll be living in Illinois. Not exactly up the road, but a hell of a lot closer to the farm she'll be to than Beaufort, South Carolina."

Mitch stopped him with a hand on his arm. "Look, Paul. I won't hold you to anything. Do whatever you need to, I understand."

For a brief moment, he thought about it. "No, I really want to try this. I felt the need to make a change before I even knew about Paula. *Paula,* can you believe it?" He started walking, shaking his head.

"When you told me the charter company was in Beaufort, I considered not coming because Sara lived here. But when I saw her yesterday, it almost felt like we were supposed to meet, like your wanting me to come here was a sign. Your job offer seems like another sign because out of the blue, it's giving me time near Paula."

He opened the door to his car and leaned his arm along the top. "Now, I'm going to be here and she's going to Illinois. Not that it matters anymore, but Sara might be heading to California with that jarhead in there. What kind of sign would you say that is, Mitch?"

"A welcome sign, buddy. *Welcome to Hell.*"

* * * *

"Can we talk about this without your getting angry?" Sara sat across her kitchen table from Matthew that evening, the paperwork for the firehouse spread before them. She really wanted his opinion, although she'd made up her mind the previous night, talking to Paul. Why Paul's endorsement meant so much, she wouldn't analyze right now.

Matthew sighed and rubbed his jaw. "I wasn't angry yesterday. I was…upset that you'd make such an important decision."

"Without you."

"It's not that I don't think you're intelligent enough to make your own decisions, Sara. I've never asked a woman to live with me before and I thought you'd talk things over before making a decision that meant you wouldn't. At least give me a chance."

163

"I didn't mean to leave you out. I was only gathering information. Then things started moving so fast, before I knew it Nicole and I were measuring floor space and talking about where to locate the front door."

He folded his hands on the table. "That's what I mean. What do you know about Nicole Brown? You only met her a few days ago and you're willing to buy a building with her?"

"I know it seems strange because I don't normally take to people so quickly, but there's something about Nicole. I felt at ease with her immediately, and I just knew that she was someone who would be a friend. And her husband's wonderful. We laughed like crazy people the other day."

"You like her. That's great but it won't keep her business from going under. Then what will you do?"

"Rob Taylor brought us together. I don't think he'd recommend a relationship with someone who's a poor business risk, do you? Besides, Nicole ran a similar shop near where they lived on Long Island. She's much less a novice than I am. I'm only running a business the way I was taught by Barbara. Nicole has actually started her own and grown it. She'll teach me a lot, you wait and see."

He sat back, his eyes hooded. "That sounds like you've made up your mind."

"I-I guess I have. But that doesn't mean I don't want your opinion. Maybe there's something in all of this—" she swept her hand, indicating the paperwork, "—that I just don't see."

His back rigid and jaw set, he picked up the contract with the city. "You have to submit renovation plans to the city council and have them approved." He looked up. "Have you gotten estimates for renovations yet?"

"Yes, preliminary ones, but I want to talk to Nicole and John—that's her husband—about some new ideas."

His head dropped to read further. "The price sounds low. And you make no payments for a full year? What kind of deal is this?"

Sara clasped her hands and smiled. "A great one, don't you think? John used to be an analyst on Wall Street and he and Rob worked out a proposal for the city.

The council doesn't want to tear down the building, but they don't think people are going to jump at using it, either. They approved our offer in an emergency meeting day before yesterday. Rob has set it up so if the council also approves the renovations, the loan is automatic."

Matthew stacked the papers. "Is there anything about this that worries you, Sara?" His mood hung in the room like fog, muffling sound and hindering sight. His expression was unreadable. She heard herself speak but wasn't sure her words traveled the few inches to him.

"Well, of course. I'm worried I won't make it. I'm full of doubts. This move will take almost every cent I have, and there's no guarantee of more business or even that my old customers will follow me downtown. I'm petrified of failure."

"But..."

"But not as petrified as I am of not taking the chance. There are few things I've ever done on my own, where I had to trust my own instincts. They haven't always turned out so well, but I have to try this."

Matthew reached across the table to take her left hand, rubbing the spot where her rings had always been. "You raised a child on your own. That took a lot of courage and you did a great job."

"I raised Paula with huge amounts of help from my parents. Aunt Barb provided a place for us to live. I got my degree at a school where I could stay at home and then started working with her. We weren't rich by any means, but I never *had* to earn a living, never had to face the future alone. I've led a very comfortable existence. I'm not complaining, but that's not a very exciting thing to say about a life, is it?"

"I still don't see why you couldn't accomplish the same thing out west with me."

"Because it would be out west *with you*. I'd be changing what I lean on." He stiffened and she grasped his fingers with her own. "You know I didn't mean anything bad by that. You have no idea how much I'll miss you. How much you mean to me."

He relaxed marginally but didn't meet her eyes. "Aren't you going to lean here? Like on that Paul guy."

"I'm the last person Paul will want to be around. He came over last night because he was alone. I took him back to his hotel and showed him the firehouse on the way. Believe me, he doesn't want anything to do with me."

"I doubt that. He's Paula's father and that bonds you, whether either of you want it. Will you tell me about him?"

She closed her eyes for a moment and shook her head. "I can't explain Paul and me. Half the time I don't understand us myself."

"You weren't married, were you? To anyone."

His voice was soft, not accusatory, but still she caught her breath. This was the second time she'd ever made the admission. It couldn't be as hard as the first, that morning to Paula and Paul. "No. How did you know?"

He shrugged. "I've had the feeling for a while. If I'd asked you to marry me before he came around, would you have?"

There was no pain in his eyes, just the plea for honesty. How could she give him anything less than he'd always given her? "No."

He nodded as though confirming what he'd already known. "Then that explains Paul and you."

"Matthew." She tugged his hand until he looked up. "Forget about Paul. My staying here has nothing to do with him. Nothing. Haven't you ever wanted something and known immediately that the chance of getting it was worth the risk?"

Finally, he smiled. "Yes, about four years ago. I met a woman in the produce section of a grocery store. We talked about peaches for a few minutes. They reminded me of the color of her cheeks, but I didn't tell her that. I suggested as casually as I could that we get some coffee, and when she agreed I thought I'd won the lottery. Marines aren't often thought of as poets, but I wrote love poems to you in my mind. I should have gotten a few down on paper. Maybe you would have seen me differently."

She started to cry. He pushed back the chair and stood.

"You said you wanted my opinion, and here it is. If I weren't being transferred, I'd say this is about the best deal anyone's ever imagined. It sounds like maybe you have a good partner in Nicole and plans that might work. The money sure seems right."

He pulled her out of her chair and into his arms. "Since this means so much to you, you'll probably make a success of it, Sara. But if you change your mind—about anything—all you have to do is call. I may not be able to stay in Beaufort, but I'm not leaving you alone. Not until you tell me to. I don't give up what I want that easily."

Cradling her face, his big hands were strong and warm. His kiss sent sparks of fire to her toes and back up again. And then he left.

Why can't I be in love with Matthew? He's perfect in every way, except he's not—

She wouldn't let herself finish the thought. Instead, she gave herself the advice she thought her new friend Nicole would give. "Sara, the past is past. Just get over it!"

Chapter 12

Supper was finished, the kitchen cleaned. Luke had gone out for the evening and by unspoken agreement, Mark, Becca, and Paul had adjourned to the dining room table, where generations of Steinerts had celebrated Sunday dinners and holiday meals. It was also where important family matters were discussed and decided.

The moment Paul dreaded most had just passed, explaining to Mark and Becca why he had to leave. Mark had been shocked speechless. Becca had surprised Paul with her calm acceptance, almost as though she'd expected him to come home with such news.

"Are you sure about this? I thought you just needed a break to clear the air between you and Sara, get the past out of your system. I didn't really think…" Mark looked confused.

Paul knew how he felt. The last couple of days had proven to be life changing and he hadn't been prepared, himself. Taking the farm responsibility fully onto his shoulders would certainly be as life altering for Mark.

"The restlessness you noticed in me wasn't just Sara's visit, although that's what set it off. Seeing her made me remember being young and having dreams. I was never cut out to be a farmer, Mark, never wanted to be one. You know that."

Mark nodded. "You always had an over-defined sense of duty. We needed you when Dad got sick and you came." He looked down to smooth his thumb across a worn spot on the table, evidence of all the years that same place had been rubbed. "I've always been grateful to you. I know you gave up a lot, and I don't know what would have happened otherwise. I guess I just thought you stayed because you wanted to."

"I never resented being here, never. But when you and Becca got married—" he smiled at his sister-in-law, "—I should have left. I always found some excuse not to, but it's time now. It won't be long before Luke brings home a girl and starts the next generation of Steinerts. I don't want to wait until it's too late and I have no choice but to hang on here."

"If I'd known you were unhappy—"

"I *wasn't*, not at all. I was too damn lazy, or too much a coward maybe, to do what I knew I should have. Now I've been pushed into making a decision, and there's only one right choice."

He stared hard at Mark. "I don't want you to think I went to bed every night thinking about Sara or woke up every day wishing I was someplace else. That's not the way it was at all. I haven't been unhappy, not like you mean. I've loved the years working with you and Luke. I really have. And I think we've done Dad proud."

Without a word, Becca got up and went to the living room.

Paul spoke to his brother in a low voice. "You said that I had a sense of duty. That's not true, Mark. I probably should have stayed home instead of joining the Navy. You were too young to handle much, and I knew Dad wanted me here. But I wanted to go and I found a way that no one could get too angry about. I used duty to country as a way to escape duty to family."

"Paul, that's not the way Dad or any of us saw it, you know that. He hated that you went to Vietnam, but he was proud of you. God, you should have seen his face whenever a letter came."

Tears filled Paul's eyes, but he quickly blinked them away. "I tried to make up for it by coming home when he asked. Tried to clean up the mess I'd made of my life for him, when I wouldn't do it for myself. But Mark, I failed the woman I said I loved. I had an obligation to Sara and myself to find out what happened, to make sure she was all right. Because I didn't, Paula grew up without knowing who I am, who *she* is. I can't let her live the rest of her life like that. But I hate like hell leaving you with everything so suddenly."

Mark's face filled with determination. "Don't worry about it. Luke and I can handle things, and that Lintz boy has been asking about whether we have any work. Maybe he'll hire on when we need extra hands." He gave a soft chuckle. "On the bright side, Luke'll miss you like hell, but he'll love moving out of the house and into your place. It's just out back, but to him it'll be like living in town."

Paul laughed too, then studied his hands, folded on the table. When he looked up, it was to find his brother silently examining him.

"You might not have been unhappy exactly, but you were lonely, weren't you?"

"What kind of question is that to ask?" Paul squirmed in his seat, his face flushed with embarrassment. "I'll tell you this. If I *was* lonely, it was for something I didn't even realize. I want you to know, Mark, I've never envied you, except maybe in the general sense. That you had a good wife and family, sure, but I never begrudged you Becca or Luke."

He snorted a soft laugh. "In fact, I never truly understood what you must have felt, having a child, holding him, seeing his features change to resemble your own, being proud. No one on the outside *can* understand it. But when I looked up and saw Paula—"

His voice broke and it took a beat for him to continue. "It's irrational, but true. I didn't even know her and I loved her. For one moment, my heart broke. I was a *father*, and finally I knew some small part of what you must feel when you look at Luke. Except I'd missed it all, her whole life. I have so much lost time to make up for. So much of her to learn."

"While you're getting to know your daughter, you might remember that you once loved her mother. Maybe she hasn't changed so much as you think. You're not old, Paul. There's no reason on God's green earth for you to be alone."

Paul nodded. "I know, but I think too much time has passed. Sara's a bridge I've already burned. This move isn't about the two of us."

He recalled the night they'd shared, when he thought he'd grabbed a piece of the past and things could be worked out. When what mattered in life could be found in her arms.

Maybe two nights were all he'd ever have with her. One night to create a daughter and another to discover her. Two nights weren't much, but they'd been more than enough to set the world spinning in new directions.

"And now," Mark said, as his wife came back into the room carrying a stack of books, "I think we'd better start planning all of our winter vacations. What do you say, Becca? The beaches of South Carolina sound a far sight better than January days of twenty below zero, don't they?"

"I hope you're getting a two bedroom apartment, Paul," she quipped.

The light laughter was a welcome relief.

"Look what I found, you two." Becca deposited photo albums in the center of the table. "I've been meaning to sort through these for a while and now's the time. I'll make some coffee then I think we should pick out pictures for you to take with you. Some for your apartment, but mostly for Paula. Then while you tell her about her grandparents, she can see what they looked like, right?"

"That's a great idea," Paul said.

"And maybe while she's living in Illinois she and her husband would like to come for a visit. Please tell her we would welcome them. Will you do that, Paul?"

"I sure will. Thanks." His voice hoarse with emotion, he feared he wouldn't be able to stop the moisture from filling his eyes this time.

This was *his*, the family and place he'd felt responsible for, for so long. What came next—an unfamiliar job in an unfamiliar town, and especially the prospect of a relationship with his daughter that was anything but certain—carried a healthy dose of anxiety as well as excitement.

He needed to take this chance. He *wanted* to take this chance. And yet…

He looked away, blinking hard. "Damn!"

Prudently, Becca turned away. "I'll just go and start the coffee."

Mark squeezed Paul's arm then got up and headed for the kitchen. "I'll help, honey."

* * * *

"Well. It's about time you came to see me."

"Hello, Mother." Sara wasn't past her anger, but news of Paula's engagement was more important than her personal feelings. Still, she'd waited until Monday evening to make her appearance.

"Hello, yourself." Her mother held a twisted handkerchief in one hand and her thumb scraped the tips of her fingers at a steady pace. She stood perfectly straight, not a hair on her head or a fold of her clothes out of place. However, her austere expression didn't mask the look of anxiety in her eyes. They hadn't spoken in more than a month. She had to know what kept Sara away was more than a minor irritation.

"I'm here with news. May I come in?"

Mary Ellen stepped aside and swung the door wide. Sara strode through and into the living room. Her mother joined her, offering neither food nor beverage. "What news do you have now that's important enough to bring you by? You've chosen to ignore my phone calls for weeks, so it must be something big."

"Paula and Dan were here Saturday. Dan proposed, and Paula accepted."

The aloof façade broke and her mother beamed. "How wonderful! I was beginning to think they'd never make a decision. Oh, I wish Paula had found time to come by. There's so much to plan! They'll be married in June, of course, after the school year is finished."

"They're planning a ceremony before the first of the year."

"*What*? Why?" Her hand flew to her chest, the handkerchief a white flag against the coral of her blouse. "Good Lord! Don't tell me she was so stupid as to get—"

Sara smiled but without humor. "Don't worry, she's not like me."

Her mother dropped into a chair. Now that she wouldn't have to look up to address her, Sara sat, also. "You knew Dan was applying to law school. He's been accepted at a very good school in Illinois. He starts in January and they want to be married before he has to leave."

"But, PB can't go, she has her job, her home. Why, Illinois is too far away. We need her here."

"Nothing is as important to her as being with Dan and thank God she feels that way. If she can make arrangements with the school board and her principal, she'll be gone right after the first of the year."

"How can I not have known any of this?" Her eyes flashed fire. "You knew all this time and never told me."

"I've known for a little while, since just before going to Iowa. But Paula's business is hers to tell."

Mary Ellen's chin rose. "Then why didn't she inform me about her upcoming marriage herself? Everyone is going to talk, you know. Becoming engaged in November and married at the end of December, people will be counting the months, regardless."

"Mother, Paula couldn't care less about that. She loves Dan and he loves her, and what your friends think or don't think doesn't mean a hill of beans to her."

Mary Ellen's fingers rubbed together furiously. "No. It just isn't done. I'll talk to her. I'll make her and Dan see that he should go on without her. They can plan for the wedding and marry next year. And PB can stay close to us."

"You will *not* say or do one thing to change Paula's mind."

Sara took a hard look at the woman sitting across the coffee table. Her back was rigid but her hand trembled. Sara wondered what held her together. "As for why Paula didn't come to tell you herself, she found out what you and Dad did to Paul and me."

"That was so long ago." Mary Ellen flapped her hand in a dismissive gesture. "You said yourself, the results would have been the same no matter what I did."

"I was wrong. I didn't see Paul's parents when I went to Iowa, I saw *Paul*. What you did changed everything, for all of us. I don't think I can ever forgive you."

Color blanched from her mother's face. "That isn't possible. Your father personally had word from the Department of Defense. That boat was hit with all hands lost."

"It was. But Paul had left it that morning. If Dad had waited a week to get the report, he would have known that. Paul's been living his life in Iowa while Paula and I lived ours here. Isn't that funny?"

Mary Ellen slumped against the back of the chair. The hand she brought up to cover her mouth shook and tears glistened in her eyes. "And-and Paula knows about him?"

"Yes. Because of what you and Daddy did, I shrank from living, not trusting my own judgment. Because of *that*, Paula grew up without a father. Like me, she's a bit resentful and that's why she didn't come to tell you herself about her engagement."

Her mother covered her eyes and moaned in a soft undertone, "Oh, Lord. Oh, Lord. Oh, Lord."

Sara saw a mental picture of her mother standing at her father's grave, dry-eyed and in complete control. She'd looked the same when Sara's grandmother died. In fact, Sara couldn't remember ever seeing her mother distraught. Until now.

She sighed. Maintaining her resentment in the face of her mother's emotion was impossible.

She moved across to sit on the arm of the chair and pulled Mary Ellen against her. "It's going to be all right."

"Will you ever be able to forgive me, Sara?"

The question is, will I ever forgive myself? "I'll try, Mom. I'll really try."

* * * *

"I had no idea things could move this fast," Sara told Nicole the next week as they exited the courthouse. The city council had just approved their renovation plans, and in the next day or two, she expected the bank to follow suit. Rob had arranged for their loan to be automatically approved if the city okay'd their plans.

"It pays to know someone with influence," Nicole said with a laugh. "So, with John working with the council and Rob Taylor at the bank, I'd say we're set. How does it feel to almost be the owner of a historic firehouse-soon-to-be-art-gallery-and-coffee-shop?"

"Scary." Nicole stopped her with a touch on her arm and stared. Sara grinned. "And great. Exciting. Exhilarating!"

"That's more like it. Now, John is meeting us at the house for a little libation." She waggled her brows. "Not champagne. That comes after we have the loan and can actually start work. But a little something to celebrate the first step."

"Celebration is good." Sara wanted to do a happy dance there in the parking lot. If she'd been wearing a tam, she would have tossed it in the air, *a la* Mary Tyler Moore. Taking a step toward independence felt good, felt right, felt...

"I'll follow you," she said to Nicole, "but I want to call my daughter and share the good news first."

"Sure. I'm parked over one row. Blink your lights when you're ready to go."

Sara sat behind the wheel and punched Paula's number in her cell phone. "Paula?"

"Mom, hi. I can't talk right now, we're, uh, going out to eat."

Irrational disappointment struck. "Oh, that's all right. I just wanted to tell you that our renovation plans have been approved by the city council. Isn't that great? That was a major hurtle, and we flew right over it."

"Wonderful, that's really good. I'm sorry I can't talk now, though, we're, uh, meeting someone."

"Oh, okay." Deflated, there wasn't anything left to do but say goodbye. "Well, I'll just—"

"We're meeting Paul, Mom. I wasn't going to tell you, but I think it's best to keep things in the open. I hope you're not upset, but he called, and he came up to take us to dinner. You know, in honor of the engagement and all."

"Oh." Her feeling of aloneness made no sense. She'd wanted Paula to see her father, had encouraged it. She just hadn't expected that he'd make the move to Beaufort so fast, or the move into their daughter's life. "Well, of course I'm not upset. Don't be silly. Have a wonderful time."

Paula blew a breath into the phone. Relief or something else? "Thanks. I have to run. We're meeting him at the restaurant and don't want to make him wait. Bye."

"B—" Before she got the single-syllable word out, Paula hung up.

"That's just great," Sara grumbled. "She doesn't want to make *him* wait." She started the car and flashed her lights. When Nicole drove out of her space, Sara moved in smoothly behind her. They eased into the turn lane, then sat at a red light. "He made me wait decades before giving me a single thought, but *please*, don't make him stand in a restaurant lobby for two minutes."

They made the turn into traffic and headed toward the bridge to Lady's Island. Her friendship with Nicole had grown very quickly, but this would be the first time in her friend's home. She wouldn't allow childish disappointment in Paula's reaction to her news cloud the whole evening.

The gallery would be new in almost every respect. The name would remain, and so would the cadre of artists her aunt and she had recruited for their uniquely focused view of low-country life. But she'd also found sculptors and artists who used glass and paper as their media. And, her idea of contacting artists in other Beauforts had paid off. She'd quickly contracted with two people in Beaufort, North Carolina, and was in negotiations with a watercolorist in Beaufort, Missouri. A painter in New Jersey hadn't responded yet, but promises of new expressions had already changed the gallery to a place that was no longer Barbara Noland's, but hers.

Her bad mood dropped away. Champagne or not, she'd celebrate with friends tonight. When she and Nicole raised their glasses in a toast, she'd allow herself to feel the self-satisfaction of taking the right steps toward a promising future. And she'd enjoy the nebulous pleasures of ownership and the vision of success edging closer.

She deserved them.

* * * *

Less than two weeks after bank approval, the firehouse had undergone so many changes Sara could hardly keep track. She looked around the upper floor in amazement. For the past hour and a half, one man had been cutting holes in the roof, and two others had been fitting them with skylight windows. The additions transformed the whole room.

The sound of the saw finally stopped and the ceiling, with its new, false beams, framed another rectangle of bright sky.

"That's the last one, Ms. Richards," the man called from the roof. "We'll be finished up before you know it."

"Fine, thanks," she hollered back. The opening skylights had cost a small fortune, but the light and air they admitted would make all the difference to the upstairs area.

She climbed back up the step ladder with a new stencil. She'd painted the walls taupe and the ceiling eggshell white. The job had taken a week, but it brightened and opened up the whole space. Now she was stenciling quotations about art, food and coffee on the beams. The green and gold lettering was a minor adornment, but enough to draw the eye up and add flavor. Sara did the tedious work herself not only because she enjoyed being artistic, but she liked saving money more.

As the renovation kicked into high gear, so had the out flow of cash. The estimate for the work had stunned Sara. Small changes since then had only added to the expenses. But the building would be transformed. The interior would be as much a work of art as the pieces hanging on the walls. Every day, Nicole gushed over something new involving the downtown rebirth of The Lady's Cup. Their work would be worth every penny. She had to believe that. She *did* believe it.

However, excitement didn't produce cash. Granted, they had that wonderful year before the mortgage payments started, but she worried about money being tight.

Knowing both Paula and her mother would be disturbed, Sara hadn't told them that she'd used her house as collateral on a line of credit. She prayed she wouldn't need the extra funds, but she'd rather deal with the anxiety of having the note, than the worry about trimming her dream in order to save a few pennies.

For one use or another, her savings were already earmarked for the gallery. Taking advantage of the equity in her home was one more step in her commitment to making the new venture a success. With her whole heart, she was in.

Blowing out a breath, she mumbled, "Give it your all." She taped the template in place and picked up a brush. "Hmm, '*Art is born of the observation and investigation of nature.* Cicero.' That's fitting." She swirled the brush in a pot of dark green stencil paint and daubed it over the template.

"Sara! A good-looking man down here wants you!"

Nicole Brown was the least inhibited person Sara had ever met. That aspect still took Sara aback, although she found everything else about her friend to be refreshing.

"It's not Matthew!" Nicole yelled.

Sara picked up another brush to paint 'Cicero' in dark gold. "It must be your handsome husband then. Hello, John!" she called back.

"It's not John, either," came a voice from below her. A voice she'd heard in her dreams too often lately.

She stared down, meeting his eyes looking up. "Paul." Keeping a tight grip on the ladder, she climbed down.

On the floor, she wiped her hands on her jeans, suddenly self-conscious of wearing a paint-spattered shirt of Matthew's that he gave her the weekend they'd painted her dining room. "This is a surprise."

"Guess you don't mind heights," he said, smiling. Hands tucked in his pockets, he turned a slow, tight circle, taking in the upper level of the firehouse. His hair had grown since she'd seen him at the beginning of the month, and his tanned face bore signs of being out in the weather.

"I see the ramp idea worked out well," he said.

"Yes, it did. The slope is gentle enough no one should have trouble getting up here. Over there—" she pointed to the back wall, "—the new appliances are going in and as you can see, the skylights will be finished today." She glanced up to see that the carpenters hadn't stopped work to watch them. Her money worries set aside for the moment, excitement once again stirred in her stomach. "You should get Nicole to show you where her dumb waiter is going, too, thanks to your suggestion."

"I just met her downstairs. She seems like quite a character."

Her hand seemed to settle on his arm naturally. "Oh, she is! I'm sorry—you hadn't met her yet. I feel as though I've known her all my life, so I forget others haven't."

"That's okay. Paula's told me a little about her and how things are going here."

"Has she?" Paula had mentioned that she'd seen Paul a couple of times but was silent on what they talked about. "Have you settled in to your job?"

"Not nearly! But I'm settling into the area. I've got a decent temporary place to live, and good people around to show me the ropes at work."

"Is there much to learn?"

He laughed outright. "Good God, if I'd known how much, I would have stuck with corn and cattle. But it's interesting."

"Well, I'm sure you'll be very good at whatever it is."

"Thanks. I'm having fun so far."

"Listen, tomorrow's Thanksgiving. Would you like to come to dinner? I mean, you're here alone, and all."

A serious expression took the place of his smile and his eyes bore into her. "Thanks, but I'll be fine. I've got work to do that'll occupy the day."

She jerked back. "You're going to work on Thanksgiving? But why not come over and eat with us? You have to eat."

"Thanks, but no. I don't think it's a good idea."

He might as well have slapped her. But then, what had she expected? He'd been in town several weeks and hadn't contacted her, hadn't even been by to see how things were going with the new gallery space until today.

"I was being neighborly, not trying to invade your privacy."

"I appreciate it, but I'd feel better if we kept our distance." He shuffled his feet, more interested in following the path of a spider as it crossed the floor than in meeting her gaze.

"Keeping our distance is one thing we've proven to be very adept at." She picked up a set of handmade stencils and selected the next she'd use.

"Sara, I came here for the job and to be near Paula. Because of Paula it's natural that we'll see each other now and then. But after she and Dan leave, I'll have my life and you'll have yours. Unless you plan on doing a lot of fishing, I doubt we'll have cause to be around each other much."

Except she'd already seen him around town. In the grocery store, coming out of the bank, buying gas for his pickup.

"Oh, I won't have much trouble staying out of your way. It's you who seems to have a problem staying out of mine."

His jaw tightened. "Listen, I just stopped by to let you know about something."

"Okay."

"I wanted to explain before you receive the paperwork from my attorney. If anything should happen to me, Paula is taken care of in my will. My brother gets my half of the farm, but I've left her my capital and investments. She's also beneficiary on my insurance policies. Not that I expect anything to happen, but you never know what life has in store, do you?"

"No, you certainly don't. I'm sure Paula will be very surprised." Her tone was sharp, an inadvertent admission of her true feelings. Pleasure that he wanted to be part of their daughter's life warred with sudden possessiveness.

What right did he have to come down here, sweeping their lives into chaos? He hadn't even wanted a child, he'd said so in Omaha, in no uncertain terms. He didn't know Paula, yet after only a few weeks he wanted to be Father of the Year.

Oh, sure, he hadn't been there for years of dirty diapers and sickness, but now here he was waving an inheritance around. All she had to offer—maybe—was a small art gallery. A gallery getting her deeper in debt with each skylight cut and square foot of wood flooring laid. It wasn't fair.

She took a breath, immediately regretting her jealousy. Paul was good to do this. No, considering he'd only found out about his daughter, his action was more than good. "That's very generous," she said more gently.

"She's my daughter." He stated the fact with pride, but his words fueled her irritation again.

"She's *our* daughter. You might manage to forget the minor part I played, but I can assure you, I was present both at her conception and her birth." *And every year in between. No "accident" was ever loved more.* Paul's word, not hers. That's how he'd described a baby if they'd had one while he was overseas, and she'd never lost the pain in her heart when she remembered.

He blew out a hard breath. "Well, of course. I didn't mean…" With one hand he swept off the cap he wore and with the other, raked his hair. "Anyway, as I said, I've already contacted my attorney, but now you know and Mark knows, in case there's a screw up."

"Right," she muttered.

"Will Dan and Paula be at dinner tomorrow?" he asked after a moment's silence.

"Yes, of course. And my mother."

"And Matthew?"

"No." She smiled tightly. "Although we'll miss him this year."

"I see. Well, let Dan know that if he wants to escape a house full of women, he's welcome to come and watch the football games with me. I'll call in the morning."

"So work doesn't interfere with football." *Why the hell did I say that? I offered dinner, he refused. If he starves, it's none of my business.* "If you don't want to eat with us, just say so. There's no need to make up a story about work."

"You're right. I won't do it again." Paul looked at his watch. "I've got to get back. I'm glad to see things are going so well." He flashed a brief smile and left without a backward glance.

Sara tossed the plastic templates on the floor, not caring that they scattered. "I'm looking at the backside of you, Paul Steinert, and I hope that's the last part I see of you for a long while."

Chapter 13

Thanksgiving afternoon Paul opened the door at the house where he had a temporary room. "Come on in," he said then raised his brows in surprise as Paula followed Dan through the door. "I didn't know you were coming, Paula."

"When I told her you were showing me the charter company, she refused to stay behind."

Paul smiled his pleasure that his daughter had an interest in his work. They moved into the living room and took seats.

"I thought I was escaping women and wedding talk," Dan grumbled. He sent Paula a withering look. "You know I agreed to bring you with me only if you promised not to mention petit fours, waltz length gowns, or wreaths of flowers for your hair. We're weeks away from the wedding and I've already had my fill of girly talk."

She ran her thumb and index finger across her lips, zipping them. Paul's breath caught in his throat. As much as Paula looked like his side of the family, that sassy gesture was pure Sara.

"Good," Dan said. "You may remain."

"*Thank* you, Master. Although I'm sure Paul would be fascinated to weigh the merits of Swedish meatballs over rumaki, wouldn't you, Paul?"

"Ru what?"

Dan laughed. "I rest my case. Just tell me where to be and when to be there, and leave me out of everything else. I'd rather exist in masculine ignorance when it comes to the details of the wedding."

"Fine." Paula flipped the ends of her hair over her shoulder and turned up her nose at Dan. "Paul, Mom sent a bunch of food for you."

Dan stood. "That's right. I'll go out and get it and the beer I brought for later."

"Ah, I wish she hadn't done that. I'm fine." Damn! Somehow eating food Sara had cooked seemed very intimate.

"You can't tell Mom not to send food. Nesting is in her blood. We'll be going home tomorrow with a ton of turkey and fixings."

"And a pound cake, I hope," Dan said, coming in with a six pack of Budweiser, three plastic containers and a plate wrapped in foil. "Sara makes the best pound cake in the state."

They traipsed into the kitchen where Paul found space for everything in the refrigerator.

"Is she trying to feed an army?" he mumbled, putting the food away.

"Matthew's gone this week. She's used to cooking and having someone help eat leftovers."

The jab hit home, although Paul tried to conceal the fact.

"Please remind your mother that I'm not Matthew." He closed the refrigerator door and looked at Paula. "Maybe you should buy her a 'Cooking for One' book for Christmas."

Paula flushed and glanced away. "Sorry. I didn't mean to make you uncomfortable."

"No, I'm sorry, Paula, really. Sending the food was very nice of your mom. Please thank her for me," he said. If he were minding his manners, he'd thank Sara himself, but he was still reeling from their talk at the firehouse the previous day.

What he'd said to rile her eluded him, but he'd opened himself up to her temper by going to the gallery instead of calling, where he could have controlled the conversation better. The trouble was, some unidentifiable urge pushed him to see her. He'd avoided her since he'd been in Beaufort, choosing instead to receive news about her from Paula. But good sense had been overridden yesterday.

Paul checked his watch. "We've got about forty minutes before the first game. Want to go down to the boathouse? It's a short walk."

"Sounds good." Dan took Paula's hand and they preceded Paul out of the house.

186

"I can't stay too long," she said. "Nicole's coming to Mom's to discuss the—" she shot a quick look at Dan, "—thing I'm not allowed to talk about. Did I tell you, Paul? Nicole's going to handle the food for the reception. She and Mom think the firehouse will be in good enough shape for people to gather there after the ceremony."

"I stopped by there yesterday and was impressed with the progress. When is the big day? Have you set a final date?"

"New Year's Eve," Dan said. "She's letting me be a free man until the end of the year, and then it's—" He made a slicing motion across his neck.

Paul smiled. "That's a good symbolic date. Might as well start the new year as a chained man." Dan snorted a laugh and Paul grinned. "Did I say chained? I meant changed."

"*Sure* you did," Paula huffed. "I forgot to tell you, Dan, so now you can both hear it together. Nicole's bringing her daughter-in-law with her today. They're visiting from New York for Thanksgiving. Anyway, she's going to make a website for Mom! Isn't that exciting? Beauty by Beaufort's finally moving into the modern age."

"About time," Dan said. "I've been after her to get on the web for years."

"I know. Matthew even offered to pay for a domain name last year, but she wouldn't hear of it."

Abrams again. Somehow he always slips into the conversation.

"Your mother's a stubborn woman. I don't know where you get your sunny nature and even temperament, darlin'." Dan ducked as Paula swung her arm in a playful slap.

"If you're stubborn, then you come by it honestly. Steinerts aren't known for their flexibility in an argument."

"Great! I'm marrying a woman with a double dose of hardheadedness."

"Dan Tanner, you'd better watch it. I've half a mind to run off to California with Matthew if Mom isn't going. He'll find me someone who treats me sweeter than you do."

It wasn't Paul's imagination that his daughter looked at him from the corner of her eye. That was the third time she'd mentioned Matthew Abrams. His temper always simmered when he thought of the years Abrams had known Paula before Paul even knew she was alive. Then there was the sore point of how close Abrams was to Sara.

"There's no doubt that he's going to California without your mother?" The question slipped out. He could have kicked himself because there was no missing the smug smile on Paula's face.

"I wouldn't say she's *never* going. But she and Nicole got such an incredible deal on the firehouse—did you know the city wrapped the first year's interest into their payments, and then delayed them for a year? Unbelievable!"

He hadn't heard. Since his return, he'd only spoken with Sara yesterday and she hadn't shared anything personal. The girl Paul knew years ago had been too wonderful for words. But she'd also schemed and tricked to get her way. The lover of his first night in Beaufort had been willing to deny him knowledge of his only child. Unlike the other two personas, the woman he'd seen in Sara yesterday was strong and sure of herself. Determined. And that made him nervous, because who knew the kinds of things a determined Sara might do?

He could deny his attraction to her all he wanted—and he did so, daily—but denial didn't kill his feelings. Instead, he became greedier. Hungry to be with her, starved for closeness. That's why being around her held such danger. His level of trust didn't rise to the level of his desire. If he gave in to his cravings and Sara lied again, it would break him.

Paula kept on talking. "Then Mom had an idea of how to bring in more business, and she's got a lot of interest from artists all over the country. I really think she wants to make a big success of the gallery on her own terms. All those years of floating by are ended. She's a woman on fire now."

Paul tried to appear disinterested. "She sure seems to be. Looks as though she doesn't need help from anyone."

Paula wrinkled her brow. "Do you think so? I disagree about her not needing anyone. Is that the boathouse?" She pointed to the top of a large structure about half a block away.

"Yes, that's it."

"It's bigger than I thought," Dan said. "How many boats do you have?"

"Five right now. Two for deep sea, one that can handle river and deeper water, and two that stay in the creek and river."

"Didn't it surprise you that your friend asked you to do this when you have no experience? I mean, as a farmer, what do you know about fishing in Carolina?"

"A hell of a lot more now than I did last month. And you're right, it surprised me when Mitch asked me to come down."

She stopped, bringing Dan to a halt one step later. Looking earnestly into Paul's eyes, she asked, "Did you come because Mom is here?"

He smiled at her. "You were what made me accept Mitch's offer, and I'm glad I did." He started walking again. Paula and Dan fell back into step. "The guys have all been great. There's no question I'm having to catch up, but it's fun being challenged."

"How many people are employed here?" Paula shaded her eyes against the sun.

"Two on the maintenance staff, five captains and seven crewmen. Then the two office staff."

"You've got your hands full, Paul," Dan said.

"Tell me about it," Paul agreed with a quick grin. "But it keeps me busy and out of trouble." He unlocked the gate blocking traffic from a parking area outside a large wooden structure. "Come on in," he said, his voice filled with pride. "Here's where I work."

* * * *

Sara and her mother had spent an awkward Thanksgiving Day in each other's company. Sara worked every day at forgiving and forgetting the mistakes of the past. However, "I forgive you" wasn't a magic wand that banished resentment and regret with a flick of the wrist.

Worse had been Paula's attitude. The pain in Mary Ellen's eyes at Paula's aloofness had caused a similar ache in Sara. So, when Paula returned full of descriptions of the charter company and the rooming house where Paul was living, Sara was happy that Paula included Mary Ellen in the conversation.

"Paul's company is really interesting. You should come with me when I go over next time."

"No," Sara said without hesitation. *Being with him a few minutes yesterday gave me heartburn. I'd probably jump in the river if I had to spend much time with him.*

Mary Ellen addressed her daughter. "If PB invites you, I'm sure he wouldn't mind." Her mother still refused to say Paul's name. If she and Paula were going to heal their rift, her mother would have to come to terms with Paul, too.

"Nana's right. In a couple of weeks I'm going to take a look at one of the boats Paul's been working on. Plan to come, Mom." She winked conspiratorially at her grandmother. "Besides, there's so little time before Dan and I leave, and I want to spend as much of it as possible with you."

Sara heaved a frustrated sigh. "I'll think about it."

Paula sighed too, mimicking her mother. "That's what you always say when you mean 'no.'"

Changing the subject, Sara asked, "Are he and Dan watching football?"

"I think that's the plan, although when I left they were deep in a discussion of fishing and river channels. They sure get along well." The doorbell rang and Paula stood. Heading toward the door she tossed back over her shoulder, "I don't think I'd send him any more food, Mom. He said thanks, but he really didn't look too happy."

He wasn't happy with the food I sent? And he showed *it?* "I swear, he's impossible," she said under her breath. Then she stood to introduce Nicole and her daughter-in-law to her mother.

In this case Paula was right. "I'll think about it," did mean no. Keeping her distance from Paul Steinert was necessary for her mental as well as emotional well-being. And keep her distance she would.

Burning Bridges

* * * *

Sara looked in the mirror for the fourth time in fifteen minutes, trying to judge whether the jeans she had on looked too tight or simply "fitted." She pulled her sweater down over her hips, hoping to minimize the way the denim formed perfectly to her body. She normally wore them without a second thought, but today nothing in the fit pleased her.

These won't do.

Paula had pressured her into joining them on a test run of one of Paul's boats. Matthew was escorting her, but this would be the first time she'd spent any time near Paul since his first night in Beaufort. She didn't want to go on the cruise, but if she went, she wanted to look right. *And good*, her vanity forced her to admit.

She reached for the zipper as Paula called from the living room. "Mom! Aren't you ready yet? We're going to be late."

When boating in the low-country, "being late" wasn't taken lightly. The depth of the Intracoastal Waterway could change by as much as ten feet with the tides, so timing departures and arrivals was crucial. Resigned, she grabbed her wool jacket and knit cap from the bed and went out to join Paula, Dan and Matthew.

As Sara walked into the living room, Paula inspected her, head to foot. Then she nodded and moved to the door, her own heavy jacket and cap already on. "You took so long we're going to drive over. Dan and Matthew are out in the car."

"I'm sorry. I had trouble deciding...which sweater to wear."

"Uh-huh. Those jeans fit you just right," Paula said with a heavy note of self-satisfaction.

Matthew pushed away from the side of the car to open the door for Paula and help Sara in. "You look great," he whispered, bending near.

She smiled her thanks. "Sorry I kept you gentlemen waiting."

"Not a problem," Dan said. "We have plenty of time." Paula shot him a sharp glance. "Or maybe it's later than I think. Is that right, honey?"

191

"Definitely later than you think, Dan," Paula murmured. He laughed.

"I don't even know why I'm coming on this trip. I have plenty enough to do, with Christmas and the wedding coming up. Then there's work at the firehouse and preparing to move before the end of the year." Sara looked out the window as Dan backed out the drive. "Look at that. I don't even have lights up yet."

"We'll take care of the lights." Paula rested her hand on Dan's shoulder. He smiled at her, briefly shifting his gaze from the road, and she returned the smile. Glancing back at her mother she said, "All of the wedding plans are in good shape. Just enjoy the day."

Matthew took Sara's hand in his. "With all the traveling I've been doing, time's gotten away from me. How about if we work on the decorations before Paula and Dan leave tomorrow?"

"That sounds good to me," Dan chimed in.

"Fine." Usually she loved when the lights went up and the house took on a festive look. This year, it meant Paula's move loomed closer.

Dan pulled into a space in the public lot nearest the marina and turned off the engine. "Not many people down here today."

"No, it's such a nice day I imagine most are out shopping for the holiday," Sara said. Paula turned a frown on her. "I'm sorry. I'll quit grousing."

Sara knew Paula noted her lack of enthusiasm and chose to ignore it. "The boat is called *The Islands*, and it's one that goes out for deep sea fishing. This is Paul's business now. We need to support him."

"You're right, and I *do* wish him well with his work. I've heard several favorable comments about him from people in town." Sara noticed Matthew remained quiet on the idea of supporting Paul.

"He really has accomplished a lot. There's *The Islands*, at the end of the dock." Paula got out and met Dan at the front of the car. Like iron to a magnet, their hands reached out and linked.

Matthew flashed her a smile as they fell into step behind Dan and Paula. "I'm glad Paula invited me to come today," he said, taking hold of her hand.

Grateful for his support, she squeezed it. "I'm glad you're going to be with me. It looks like it's going to be a beautiful day."

As they neared the end of the dock, she saw Paul's reason to be proud. From bow to stern, *The Islands* looked good. Fresh paint gave her a like-new appearance—a lady in make-up and fancy clothes. Brass trim lining the bridge and deck mirrored sunlight, and new American and South Carolina flags fluttered proudly atop the bridge. If she proved as seaworthy as she looked, Paul would be very satisfied at the end of the day.

Removed as she was from the water community, even Sara had heard about the farmer who managed Hamilton Charter. As an outsider in a closed community, Paul wouldn't be immediately accepted, so she wasn't surprised to hear a few snippy comments. The most extreme was that at his age, the farmer should be looking for a quiet pasture somewhere instead of taking on a new career. But very quickly, the negativity died away. Word filtered from the crews that Paul was both good to work for and a quick study.

Paula, who seemed to talk to Paul several times a week, always had something new to report about his activities, and her comments were usually full of praise. The note of pride in Paula's voice when she talked about Paul surprised Sara. She'd wanted daughter and father to know one another, but she hadn't expected to feel so alone—or so left out—while they explored a tentative relationship.

Her envy didn't end with Paula and Paul. Earlier in the week, as she and Matthew dined at a small restaurant favored by locals, she saw Paul across the room having dinner with a very attractive brunette.

As they were leaving, Paul spotted Sara and Matthew and stopped at their table. His hand rested easily on the woman's back and he smiled when introducing her. Rose Carter was a friend of Mitch's wife's, he'd said. Rose, petite with dark eyes that flashed with affection when she looked at Paul, smiled at Sara and Matthew and said she hoped she'd see more of them in the future.

Sara had smiled too, and said all the right things, but she ached inside. Her disquiet was irrational, yes, but there it was just the same. Knowing Paul lived and worked a few miles away had been hard—harder than she'd ever imagined. She'd managed to maintain her dignity, regardless that she felt miserable each time he turned away. She'd even done some of the turning away herself. But seeing him with another woman, perhaps grocery shopping, going to church, walking hand in hand along the river, simply *living* in her town? She'd never find peace.

And so, the anticipation of a somewhat bad day on Paul's boat quickly turned into the certainty of being a horrible day when the first person Sara saw on board was Rose Carter.

Chapter 14

Rose introduced Sara and Matthew to Bonnie Hamilton, Mitch's wife, and told them where to find seating, coffee and life jackets.

"Paul and Mitch are down with the engine," Bonnie said, "making last minute checks before we leave."

Shortly, the captain came on deck along with Mitch and Paul, said hello and took charge of getting them underway. Soon they entered the river and headed downstream.

Talk of engines, bilge pumps, and navigation channels segregated the women from the men. The ladies found places in the stern, watching the marsh grass recede as they made their way into deeper water. The men stood on the bridge with the captain. Intermittently, one or another of them dashed below deck.

"I can't tell you how antsy Mitch has been, knowing Paul is up here doing the 'fun' stuff," Bonnie said. "When Paul suggested he help check out the cruiser, he was like a kid at Christmas."

Paula tucked her hands in her pockets as the breeze picked up in conjunction with their speed. "Fun! Paul puts in lots of late hours, either working on the boats or studying so he'll feel confident with the crews. I swear, I worry that he doesn't remember to eat."

Rose stretched out her legs. She'd worn deck shoes topped by dress slacks. The collar of a mauve silk blouse peaked out from beneath a pea coat. A light pink snood trapped her hair, not only keeping it in place in the wind of the river, but ensuring she'd look as good when they docked as when they left.

Damn. Now that Sara had a chance to look at her closely, she saw Rose was beautiful. *And she even found a way to keep her hair looking good in a brisk wind. Does the woman have no faults?*

"I try to see that he eats when I'm in town," Rose said, a soft, dreamy smile playing on her lips.

Sara turned to face her. "Don't you live here in Beaufort?"

"No, I live near Bonnie and Mitch in Brunswick. I manage Mitch's real estate office there."

"That's why Rose is up here every week or so," Bonnie explained. "She's helping Paul go through the books and come up to speed on that part of the business."

"How interesting." So, for some of those late nights Paul worked, Rose was with him.

Don't go there, Sara. You have no claims on Paul.

"He doesn't need much help. In fact, I won't have to make those trips much longer." Rose said, sounding less than pleased.

Bonnie nudged her and grinned. "Not for office business anyway."

Rose smiled back and gave a slight shrug. "It's hard to believe how much he's accomplished in the short time he's managed the company. He was wasted working on a farm. I don't think I've ever known anyone as naturally adept in business."

Sara bristled at Rose's characterization of Paul's life on his family's farm. Or maybe Rose's casual familiarity stepped on Sara's nerves. "He wasn't 'working on a farm,' he was helping to run his family place. I doubt he saw that as time wasted."

Paula shot a puzzled glance at her, and Sara wondered if her comment had sounded sharp. She hated being there, hated hearing another woman talk about Paul as though he was much more than a colleague or friend. She'd scream if she had to respond politely to much more chatter.

Just when she'd decided to get up and move away, Paula tilted her head back to capture sunshine on her face and asked, "Did you find out what was wrong with your car last week, Rose?"

"Yes. Paul was right. I took it in for a tune-up and it runs just fine now. It wasn't enough he got me going, but for ya'll to follow me all the way home was just wonderful. I'm glad you could stay for dinner."

"And we were happy you called us to join you," Bonnie added. "I want to ask Dan the name of that wine he ordered. It was fabulous."

Paula must have realized the twist the conversation had taken with her question. She snapped upright and stared at her mother, *I'm sorry* written all over her face.

Too late.

Sara called on every lesson in civility she'd ever been taught, but knew her face expressed the shock waves reverberating through her.

She couldn't speak. Locking her fingers, she clenched her hands in her lap to keep their trembling from being noticed. Paula and Dan had been in Beaufort, presumably to see Paul, but hadn't called to say hello, much less to ask if she might want to join them. Paula had already met Bonnie and Mitch. And Rose. And seemed to like the woman.

None of which would have hurt as much if Paula had told her, had let her come to terms with the information before having to face these strangers. Instead, she'd had no preparation, no word of warning. No hint that her daughter kept secrets that would cut like a knife when revealed. Paula was the last person in the world Sara would suspect of betrayal.

How will I get through the day?

Bonnie stood and flexed her knees. "I think I'll duck below and get something to drink. Does anyone else want coffee?"

"I do," Rose said. "I'll come and get mine. Paula?"

"Yes, if you don't mind. Nothing in it." As soon as Rose and Bonnie left, Paula moved into the chair next to Sara. "Mom, my God, I'm so sorry. I meant to tell you, I really did, but everything's been so hectic, trying to decide what to do about the house and settling work and…. I'm *so* sorry. I didn't mean to upset you."

Sara sat there feeling the cold far more than she had a few minutes ago. Feeling the hurt of exclusion even more than the chill.

She said nothing, so Paula filled in the dead space, speaking quickly. "We came down on the spur of the moment to have dinner with Paul. I thought I'd call and tell you where we were in case you wanted to come, but Paul and Rose had just finished work and her car wouldn't start. The guys got it going, but then Paul worried about her driving all the way to Brunswick alone and after dark, so we followed her. We had dinner before driving home, that's all. It was nothing, Mom, *really*." She lapsed into silence.

"If it was nothing, why didn't you tell me? I've talked with you at least twice in the past week. My gosh, you've made friends with your father's love interest and call it noth—"

"Love interest?"

"I've seen how they look at each other." God, she hated sounding jealous and petty. Hated more that it was Paula's actions that brought her to this confession.

"I think you've got it wrong. And I don't know why I didn't say anything. I guess because Rose seems like a really nice lady and she does obviously like Paul, and I knew you'd be upset."

Sara stiffened. "Oh, you're right. This was much better." She rubbed her temple. "Why did you insist I come on this trip? Why put me in this position?"

"I didn't know until recently that Rose would be here. To tell the truth, I didn't want her to be here without..."

"Contrast?"

Paula frowned. "Comparison. Rose is nice, but she isn't Sara Richards, not by a long shot. I wanted to be sure Paul saw that clearly."

"I'm not competing for your father's attention, in case you haven't noticed. He's a big boy, Paula. And he seems to be partial to Rose, regardless of your opinion." Sara caught herself before she lost control. "I'm glad you and Paul are getting along so well. I just wish.... Well, never mind what I wish, except that if you have any more plans for your father, I hope you won't involve me."

"Don't forget I'm involved *because* of you. You and Paul," Paula snapped.

Moments passed. Paula sat back and stared at the water. "Matthew and Paul are very different."

The suddenness of Paula's statement startled Sara as much the words. "Where did that come from? I never likened them."

"I'm just saying, since I've seen more of Paul, I notice a big difference. Don't get me wrong, I love Matthew and think he's wonderful, and not just because he cares for you so much." She paused, still facing the warmth of the sun shining off the water. "He's a strong man and comfortable in who he is. Here's the weird thing, though. Matthew isn't a person who needs people. Except the Corps, of course, but that's a whole other thing. Do you know what I mean? He'd love you and want you to love him, but he wouldn't *need* you, to be happy. With Matthew, a woman would never feel complete, Mom. Paul isn't like that."

"You know him so well, after a few short weeks?"

"I've worked at it, I guess because we have so little time. We talk a lot. In fact, when we can't get together we talk on the phone." She smiled. "He's sweet. It's as though he has x-number of weeks to find out my life and tell me his. And that's how I know. With Paul, family is everything.

"Like Matthew, he's confident in himself. But he sees life as a cloth—even a strong thread is tougher when it's woven with others. He doesn't think *need* weakens or diminishes him. He sees it as a part of loving, making him more than he is alone. That's why he's had such remarkable success here in so little time, and why he wants us to keep trying to love him, even when he pushes us away."

Sara was stunned. "Thank you, Dr. Richards. And why are you telling me all this? I tried to reach out to the man. I invited him to Thanksgiving dinner, I sent food to him when he refused to come, I—"

"He's pushing because he's unsure of us. Well, maybe not me, and not Dan, for sure. So, guess who that leaves?"

Rose's voice indicated her approach. Paula turned to Sara and spoke quickly. "I think I know how you feel, and I'm pretty sure I know how he feels. Reach out to him, Mom. Let him in. Make sure he knows he can trust you and that you trust him." Worry etched Paula's face. "Or some nice woman like Rose will. He can hang tough all on his own, but I think he'd much prefer loving someone. I just thought you should know."

"Here you are." Rose handed a steaming cup of coffee to Paula. "What have y'all been talking about while we were gone? Not me I hope." She laughed a bit nervously.

"Thanks for the coffee. No, just talking about Mom's new art gallery. You'll have to go by and see the place when she and her partner open. It's going to be fabulous." Paula took a sip of the coffee. "Give Rose one of your cards, Mom."

"I don't have any with me, I'm afraid." Sara only half heard, concentrating hard as she was on Paula's earlier comments.

"Here's one." Paula pulled a business card from her pocket and handed it to Rose.

"What kind of art do you sell?" Rose accepted the card, glanced at it and tucked it in her pocket.

"Canvases in oil and watercolor, mostly. Some pastels. I'll be offering sculptures and pieces in a variety of media when we open."

"That sounds great, although I exchange Christmas gifts with a friend. We agreed years ago that whatever the gift, we'd use it or display it. A couple of years ago she gave me the print of the dogs playing poker. I was kind of hoping you might have something painted on velvet."

Sara laughed. She wanted to dislike this woman but couldn't. It was easy to understand what Paul appreciated in her.

"Paula, how are plans for your wedding coming?" Bonnie joined them after taking coffee to Mitch.

"Fine, thank you."

"I'm sure you'll make a lovely bride," Rose said on a sigh. Then her gaze flitted, meeting no one's eyes. "Paul will probably ask you himself, but, well, since it's just us women, maybe I will. Will he be allowed to bring a guest to the wedding?"

Paula straightened in her seat. "Gosh, Rose. He hasn't said anything and we're right up against the number we told our caterer. Um, it's costing quite a bit as it is, and Dan and I are insisting on paying ourselves. With Dan's tuition and my leaving work and our not selling the house, well—"

"You're not selling the house?" Sara suddenly felt adrift on an island with no communication. "When did you decide this?"

"We talked about how much we love the place and decided to rent. I'll tell you all about it later." Paula turned back to Rose. "Anyway, I know you understand—"

Rose flapped her hand. "Oh, of course. Forget I mentioned it."

In the awkward silence, Paula stood and nodded toward the bridge. "I think I'll take my coffee up there and see what's captured Dan's attention so thoroughly that he can ignore me for more than an hour."

Giving Sara a hesitant smile, Bonnie followed Paula.

A shadow fell over Sara. Looking up, she saw Paul silhouetted by the sun.

"Hello, ladies."

"Hi," Rose said before curving her lips in a smile. "How's it going?"

"Pretty well, I think." He handed Sara a lap rug. "Matthew thought you might be cold. He's below pouring you some coffee."

"Thank you." She took the coverlet and draped it across her legs.

"Would you like me to fix you a cup, Paul?" Rose stood, anticipating his answer.

He grinned. "You know me. There's no such thing as too much coffee. Thanks." He took her seat when she left.

Sara broke the ice. "It seems you and Paula are getting along."

His eyes lit up. "Isn't it great? She's so beautiful, and funny, and smart."

"I just find it interesting that you two have hit it off so well when she hated the thought of you at first, and you were so happy you and I hadn't had 'an accident,' as you put it." She hadn't meant to sound like a bitch—she cringed inside, listening to herself. Why couldn't she stop?

"I never said that."

From his shocked expression she could almost believe him. "Yes, you did. In Omaha. You told me in several different ways how happy you were that you weren't burdened with children. You said being overseas, knowing you had a child here would have been awful, a distraction."

"Sara—" His mouth tightened, and he looked out over the stern of the cruiser instead of facing her. "When I came to see you, I was angry. I told myself I wanted to clear the air, but every time I thought of you with someone else, having a baby, making a life... I don't know, I lost it. My mouth outran my brain, and I said things that hurt you. I said things *to* hurt you."

He faced her. His eyes blazed with emotion and a muscle ticked in his jaw. "A child of ours, a distraction? A burden? That was bitterness talking. I'm so sorry. I don't remember half of what I said in that hotel café, but I hope you'll accept my apology. And—" he stopped for a deep breath, "—my thanks for Paula. She's a wonderful woman, all due to you. Every time we're together I see something new in her. She's a perpetual surprise."

Sara wanted to cry but she smiled instead. "If you'd been there when she was growing up, you wouldn't have thought all those surprises were so wonderful."

The smile disappeared from Paul's face.

She sighed. Paula hadn't wanted to hurt her. She didn't want to hurt Matthew. Her mother hated having hurt Paula. Sara was tired of tiptoeing around issues in order to avoid a bruised feeling. Avoidance caused more pain.

"Don't be offended," she said. "You know what I meant."

"Yeah, I know. God, I *hate* that I wasn't around while she was growing up. I'll never forgive myself."

"Or me," Sara said, facing the admission head on.

"Neither of us," he agreed.

They sat quietly. To Sara, the engines rumbling beneath them provided a lulling backdrop to the momentary tranquility with Paul. She wondered if their relationship would always be analogous to the river near which she lived. Rushing in wildly and finding its own precarious balance, just to have what little rapport they established swept out to sea when the tide changed.

"We can't seem to get past it, can we?" His words reflected her thoughts. "I mean, what we should have done and all that we lost because we didn't."

"There's nothing I can say to fix things. I wish there was."

"Me, too."

Quiet descended between them again.

"I know this might not be the right time, but would you like to come over Christmas day?"

He didn't look at her, but stared at the expanse of water and the wake churned by the twin engines. "I'm going home for Christmas. Paula and Dan aren't going to be here, so I figured there was no reason for me to stay." He rubbed his hand across his thigh in a steady motion, as though the action calmed him. "I won't be gone long. Paula's invited me to the wedding, and I wouldn't miss that, plus we have a couple of charters lined up right after New Year's."

"That makes sense. Usually I prepare a big meal, but Mother is dining with a friend, Paula and Dan will be in Atlanta and Matthew will be gone this year. I thought if you were at loose ends..."

His look was sharp. "I'm rarely at loose ends. And don't mistake me for a Matthew substitute." Anger made his blue eyes spark.

She stared back. "Not only do I not know what that means, I never thought—"

He held up a hand and cocked his head, listening.

"Paul! Do you hear that?" the captain shouted.

"Yeah, cut the power a bit and let me check," he called back. He jumped up as if he'd been shot out of the chair. "Excuse me." Mitch was already on his way down the ladder from the bridge, following Paul below deck once again.

"How does he *do* that? Insufferable, arrogant—"

"Who? Paul?" Paula took her father's place in the chair next to her mother. "What happened?"

What always seems to happen. "Nothing. Just forget it. I'm so sorry I came on this trip."

From behind her, Matthew kissed the top of her head and handed her a cup of steaming coffee. "Aren't you enjoying yourself?"

Bonnie came up. "I think we're going back early."

"Thank God!" Sara said.

"Not because it's good news," Bonnie explained, with a cautious eye to Sara. "There was some kind of noise in the engine. Or someplace."

As Bonnie predicted, the boat made a lazy U-turn to head back, slower than when they'd gone out.

"It's going to be a late night for Paul and Mitch, I think," Matthew observed.

"Oh, no," Rose said, joining them. "I was hoping Paul would get some time off tonight."

With a touch to her shoulders, Dan bent to kiss Paula's head.

She tilted her head back to grin up at him. "It's about time you gave me proper attention."

"I couldn't be making cow eyes at you in front of the guys or they'd think I was whipped. Matthew already knows I'm a wuss when it comes to you, so now I can happily show you the adoration you deserve." He bent to kiss her lips, once, twice, then winked at her. "We're going back to the boathouse." He looked up at Bonnie. "Can you give us a ride to the marina?"

204

"Sure."

"What should we do while the men work?" Rose directed her question to Bonnie. "We can't go home without Mitch."

Paula quietly offered, "We can go back to Mom's house."

What? Sara stared at her daughter as though she were a child exchanged by the faeries.

"We can start decorating," Paula continued, "and have dinner when the guys are finished."

"Paula, I don't think Bonnie and Rose are interested in decorating my house." That was the best Sara could manage, so shaken was she at Paula's suggestion that the very people from who Sara wanted to escape follow her home. Good manners dictated that she not leave them stranded, though. She half smiled at Bonnie. "You're perfectly welcome to come home with us, of course."

"That sounds good," Matthew agreed. "We were going to get the lights up tomorrow, but we can start tonight. Dan and I can even get your tree in."

"That sounds like fun," Bonnie said.

Outnumbered, Sara closed her eyes and let the talk swirl around her until they reached the boathouse.

"Ready to go, honey?" Matthew held out his hand to help her onto the dock.

Paul stood aside, watching. "I guess I'll see you later." He sounded as unhappy as she felt.

Apparently so.

Chapter 15

Paul felt a sudden surge of homesickness when he and Mitch arrived at Sara's that same evening. A wonderland of lights met them. Matthew and Dan were entering the garage, one carrying a ladder and the other balancing a large box. Each of the bushes bordering the porch twinkled. Dangling icicle lights defined the front roofline, and a large, fragrant wreath dressed the door.

"Looks like Christmas," Mitch said.

"Sure does." They stood back to view the effect.

"What do you think?" Dan and Matthew joined them in the yard.

"Looks great," Mitch said.

Paul grinned at Dan. "I'd say we timed it perfectly to get out of all the work."

Dan chuckled. "Oh, no. We did the work out here so we wouldn't have to help the women decorate the tree. We left that job for *you*."

"Thanks a lot," Paul groused good-naturedly.

"Yep, Matthew. Our work here is done. Time to grab a beer and watch the old guys tackle the tree trimming."

"Old, schmold," Mitch said. "What's to decorating a tree? You hang a few balls, throw some tinsel at it and you're done." He stomped up the steps. "Don't drink all the beer. Paul and I'll be wanting some before you know it."

Matthew laughed. "He's obviously never decorated a tree with Paula."

"That's for sure." Dan cheerfully slapped Paul on the shoulder. "Your darling daughter is a tree decorating perfectionist. You'll be lucky to be finished by midnight."

Paul soon saw what Dan meant. Boxes of ornaments littered the tables and living room floor. There appeared to be four strands of lights wrapped around the seven-foot Scotch pine, and Paula and Bonnie were in the process of adding another.

"You'll cause a brownout when you turn that thing on," he teased.

Paula looked up, a bright smile lighting her face. "Isn't it beautiful? Matthew and Dan were only gone twenty minutes and came home with the best tree in town."

Mitch wandered into the living room, beer in hand. "When do we start hanging stuff?"

Paula examined the limbs for even placement of lights. "Not until later. The limbs have to drop first."

"So says my little tree guru," Dan said.

"Drop? If the limbs fall off, how do we hang the sparkly things?" Mitch laughed at his own joke then leaned down to kiss Bonnie hello.

Paul envied their easy relationship. Despite Mark's assertion, he hadn't been lonely at home. Not in the way Mark meant. But he was beginning to feel that way here.

He looked around. "Where are Rose and Sara?"

"Sara's in the kitchen," Dan volunteered. "And I'm not sure where Rose is."

"Using the phone in Sara's bedroom. I think she had plans for later with her sister."

So that just leaves Matthew, and I'll bet he's in the kitchen, too.

Glancing up, he saw Paula watching him with a strange expression. He raised his brows and smiled, and she seemed to relax. Something had happened this afternoon, infecting the moods of the women. The holiday spirit he saw now made him think the problem had been handled.

He sat at the end of the sofa and tipped open a box lid. Inside, eight ornaments lay nestled in tissue. A couple were ragged, Styrofoam showing through faded ribbon. A few others missed more sequins than remained. Tears stung his eyes as he realized what they were.

Paula sat beside him and pointed to a ribboned ball. "First grade. Mrs. Hoyt wouldn't let me use orange ribbon. She said I had to choose green or red or gold. So I wrote, 'Mrs. Hoyt stinks,' and other charming comments on the Styrofoam before I covered it with ribbon. Mom didn't know until it got so tattered the base showed through."

Paul laughed. "What about this one?"

Matthew spoke over Paul's shoulder. "You told me last year that was from when you were at Scout camp, right?" His tone was smug, like the know-it-all in class, certain of having all the right answers.

A storm brewed inside Paul. The Marine wasn't at fault for knowing things about Paula, but his constant reminders, calculated to irritate Paul and emphasize Matthew's more powerful position with the women, had about reached his limit. If Paul knew when Matthew was due to report to California, he'd be marking the days off on his calendar.

"Right, a weekend Scout camp," Paula said, holding up the glitter-splotched ball. "Each of us was given a glob of white glue to smear on a ball. Little trays of glitter lined the tables for us to roll the balls in. Abigail Horton, who always had nasty things to say about everybody, sat next to me. That day, she picked on me, and I rubbed my glue in her hair."

"Oh, no!" Paul couldn't help but laugh. He looked at the ornament. "You must have saved some glue because there's *some* glitter on here."

Paula looked chagrined. "I kind of rubbed the ball over her head. I didn't get much." She gazed at the scruffy ball with a half-smile. "But I did gain satisfaction in knowing that my efforts made it harder for Abigail to remove the glue from her hair. And she never said another mean thing about me."

Paula sighed. "She was a bitch, but I did a bad thing. I've regretted it many times since."

"What in the world did she say?" Paul examined the sad little ornament with almost no glitter.

"It's a secret."

"I asked, believe me," Sara said, setting a tray of snacks on the coffee table's only bare spot. "I was summoned to the camp and lectured by the counselor. They expelled her from the troop and a few mothers called and said they wouldn't let her play with their children again. What's strange is that Abigail didn't talk, either." Sara narrowed her eyes at Dan. "Has she ever told you?"

"Nope." He threw his arm over Paula's shoulders. "My little brat, I love that fire inside that inspires you to say and do outrageous things."

"You wouldn't have loved me then. I didn't speak a word of French." He chuckled, but she stared at the ball a moment longer. "I really did feel awful for Abigail afterward. Her hair was so tangled, she had to have most of it cut."

"Ouch! But you didn't know that would happen when you globbed her," Matthew said in Paula's defense.

"No, but that goes to show what can happen when people do things without thinking of consequences." Her eyes shone with moisture. Dan pulled her into his arms.

"Well," Sara said, filling the silence. She looked done in, and Paul wondered why she'd invited everyone to the house. As tired as she seemed, she kept trying to be the good hostess. "Here're some snacks, but I really think if Rose is off the phone you all should head to dinner. It's Saturday remember. Places are liable to be crowded."

"I'm here," Rose said. Mitch and Bonnie had stood aside quietly when the talk turned to family, and Rose had taken a place beside them. "And I am hungry, so I agree with Sara about going to dinner."

"You're coming with us, aren't you, Mom?"

"No. It's been a long day." She smiled, a sad affair that didn't light her eyes. "But you all have a good time."

"I'm exhausted myself, but as someone once told me, you still have to eat." Paul hoped to challenge her into coming along. He'd enjoyed hearing Paula's stories but more than that, since that afternoon, when she'd revealed part of the reasoning behind her continued anger, he wanted Sara with him. In a way he didn't fully understand, being near her was necessary for the warmth to continue.

Burning Bridges

"I can take care of myself, thanks. So, everyone, just *please* go to dinner."

Sara's intake of breath told him she realized she'd passed her snapping point. Paula's wide-eyed stare told him she was as surprised as Sara. A negative flow of emotion circulated the living room as strong as the currents streaming beneath the ocean's surface.

Her cheeks flaming, Sara addressed everyone. "I'm sorry. I didn't mean to sound so sharp. I guess I had too much wind today, and now I have a headache. I hope you understand."

"Sure we do," Mitch said, one octave below a boom. "It's been a hard day all around. It would have been a lot worse if not for Paul, so dinner tonight is on Bonnie and me, and I could eat a whole cow. Let's get a move-on, everybody." He tried herding Bonnie and Rose to the door.

Paul stood and turned back to Sara. "Are you sure?" She nodded but wouldn't meet his eyes.

What could he do but let it go? "I'll just wash up and then I'll be ready," he announced to the rest of the group. "Rose, do want to ride with me?"

"That would be lovely, thank you. I'll get my jacket."

"Let me." Sara started to move toward the bedroom.

Rose halted her. "That's all right. I know where you put them." She edged around Bonnie and walked to the coffee table. "And let me help you get this back into the kitchen."

Rose was only being kind but her patronizing tone set Paul's teeth on edge. He could only imagine the way it affected Sara. If anything could get her steamed it would be something like this.

"Thank you, Rose." Only a nibble on her bottom lip let slip that she wasn't completely composed.

Paul glanced at Paula, who watched her mother through worried eyes. Then his gaze caught the distress in Bonnie's expression as Rose went into the kitchen with Sara. *What in hell is going on?*

211

Mitch caught his attention and shrugged dramatically.

You can say that again, buddy!

* * * *

Sara had run out of things to do in the kitchen after Rose set the tray on the counter. Seeming to sense Sara's mood, Rose said her thanks for the pleasant afternoon and left Sara alone.

Pleasant afternoon, my Aunt Fanny. She'd felt nothing but tension since the conversation on the boat between Paula, Rose and Bonnie. If only Paula had told her everything. Or if she hated Rose instead of liking her.

Much as she'd tried since seeing Rose with Paul earlier in the week, Sara couldn't find a good reason to dislike the woman. She understood why Paul was attracted to her, which only made Sara feel worse. What she needed was time alone to sort through everything from the day. Then she'd organize her biases and thoughts, pack them away in neat bundles, and she'd be in control again.

In control and able to think about Paul's admission, too. So, he'd lashed out at *her*, not at the concept of a family. He hadn't really hated the idea of having a child. If she'd told him about Paula then, maybe things would have been different. Or maybe he still hadn't been ready to listen. One thing for sure, what he told her on the boat changed her perspective. He wanted Paula. He loved her. And Sara felt certain Paula returned the feeling. Self-pity aside, she was happy that they'd found each other. Eventually, when they were comfortable in the relationship, they'd make room for her. She'd have to tell Paula that tonight, before any further misunderstandings cropped up.

One by one, she placed the crackers back in the waxed wrapper. Carefully, she stacked the cheese and covered it with plastic. The olives slowly dropped into their respective bottles. She rinsed and dried the dishes and tray and put them away. And still she didn't have the house to herself.

Will they never leave? Please, just go, she shouted in her mind at the group congregated in the living room.

"Are you talking to someone?" Paul's deep voice interrupted her thoughts.

She blinked. "No." Licking her lips nervously she asked, "Why, did I say something?"

He moved farther into the kitchen. "No, you just looked like you were carrying on a conversation."

Leaning against the counter, he crossed his arms. Sara cast a look toward the main part of the house, suddenly noticing the quiet. *At last.*

Paul followed her gaze and then turned back. "They're all out deciding who's riding with who to go to dinner. Are you looking for Abrams?"

Her gaze snapped back to him. "No."

Doubt showed in his raised brows. "I came in to make one last try. Come to dinner with us."

"Why can't anyone understand I don't *want* to go to dinner?"

"What'll you do instead?" He uncrossed his arms and stood straight.

As if his height will make a difference. "I don't know why it matters, but I have homemade soup."

"Do you have enough soup for eight? I have a feeling you shouldn't be alone right now."

"*No!*" She took a deep breath. "Look, Paul, I don't mean to be a bitch, but—" His brows rose higher in surprise. "I really just want you all to go away, have a great time, laugh it up, and then go home." She rubbed her temple. "Tomorrow I'll be much more social."

"That's not going to help whatever's bothering Paula. She's upset because you're not joining us."

"And she can't tell me that herself?" Sara stomped around the compact space, ending closer to him than she'd been before. He smelled like ocean wind, oil and pure man. In that instant, she wanted to burrow into him, inhale his scent and take comfort from the heat of his body. *That* might relieve the chaos inside.

Or cause more.

"She thinks you're mad at her. Something happened out on the boat today."

Something happened all right.

"They're leaving for Atlanta before next weekend, Sara. This is a very small thing to do—"

She stepped back, astonished. "Are you lecturing me about my own daughter?"

He took a step forward. "Yes, I guess I am. You should forget whatever petty problem is worrying you and be with our girl tonight."

She poked her finger at his chest. "Maybe it isn't Paula but you I want a little time away from, you and your friend." Her voice had dropped to a furious whisper she was sure only Paul heard. God, she *hoped* only Paul heard. Everyone *was* outside, weren't they?

"Mitch?" He looked honestly perplexed.

Can he be so stupid?

He raked his hair with his fingers and the exhaustion he'd casually remarked on shown clearly in his eyes. "I have no idea what you're talking about, so I'll move on to the other reason I came in here." His glare spoke volumes. "Then I'll give you time alone, I promise."

"Fine." She gestured for him to continue.

"Bonnie told me the subject of guests for the wedding came up today, and that Paula said adding people now would cause trouble. I should have mentioned this last week, but I didn't realize there would be a problem."

She'd been dreading the question yet all the while expecting it. He was dating Rose, obviously liked Rose, and having her on his arm at a family wedding—no, not a family wedding but his *daughter's* wedding—would be tangible proof of his affection. How would she arrange her life to ensure she never saw the two of them?

214

"After Bonnie cornered me in the hallway, I talked to Paula. She looked like she wanted to cry and told me I needed to talk to you." He huffed a breath. "So, I'm talking."

"And I can't believe you just instructed *me* in proper behavior. I'm sorry, it's too late. To add anyone else now would be inconvenient and costly." *Selfish, selfish, selfish!*

He narrowed his eyes. "Is Matthew invited?"

"Yes, but he's like family." She tilted her head back, daring him to claim Rose was as important.

Glaciers held more warmth than his eyes. "'Like family'! Ever since I met Paula, Matthew's intruded. He's had time with my daughter—and yes, I said *my* daughter—that I'll never have. They've shared jokes, meals, and love for the same woman." He held up a hand. "Don't try to deny it, any idiot can see how he feels about you, *and* Paula. I swear, sometimes I forget that *I'm* Paula's father and not him. I'm telling you, Sara, I may be the outsider, but that doesn't make my family outsiders, too."

The toes of his shoes touched the toes of her shoes. His mouth hovered inches above hers. Their breath mingled. "As far as I'm concerned, that damn Marine can lose his invitation to make room for *real* family. I'll pay whatever it costs for the other two spots, but if I'm coming to this wedding—and I *am*—then so are Mark, Becca and Luke."

Not Rose? "Why the hell didn't you just say the guests were your family? Of *course* they're invited."

For a beat they stared, wordless. Her breath quickened. His eyes dipped to her mouth then lower, to her breasts. When he raised them to lock with her gaze, they'd dilated and darkened.

"I'm going to kiss you, Sara."

Her heart pounded so hard he should have heard it. Maybe he did. "I want you to."

His mouth lowered until she felt the soft texture of his lips, like a butterfly kiss. Her tongue darted out for a fleeting taste. Paul raised his head to search her eyes, then took her lips again.

The kiss turned fierce in milliseconds. His tongue, hot and probing, claimed her mouth, intoxicating her, branding her. He slanted his mouth, taking ownership, demanding a response.

She gave it, pushing his tongue back, blazing past his lips and exploring his mouth as though on a search for hidden treasure. He tasted like coffee. And cheese, and a hint of chocolate, which he'd sampled from her snack tray.

Her senses spinning out of control, she grasped his shoulders to keep from folding like cardboard. His arms wrapped around her waist and plastered her to him so that his erection pressed like a steel rod into her stomach.

She couldn't breathe but not because he held her too tightly. Paul couldn't hold her too tightly. They could merge into one being and still not be close enough. No, wanting him consumed her entire being. All she knew, all she could ever know.

He broke the kiss but didn't release her. She dropped her hand to lie over his heart and found a battering ram much like her own.

"Who did you think I meant? About the wedding?" His voice was hoarse, hardly a voice at all.

"Rose."

There was still danger. He could say, "Oh, yeah, I meant to ask about her, too." In which case, Sara was totally lost because their kiss proved what a fool she'd been all along. Her heart had never forgotten Paul. She needed him past, present, and future.

He cocked his head. "Does Paula *want* to invite Rose? I didn't think—"

"I don't know what Paula wants but I know *I* want to kiss you again. Do I need to go out and scrounge up some mistletoe?"

His smile was slow and so sexy she couldn't believe she'd survived all these years without the thrill of it.

"Hell no," he growled. One hand splayed across her lower back while the other wrapped around her nape, holding her steady for his mouth.

He didn't devour her but took licks and nibbles instead. Just as she was returning the favor, someone cleared his throat. Paul raised his head and turned toward the hallway.

"Sorry to interrupt," Dan said, "I came in to check on you because everyone's getting antsy to go. Uh, are you still coming, Paul, or should I say you have other plans?" His grin shouted what he thought.

"I'll be right there." When Dan didn't move, he added, "I promise."

Dan swung around to leave. Behind him, Matthew stared at Sara. "I can see you don't need me to stay, Sara. I'll talk to you later."

Her heart went out to him. Moments ago, she'd contemplated how she would handle seeing Paul with Rose, and now she'd hurt her best friend in the same way.

"Matthew, I—"

Paul held her with steel bands instead of arms. "See ya, Abrams."

With a look full of fury, Matthew spun around and walked out.

"Come to dinner with us," Paul murmured against her lips.

"I really do have a headache and now...I have a lot to think about." She smiled.

"I hope your thoughts include me."

"You know they do."

"I'll come back after seeing Mitch off."

"Paul, the kids are staying the night."

He chuckled. "I doubt Paula will be traumatized if her parents spend the night together. You know Dan's already told her what he saw."

"Paula and I need to talk when they get in tonight." She stroked his upper lip with her fingertip. "But come back for breakfast in the morning?"

"Can't. I didn't finish work on the engine this afternoon."

"Then tomorrow afternoon, to decorate the tree. Paula and Dan will open their gifts since they won't be back before Christmas."

"Tomorrow afternoon." He kissed her forehead, nose, mouth. "I guess I can wait until then to have more of this."

"I'm not sure I can. You'd better go before they send in a search party."

"Okay." He gave her a light kiss. She gave it back.

He stepped away. The absence of his body heat chilled her. Stopping in the doorway, he turned and grinned. "Don't forget me."

As if.

* * * *

The smell of bacon filled the house, crisp the way Paula liked it. Sara had the ingredients ready for Paula's favorite omelet and biscuits ready for the oven. In two weeks, her daughter would be gone. Months, and more than a thousand miles would separate them. She didn't know how she'd survive.

With work. The gallery renovations had progressed to the point where display stands for the glass and sculpted works were in place. Track lighting provided a way to move small halogen fixtures to various places in each room, and add more, if the need arose. The ash wood flooring brightened the large area and brought the whole space together in sleek, cohesive sophistication.

Carpeting upstairs kept noise to a minimum, while the skylights flooded the room with natural illumination. Sara's mood lightened whenever she strolled up the ramp to the upper level. She'd never been so proud of anything in her life, as she was the new gallery. She smiled. Except Paula. Nothing could ever touch the pride and love that infused her every time her daughter came to mind.

218

Burning Bridges

Paula inevitably prompted thoughts of Paul. He loved her. There was no way a man could kiss a woman the way he had and not be completely, absolutely, intensely in love. Or maybe that was her mindset. Her smile changed to a grin. She had been very happy with their kisses and even happier with the way he looked when he said, "Don't forget me." As though he knew she wouldn't. More, as though he finally believed she hadn't.

He'd wanted to stay with her, and not just to share soup. His erection pressing against her belly had sent spiraling urges through her, coalescing between her thighs. If not for her need to talk to Paula about the afternoon, she couldn't have stopped herself from agreeing that he should return. "Paula and Dan won't be here tonight," she sing-songed, and grinned again, feeling closer to seventeen years of age than…"Oh, what's age anyway? Think young, Sara."

At the sound of the bell, she gave up her daydreams. She checked the dining room table again, wanting everything to be perfect today.

Matthew leaned against the doorframe when she opened the door. "Good morning," she said. The image of his face when he spotted her and Paul in the kitchen popped into her mind. It seemed unfair that she'd been so happy in the face of Matthew's pain.

"Morning, Sara." His eyes widened and narrowed as though trying to focus. He reeked of stale whiskey. His clothes were dirty and one sleeve had been torn.

"Matthew, you're not well." She took his arm and pulled him into the house. He walked without stumbling, and his words weren't slurred, but his actions were slow, carefully executed, like illusions he struggled to maintain.

"Paula here? Want to say good luck."

Sara pulled out a chair in the kitchen and he fell into it. "She and Dan are out for their morning run. You need some coffee." Taking a cup from the cabinet, she glanced over her shoulder to make sure he still sat upright. She slipped an ice cube into the hot brew so he could drink right away.

"What happened, Matthew?"

He looked at her and grinned. "I got drunk."

She examined the ripped sleeve. "Were you in a fight?"

The cup didn't quite make it to his mouth and coffee dribbled down the side and onto his shirt. Dropping his head and tucking his chin into his neck, he looked down at the front of his dirty—and now coffee-stained—shirt. "Nah. I think I fell."

She took the cup and set it on the table. "Do you want something to eat?"

He shook his head. "Just came to say goodbye. I love you, but you still want that damn farmer. He doesn't love you, Sara. You better watch out." He tapped his cheek in the vicinity of his nose. "Matthew knows."

"You know you're one of the most wonderful people I've ever met. If there was any way in the world I could be what you want, I would." She stroked his hair and cradled his cheek in her palm. "But Paul and I have a history, and a daughter. I can't help it, Matthew. I love him."

His eyes filled with tears. *Oh, God, what will I do if he starts to cry?* Her own eyes filled, with the thought.

"I don't want you to love him."

"Sometimes I wish I didn't."

He sniffed, then seemed to come together. With great effort he stood and moved toward the front door. His steps were remarkably steady and if she hadn't been close enough to see his shirt or smell his breath, she might not have known he was drunk.

"I can't let you drive," she said.

"Got a cab waiting. You tell Paula I said good luck. Dan's a good guy." When he looked at her, his eyes were clear and focused. "But not that farmer. He's gonna break your heart, the damn farmer."

A horn blared. "My trusty steed." His grin made her want to smile and cry at the same time.

She opened the door and touched his arm. "Will I see you before you leave?"

"No. Leaving Friday." He laid his hands on her shoulders. "All my years in the Corps, only time I was sorry to go."

"Matthew, if I could make things different, I would. I'll always remember you with love and joy in my heart."

Tears filled his eyes again and she was glad when he took her in his arms so she couldn't see them. "I'll always love you. Always. If you ever need anything, if Paula ever needs anything, you call. Okay?"

"I will. You'd better go."

The kiss he gave her was short then he eased away and walked to the cab. He didn't wave or look back.

Watching the cab pull away, she caught sight of a truck just like Paul's round the corner. She wished he'd come for breakfast and stay the day, but she understood how important his success at Hamilton was for him, personally.

Her thinking switched from the man she loved to the daughter she loved, when Dan and Paula came up the street from their run. Walking at a jaunty pace in the chill air, wearing skimpy little shorts and tops, Paula said something to make Dan laugh. Then she faced him, prancing backwards until he sprinted forward. Letting out a yell, she spun around and gave chase but he reached the house seconds ahead of her.

"That'll teach you challenge me, darlin'. Hey, Sara," Dan said, slipping into the house.

"Next time, big boy. Just wait." Paula called, and winked at Sara. "Do we have time to shower before breakfast, Mom?"

"Sure. I'll start when you're ready."

Paula pecked her mother's cheek and followed Dan to their room.

The day had started almost perfectly. Only if Paul had come by could it be any better.

* * * *

How could I have been such a damn fool again? *I never learn.*

Paul sat parked in Sara's driveway that evening. Below the icicle lights he'd admired the previous night, the living room window revealed a domestic scene. Woman, laughing on the sofa, watching a younger man teasing a cat with a strand of tinsel. Younger woman propped on the arm of a chair smiling at the other two. If not for the treachery he'd witnessed that morning, he would have been rushing to be part of the picture.

Unable to face a whole day without seeing Sara, he'd driven over early that morning. Thoughts of the kisses they'd shared filled his mind and his heart. She hadn't said it, but she had to love him, and knowing that, he knew they could work out any problems they had.

A few doors down from her house he'd had to stop, because what he saw didn't mesh with the fantasy he'd spun on the way over. Matthew Abrams, the guy who was supposed to be *out* of the family picture, was exiting Sara's. In the same clothes he'd worn the day before. They hugged and kissed, and...

He didn't stay for more. What he'd seen was enough to make him dangerously distracted. Abrams' arms around her, her face upturned for a kiss— the image haunted him.

Sara had told him not to come back to her place last night because she had to talk to Paula. Instead he saw with his own eyes that she'd had other plans. Paula and Dan probably thought Abrams was there for a quick visit. Or damn, maybe they were used to his spending the night.

Giving up work, he'd climbed in his truck to wander the roads threading the islands. Not caring where he went, he made indiscriminate turns and drove for hours. When the clock indicated he had no choice, he paid attention to his surroundings and wound his way to where he sat now.

While he stared, Sara looked out the window, smiled, waved. Paul got out and dragged himself toward the house. Before he made it halfway, she was there. The fragrance of a light perfume as well as the spicy aromas of the kitchen surrounded him. That alone was nearly enough to knock him to his knees.

Her face wreathed in a smile, she stepped right up to him and wrapped her arms around his neck. "I'm so glad you're here," she whispered in his ear.

It took a few seconds before she moved back. There was no way he'd embrace her, not after she'd held Abrams the same way that morning.

"What's wrong?" She honestly appeared puzzled.

"I've thought about you all day," he started, then stopped to catch his breath. Coming to the house tonight was among the hardest things he'd ever done. Loving her as he did, needing her with everything in him, how could he sit nearby, laugh, make pleasant conversation and not scream that she'd destroyed him? Only for Paula would he make the effort.

She nodded, sharing a faltering smile. "I've thought of you all day, too."

"Right." Looking away to avoid the questions in her eyes, Paula's intense gaze met his. He felt her silent questions through the window. It would be easier to focus on Sara after all.

"Last night was a mistake. I was caught up in the holiday lights and hearing Paula's stories. Anyway, nothing's changed between us. We'll have to be together a bit until after the wedding, and I think we should try our best to be pleasant. But then, I don't want to see you. Don't call and offer dinners or home baked cookies or a walk along the river, because I just can't do it."

Her face paled and tears filled her eyes. "I don't understand. I thought—I *know*—you meant it when you kissed me."

"I was homesick for a few minutes and I got caught up in the moment. That's all."

She looked away from him. Seconds later, visibly in command, she met his gaze again. "Are you staying this evening?"

"Yes. For Paula. I have a couple of gifts to get out of the truck and I'll be right in."

Without a word, she turned and went inside. The closing door cut off the light from the house and he shivered. Paula watched him a second more but left the window when he glimpsed Sara walking past the living room to the hall. Dan stepped to the window and shot a worried glance his way, then he, too, went down the hall.

If he swallowed his pride and believed Sara's lies when she spoke of love, he could make this family his. But he couldn't. So, once again, he was the outsider.

Chapter 16

"Mom, let me in." Paula stood outside the bathroom door. Her daughter's curiosity was strong under normal conditions, but the confrontation between her and Paul moments ago would have Paula anxious as well as interested.

"It's okay, I'll be right out." First, Sara needed to figure out for herself what had just happened.

For a brief moment, when Paul said the previous night's kisses were a mistake, she'd wanted to cry. Her eyes had stung and she clamped her mouth shut, knowing she couldn't speak without starting the flow. She no longer felt the need for tears. Later, alone in bed, maybe then her emotions would overwhelm her, but not now.

She looked in the mirror. Her cheeks flamed red with anger, and a muscle ticked along her jaw line. How dare he use her that way! He knew things had gone wrong earlier in the day, he'd said so. And he knew how overwrought she was over Paula's move. So why, if he had to lure her into lowering her defenses, why couldn't he have waited a few weeks, when she'd be past those things? Why choose last night to trick her into giving her heart? Again.

She spoke to her reflection. "You're an idiot. The man has been anything but reliable in the past. Why would you trust him now?"

"Mom?"

"Just a minute, Paula."

Dan's low voice came from the hall. Paula answered him and a second or two later she heard them move away from the door. Thank God she and Paula had set aside time last night to talk. In her euphoria, she'd confessed her jealousy of Rose and of feeling left out in the developing relationship between Paula and Paul.

Paula explained that at first, she was nervous being with her father. She wanted to determine whether a bond could be forged without worrying about saying or doing something to hurt her mother. Then, Paul and Sara had seemed so uncomfortable with each other, Paula thought it would be easier on them if she visited separately. In the end, they hugged, cried a little and went to bed far happier than either had been that afternoon.

Sara took one more look in the mirror. Fluffing her hair, she checked her lipstick and straightened the cardigan over her blouse.

She understood now that Paul thought of Rose as a friend. After Paula left and Sara opened the gallery, she'd work on preparing her heart for seeing Paul with another woman. She'd lived most of her life without him, and she could do it again. "Anything is possible," she murmured to her mirror image.

Her daughter was starting a new life and so was she. Whatever came next, Sara would handle it.

* * * *

Paul and Dan stood when Sara swept into the room like royalty. God, she was beautiful, and so composed no one would think anything had transpired on the front lawn.

"Mom, you look great!" The approving tone in Paula's voice told him she'd been worried. He had, too, but it appeared there was no reason.

What does it mean that she's not upset? I just wrote her off and she acts like it was nothing. Was she really only playing me, getting me in place for when Abrams left?

"Let's do the tree before anything else in case Nana leaves early," Paula said. "She should be here any minute."

Dan leaned toward Paul. "Both Paula and Mrs. Noland are tree dictators, so pick your poison before we get started. I'm smart enough to back Paula but you might want to butter up Mrs. Noland."

Not damn likely. "I think Mrs. Noland has already dictated my life enough," Paul murmured back. "I'll go with Paula."

"I agree." Dan lifted his glass in a toast. "Besides, Mrs. N likes too much tinsel." Paul laughed.

"What are you two talking about?" Paula demanded.

Dan adopted an innocent expression. "Nothing, sweet. What are we doing for dinner? Pizza or Chinese? I'll order now for delivery in about an hour."

226

"Pizza," Paula said, opening the lids on the ornaments' boxes.

"Pizza is fine with me, Dan." Sara sat on the sofa at the end opposite Paul, checking each ornament for a hanger.

"Same," Paul said. "Can I help pay?"

Dan shook his head. "No, this is our treat."

Paula laughed. "That's why if you'd said Chinese you would have been overruled."

"So I had no choice. Why even offer Chinese?"

"Mom loves it," she said, "but on tree decorating night she never gets it. Sorry, Mom."

"I've learned to live with pepperoni and mushrooms once a year." Sara smiled at Paula. She'd still said nothing to Paul.

A few minutes later, the doorbell rang and Paula admitted Mary Ellen, laden with gifts. After she'd said hello to Sara and Paula and Dan, she faced Paul. The house fell silent except for the carols playing on the stereo and the crackling of the wood in the fireplace.

The first thing that crossed Paul's mind was that he hated this woman and wished her a long, painful time in Hell. Because of her he'd spent his life alone, without the woman he wanted and the child he would have loved. Time wasted after Nam when his life had no direction, years of working and saving, but with no wife to share his accomplishments, and the many sleepless nights he tossed in bed cursing Sara, all of this and more he laid at Mary Ellen Noland's feet.

"I owe you an apology, Paul Steinert."

Someone gasped and he didn't think it was him. This wasn't what he expected.

"And I owe PB a loving apology. Sara and I have already talked through this, and I think—I hope—she's forgiven me." She looked from him to Paula. "I hope in time you will also, PB."

227

"Nana." Paula stepped up and hugged her grandmother. There were tears in Mary Ellen's eyes when she pulled away and looked at Paul.

"I don't expect it will be easy for you, Paul, but if you're going to be a part of this young woman's life, I hope you can find your way to be part of mine, also."

"These past weeks have been wonderful, but I won't lie and say everything is all right just because I've found Paula now. But yes, I do intend to be a part of her life, so I'll try."

She nodded. "That's more than I could expect. Thank you." Seating herself in a wingback chair near the window, she asked for a glass of wine.

"While we decorate, tell me about the wedding plans, PB."

"It's New Year's Eve, Nana. I'd suggested New Year's Day, but Dan didn't want to chance missing the bowl games." She placed a red bulb and pointed out a bare limb to Dan.

"Maligned again," he cried. "If you'd promised we'd be finished with everything by one thirty at the latest, I would have been good with that."

Paula laughed. "Nicole is providing food for the reception which will be in the new gallery. It's just beautiful! The service will be small and elegant."

"Of course," Sara said around a smile.

Her mother smiled, too. "It sounds wonderful."

"It will be," Paula said confidently.

When the ornaments were hung and the tinsel carefully applied, Paul placed the angel on top and they switched off the room lights and lit the tree.

Paula shone like a golden angel herself, in the soft glow of candles. Paul cast a side glance at Sara. She held herself still watching their daughter. He wished he hadn't come to the house this morning. If he hadn't known about Abrams sneaking out in the early hours, he'd feel at home right now. He'd hold a sprig of mistletoe over Sara's head and steal a kiss, then he'd sit there with her in his arms as though he did it every day.

Burning Bridges

He picked up his wine and took a healthy gulp.

He was crazy around her, absolutely mad. She was like a disease for which there was no cure. God knows, he hadn't asked to fall in love with her again.

At that moment, he decided to work until spring and then leave Beaufort. The company would be in good shape, and he'd help Mitch find someone else. Away from here, away from her, life had to be easier.

"How's the gallery coming along, Sara?" Mary Ellen asked.

"Very well. It'll be lovely for the wedding reception and I think we're on schedule to open the second week in January. Jennette's been packing the inventory in the old place and we should have everything moved before the first."

She stepped to the tree and moved one of Paula's childhood ornaments—a round piece of ceramic with a Christmas tree painted on it—higher up on the tree. Paul wondered what the story behind it was.

"The renovations have turned out great. Nicole is preparing samples every day to determine what she wants to sell. I'm going to weigh a ton if she keeps begging me to test items. Her husband refuses to try anything else." Sara chuckled, the low, rumbling sound that turned his insides molten. "Come down this week, Mother, and I'll give you a tour."

"I'll do that. The renovations were terribly expensive weren't they? I know you were just getting back on your feet. Are you all right financially?"

All motion stopped; all eyes focused on Sara.

"Oh, dear, I shouldn't have asked. I just assumed, we're all family—" Mary Ellen glanced Paul's way, "—pretty much, and I didn't think it would matter."

"Don't worry. Someone dear made sure I was taken care of. I'm so proud of the new space. It's totally different from what we had before, but I think Barbara would approve."

So, *someone dear* had helped her out. A certain Marine colonel, no doubt. No wonder she'd kissed and hugged him.

229

Mrs. Noland tapped her glass against the edge of her dessert plate. "I know you've ordered your usual dinner." She wrinkled her nose. "So, I'm going home a little early. I'm leaving your present under the tree, Sara. These are for PB and Dan." She indicated three packages beside her chair.

"Nana, aren't you going to be with Mom for Christmas?" Paula's voice sounded worried.

"No, my bridge partner is going to be all alone and I said I'd spend the day with her." Mary Ellen frowned up at Sara. "You're not going to be alone, are you, dear?" Her eyes shifted to Paul and back. "I assumed you'd have company."

"Paul is going home for a few days, but I'll be fine everyone. A day without cooking a big meal will be like a mini-vacation." She winked at Paula. "Maybe I'll bring home Chinese the day before."

After giving Sara another worried look, Paula sat on the floor next to Dan and ripped off the paper on her gift.

"What beautiful scarves and gloves, Nana, thanks."

"Thanks, Mrs. Noland."

"Chicago is a lot colder than here," Mary Ellen explained.

The third item was a photo of Sara and her parents. "Nana, this will go in a place of honor in our new home." She handed the frame to Dan. "Speaking of homes, one of the things I hated to leave was our beautiful house. Dan and I have decided to rent it while we're gone. The man who's taking over Dan's classes is going to live there, and he wants to keep the furniture, too. If we come back to Charleston, then we have a place. And if we don't—" she smiled at Dan, "—then we have time to decide what we want to do."

"That's sensible," Paul said.

Dan held up his hands in surrender. "What else could I do? The woman would not leave the house." They laughed.

"There's one more present," Mary Ellen said. "It's for Paul."

"What? I never expected this."

Paula handed him the wrapped package. Inside he found a double frame.

On one side, a teenaged Sara posed in front of a different Christmas tree, holding up something. She wore a pink bathrobe and a huge smile. The facing photo showed Sara holding a newborn Paula. Her smile was just as large, if more weary. He was nearly overcome with emotion.

Finally, he managed, "I can't tell you what this means. Thank you."

"Sara came over this afternoon and chose the pictures. She wanted to give them to you but I asked if I could, as a gesture of…peace, I suppose."

Paul looked at Sara. "Thank you."

"You're welcome." She smiled at her mother. "Thanks, Mom. The frame looks great."

"And now, children, I'm going." Mary Ellen hugged Paula then Dan. "Have a great Christmas. We'll see you very soon for the big day."

Paul stayed in the living room while everyone else accompanied Mary Ellen to the door. Sara was the first to return.

"Are you holding the ticket for the concert where we met?"

She smiled at the photo. "Yes. I was so thrilled. It was a big surprise."

"You couldn't have chosen pictures that mean more."

"I'm glad you like them, though I had the idea before I knew last night was homesickness playing a trick on you. I only ask that if you ever don't want the pictures to please let me have them back. They aren't copies."

"Sara—"

She bent and looked out the window. "Pizza's here." And suddenly, he was alone again.

* * * *

231

Leaning her head against Dan's knee, Paula put an unfinished slice of pizza back in the box. She took a sip of soda. "Do you know why I was so anxious that the tree look perfect?"

"No, why?" Sara took another bite. Hot pepper flakes and pepperoni warmed her mouth and throat.

"It's my last Christmas at home like this. Holidays won't be the same, ever again." She sounded so like a child that Sara had to remind herself that Paula was an adult and not ten years old.

Tears she'd avoided all day rolled down Sara's cheeks.

"Mom, I'm sorry. I should have softened that statement. But you know you've been thinking the same thing."

"I know." Sara wiped away the tears with her napkin. "Everything has happened too fast."

Paul looked as though he would reach for her, so she pulled in her arms and scooted an inch or two farther away. Seeming flustered, he hesitated then picked up his beer and took a big swallow. That he would try to hold her, even to comfort her, after what he'd said earlier confused her.

"I know we haven't exchanged Christmas gifts yet, but I want to talk wedding gifts. After all, we only have a week or so to go." Paula sat on the floor at Dan's knee. Squared formed a furry comma in her lap. She looked over her shoulder at Dan, grinning. He rested a hand on her head, casually running his fingers through her hair.

Were Paul and I ever that relaxed, that confident with each other? They might have been, given time.

"Rather brazen, bringing up gifts, don't you think?" Sara raised her brows at Paula.

"Yes." She grinned. "First, from Paul. For your gift, I'd like you to give me away."

Sara quickly turned toward the other end of the sofa. The beer bottle was halfway to Paul's mouth when he froze, appearing stunned.

"I thought I heard Dan's father was going to do the honors." Paul finally croaked out.

"He was. But when I explained I'd like you to walk me down the aisle, like the sweetheart he is, he agreed you should. So, will you? I'd really like my dad to give me to my husband."

"Paula, I'd be honored." Paul cleared his throat, but his eyes sparkled with moisture when he swiveled and looked at Sara. "Did you know about this?"

"No."

"Next, I thought after what Dan told me last night I wouldn't have to request this gift, but tonight, I'm not sure."

"Paula…" Dan tugged her hair to get her to look up.

"I have to. It's important."

He shrugged. "Okay, shoot."

"I don't know if you realize, but being in the same room with you two is hard. You don't actually fight, but the tension is thick. For me—for us—can't you spend some time together and try to work out whatever your differences are?" She shifted her gaze to Sara. "After we talked last night, I knew I should have tackled this from the beginning and not waited."

Paul spoke. "Paula, none of what's between us has to do with you."

"But it does. I grew up without a father. Both of you were responsible for that. I still had a great childhood, full of love. But it could have been even better, because seeing how much you two still care for each other, I can imagine what it would have been like if you'd stayed together. Mom, you let Dad down, and Dad, you did the same to Mom. But y'all, look at me." She held out her arms. "It was a hell of a long time ago. I'm no child. Can't you put the past behind you and start over?"

Sara said, "I thought we had," at the same time Paul said, "It's more complicated than that."

"Well, for my wedding I want you to *try*. I'm tired of walking on eggshells fearing I'll hurt one of you. I'm not daring to hope you'll actually rediscover the love I think is still there, but it would be nice if you could be pleasant."

She glanced up at Dan again. "I know I'm getting to this a bit late, but we've decided we want children after all. More than one, hopefully." Looking at Sara and then at Paul, she said, "They'll want grandparents who can be in the same room without acting like they want to strangle each other."

Sara didn't know what to say. Paul was speechless for the third time in less than an hour.

"Well?" Paula bristled with impatience. If Squared hadn't been in her lap she might have tapped her foot.

"I'm sure we can come to an agreement, can't we Paul?"

A face filled with resignation looked back at her. She took that as a yes.

"And now it's time for your presents," Sara said.

In her room, Sara pulled two large packages from the closet shelf and then crossed the room. *Paula's request isn't unreasonable*, she thought, taking the card addressed to Dan and Paula from her desk drawer. *So why did Paul looked as though he'd rather jump out of a plane without a parachute? What's happened between last night and today?*

Paula calls her father "Dad." Did he even take it in? It's wonderful that she wants him to walk her down the aisle.

Almost as wonderful as their planning a family! What a surprise that is, after years of denying she wants children.

"You're talking to yourself again." Paul intercepted her before she made it back to the living room.

She smiled. "I guess I am, but tonight I'm not mentally screaming or wishing I had a voodoo doll."

His eyes widened in surprise. "I, uh, wanted to talk to you about something."

"Now?"

"Yes. I should have told you before, but as Paula said, we don't really handle being together too well."

They had last night, but this wasn't the time to bring up the change in him.

"A week or so ago, we drove their car down to Brunswick. It's not in great shape, although Dan keeps the maintenance up."

"Teachers don't make a lot, and they haven't needed a great car in Charleston."

"Right. But they will for the trip and the years Dan's in school. I'd worry if they take what they have into a Chicago winter. So, I thought I'd give them a car. We can look for a good model when they get back."

A car. Suddenly, the down jackets she had in her arms seemed insignificant.

"I was planning to give them a check for a wedding gift, but this is separate and is something they need. You acted a little funny when I told you about the will, so I wanted to let you know first."

Mindful of Paula's request that they try to be civil, all she said was, "Thanks." Using the jackets to push by him, Sara deposited the wrapped packages on the floor in front of Paula.

When she and Paul sat once more, Paula ripped the paper off. "A down jacket! Thanks, Mom. I'm afraid we'll need this. Dan, sweetheart, is it too late to apply for law school in Miami, or someplace warm?"

"I checked the temperature this morning. Chicago will have a high of nineteen degrees. These will really come in handy, Sara, thanks."

Excitedly, Paula said, "Speaking of school, Dan received a letter earlier in the week. He scored so high on his entrance tests and his application is so impressive, they'd like him to mentor a couple of other new students. Isn't that great? They're giving him a break on tuition if he'll do it."

"Congratulations!" Paul offered Dan his hand.

"It's not much of a break in tuition," Dan said, winking at Paula, "but every bit helps. Paula says they made the offer because of my application and scores. Really it's because I'm older than most applicants and they want to use my life experience." He scowled. "God that *does* sound old!"

Sara laughed. "It's a wonderful vote of confidence in you, and you deserve the recognition."

"Thanks." He picked up Sara's card and slid his thumb under the envelope flap. A check fell out when he opened the card.

"Mom! This is for three hundred dollars. You can't afford this."

Sara ducked her head when Paul turned to her. "It's to help pay for the trip. You know, food, hotels and such."

"It's great. Thanks so much." Dan took the check from Paula and slipped it in his wallet.

Paul handed his card to Dan.

Dan opened the card held up the enclosed slip of paper. "IOU a car that will make the trip and get you through your time in school."

"What?" Paula took the paper from Dan. "Oh my God! This is so wonderful, Dad, thanks!" Dan leaned over Paula's shoulder and read the paper again.

He shook his head. "Paul, I don't know what to say."

Paul's brows creased. "I hope it's all right. Your car is fine for short little trips in good weather like you have here, but—"

"No! I just mean, I'm overwhelmed. This is great."

"Good. When you get back after Christmas we'll go and find what you like." Paul glanced at Sara. "Between your mother and me, I think we've about got the trip covered."

Paula gave Sara one of the wrapped gifts from under the tree. "I hope you like this, Mama."

Sara smiled. "You know I will, whatever it is." Another double frame hid under the wrapping paper, this one sterling silver. One side held a photo of Dan, Paula and Sara. Dan had his arms around both women.

"This is Thanksgiving. I wondered why you never gave me a copy."

"Because I'm devious, that's why." Paula pointed to the other side of the frame, which was blank. "I thought the four of us could get a picture at the wedding or reception or something."

"Wonderful idea. Thank you, both." She immediately displayed the frame on the mantle.

Dan left the room. Moments later he came back carrying the Marilyn Yates painting Paul had admired at the gallery, his first day in Beaufort.

"We're giving this to you while Dan and I are here, but it's really from the three of us," Paula said.

He beamed at Sara. "You remembered."

"Sure. I know you don't have a good place for it now, so you can store it here if you want. That would be more convenient for me than at either gallery."

Dan leaned the painting against the coffee table.

"Thanks, you guys." Still smiling, he examined the piece. "This will always remind me of South Carolina."

Paula laughed. "As if you need reminding. All you have to do is look out your window."

"There's one more thing." Paul handed Paula a flat, rectangular package.

The photo album filled with pictures of Paul's family caused her to burst into tears.

"Stop," he said, "or you'll make me cry, too."

She opened the album on the table where everyone could see, and slowly leafed through it. Paul had marked each photo with dates, names and information about the people.

"It's a pictorial history." Dan stood behind Paula and read over her shoulder.

Near the back she pointed to a young man standing in jeans beside a pickup truck. "Who's this?"

"Your cousin, Luke, my brother's boy. They'll be here for the wedding. I hope you'll visit them, too."

"Wow, honey, you really do resemble the Steinerts. Look at your grandfather." Sara glanced up in time to see Dan send Paul a silent, *thank you.*

"Look at this." Sara pointed to a picture of a sailor, grinning at the photographer. A huge ship filled the background.

"That's your dad, the same year I met him," Sara told Paula.

"Really? Pretty darn handsome." Paula gave him a wink. "Just like now," she teased.

Sara merely touched the photo and smiled.

* * * *

"A night of pictures," Sara said after closing the door behind Dan and Paula. "Painted, sepia, all kinds."

Paul held the Yates at arm's length admiring again the color and form. And the feeling of freedom that had lured him to it the first time. "This is great of you, Sara. I've thought of this painting many times in the past weeks, so you know I really like it." He placed it between the wall and wingback chair.

"Paula and Dan were excited about the car. That is so thoughtful. I was silly to be tiffed."

"Tiffed? That's a word?"

Picking up empty glasses she peered at him. "Irritated, ticked." She headed for the kitchen.

He followed, carrying dirty plates. "Why would you be tiffed? It's just a car, a thing to get them around. I want them to have a safe, reliable one."

A dishrag dangled into the sink from her hand braced on the counter. "A car is a big deal to people who can't afford to give their kids such things. Just like the will. I feel like I've worked all these years being Paula's mother and you waltz in throwing money around after a few weeks. Like you're trying to buy her attention."

Rubbing his chin he said, "I understand 'tiffed' now." He set the plates beside the sink. "Look, first I didn't 'waltz' in here, I stumbled in. Second, I'm sure not trying to take over your position or make you look bad. Paula doesn't get anything from the will until I die, and I hope that's a hell of a long time from now. The car, I've explained. It's a safety issue not a 'how can I outdo Sara' thing."

Taking the dishrag from her hand, he wiped the table and put the packaged food in the refrigerator. "Third, fair warning, I plan to give them a large check for their wedding gift. They have a lot of expenses ahead of them and they'll need the extra money." He tossed the cloth into the sink and stood before her, arms crossed. "And fourth, you have money yourself, from 'someone dear.' Is that Abrams?"

She snapped back as though she'd been slapped. "Why is it always Matthew? You're obsessed with him."

"*I'm* obsessed with him? What about you?" The image of her arms around Abrams' neck, his arms around her and his lips coming down to meet hers popped into Paul's mind.

"I suppose you're going to blame your flip-flop between last night and today on Matthew, too."

"Damn straight. He's been the cause of every *tiff* since I've come to this town."

"He's leaving this week for a different state. Who are you going to blame for your irritations then?"

The same person who's been to blame all along. "I guess you, Sara. Every time I think I can trust you, som—"

"Oh, and you're Mr. Reliable? I reach out to you time and again and all you do is play emotional games."

His hands clenched, opened and clenched again at his side. He took a deep breath, but it did nothing to calm him. "It always comes down to this, doesn't it? I try to bridge the gulf between us, and maybe you do, too, in your way, but we'll never trust each other enough. That's why when Mitch's company is in good shape, hopefully this spring, I'll be going home. If I stay here, we'll just get in each other's way, and that won't be good for either of us."

He walked into the living room to pick up the gift Sara's mother gave him. Sara trailed behind him. At the front door he turned. "Thanks for a good evening." He held up the frame. "And for this. It's really special."

"You're welcome."

"Well—" he hesitated, fighting the urge to hold her just like he always did, even at his most irritated, "—guess I'll see you at the wedding, if not before."

She said nothing, just reached behind him and opened the door.

Before he made it to his truck, Sara called to him. "Here's something you can rightfully blame Matthew for. He promised me you'd break my heart. And he was right."

The door closed, leaving him surrounded by a darkness that matched his mood.

Chapter 17

Traffic was heavy for a weekday, three days before Christmas. Since leaving Charleston, Paula had worried enough when Dan was driving through downpours, but a short distance out of Augusta, the weather turned more ominous. Rain changed to sleet, and their reasonable pace degenerated to a crawl.

"Sherman reached Atlanta in less time than it'll take us," she quipped, trying to hide her uneasiness.

"Maybe. But he didn't have a—" Dan deepened his voice to sound like the newscaster they'd heard that morning "—'major winter storm' to contend with. We're braver than ol' Sherman. Faced with sleet and snow on Georgia roads, he would have hightailed it and never made it to the sea."

"Hmmm."

Dan threw her a quick glance. "Are you nervous?"

She forced her white-knuckled fingers to relax. "I guess, a little."

"Me, too, but don't tell anybody." He flashed his brilliant smile, the one that melted her heart.

"I'm glad you tricked me into marrying you, Dan. I love you so much."

"Tricked you? My God, woman, I thought you'd never decide to marry me. I was des—"

"Dan! Look out!"

* * * *

Sara wrapped brown paper around a small beachscape, preparing to crate it for transfer to the new gallery in a week. She couldn't help but glance out the window. The storm hadn't diminished in strength since she'd checked two minutes before.

In a phone call last night, Paula said they planned to leave early enough to arrive at Dan's parents' home in Atlanta before the predicted storm was too severe.

But the front moved in faster than forecasters predicted, and weather reports on the radio confirmed Sara's fear that conditions would be bad for their whole trip.

She checked her watch. Three-fifty. If Paula and Dan left when they'd planned, they should be in Atlanta by now, even accounting for nasty weather.

Her cell phone rang, and she ran to where it lay on the counter to answer, thinking it would be Paula saying they'd arrived safely.

"Beauty by Beaufort."

"Sara? This is Alice Tanner."

All-encompassing fear filled Sara's stomach. "Alice? How are you?" How did her voice sound so calm when panic wracked her mind?

"Fine, thanks. We just wondered if you've heard from Dan and Paula. Dan called several hours ago and said the rain was terrible and traffic was heavy, but we haven't heard anything since."

"No, I'm sorry, they haven't called me. In fact, I thought this might be Paula. According to the radio, the weather is awful."

"Yes, there's sleet south of here. Snow, closer to Atlanta." The calmness in her voice couldn't hide her anxiety. "Well, I'm sure that's what's holding them up and they'll be here soon."

"No doubt, with an interesting story."

Alice Tanner's laugh sounded strained. "You're right. I'll ask Paula to call you when they arrive."

"I'll keep my cell phone with me. Thanks, Alice."

"I'm sure they're fine." Was Alice trying to convince Sara or herself? "Merry Christmas, Sara."

"I know you'll enjoy visiting with the kids, Alice. Merry Christmas to you, too."

She hung up. *Ohmigod, ohmigod!* If anything happened to Paula she'd die. As it was, terror, irrational and stark, struck with a force she'd never imagined.

Without thinking, she touched the number pad.

"Hamilton Charter Fishing."

"Paul, thank God." He was there and he'd make her believe her alarm was unwarranted. That she was being silly.

"Sara?" His deep voice soothed her, though an edge of uncertainty crept through.

"I need you. I'm at the old gallery but I'm heading right home. Can you come? Please?"

"It'll take me a minute or two to close up here and then I'll be on my way." His tone took on the firmness she needed. "Try to stay calm."

She wanted to say goodbye or thank you or something, but he'd hung up. That didn't matter. He was coming. Paul would keep her from going crazy while they waited, and if there was any bad news, he'd be there.

But there wouldn't be bad news. She couldn't go on if...

Stop it! The kids are fine. The weather has held them up, that's all.

Taking a quick look at what remained to be done, she felt a twinge of guilt over not staying and packing a few more paintings. After all, Paula would call her cell, so it wouldn't matter if she were at the gallery or at home. But she wanted to be home, needed to be there when news came, regardless of what it was.

The phone rang again. She grabbed it up. "Paula?"

"Sara, it's Matthew." He hesitated. "What's wrong? Is everything all right with Paula?"

"Oh, Matthew, they're late getting to Atlanta and they haven't called Dan's parents, and..."

243

"This rain is flooding a lot of roads in the area, but I'll find a way around. I'll be there as soon as I can."

"No. It's okay." She heard the hiss of his breath, knew this would hurt. "I'm on my way home and Paul is coming."

He was silent for seconds. "I see. I'm leaving tomorrow and I'd like to know Paula's all right before I go. I'll call later, okay?"

"Thanks, Matthew."

"Goodbye, Sara."

Without wasting another minute, she transferred incoming calls from the gallery's landline to her home number and dashed to the car. In a few minutes, she'd be at the house and a few minutes after that, Paul would be with her. And after that…she'd have to deal with whatever fate threw her way. But at least she wouldn't be alone.

* * * *

Paul hardly slowed before swinging his truck into Sara's driveway. Running for the porch, he tried the door before ringing the bell. The handle turned.

"Sara!" She rushed from the kitchen and straight into his arms. He tightened them around her. "What's wrong?"

"Dan's mother called. Dan and Paula haven't arrived yet. Paul, it's been more than twice the time it normally takes them. I-I'm scared to death."

Fear settled over him. *They have to be all right, they* have *to be.*

"Ah, honey, you know how slow traffic is in this weather. They're fine." He eased her away. "I'm getting you wet. Let me take off my jacket."

Under the ruse of shaking off water from his jacket, Paul stepped onto the porch. Never had he been so frightened. Never. He'd been shot at, dead drunk in the worst part of San Francisco, and once had to rush Luke to the hospital after a tractor accident. But he'd never wanted to crawl in a hole and hide in sheer terror like he did right now, at the possibility that something had happened to Paula.

Burning Bridges

He held his jacket by the collar and gave it a good flick of his wrist. If bad news came in, how would he ever hold it together for Sara? How would he comfort her when he'd want to fall apart himself? He took a steadying breath and went back in.

"I'll let this dry here," he said, draping the soaked jacket over the umbrella stand in the entryway. He set his hat on top.

The phone rang. Sara jumped, then stood frozen. Paul took the phone from her hand and pressed the Answer icon.

Forcing himself to sound calm he spoke. "Hello?" Sara watched him, her hand to her mouth and her eyes wide. He winked at her. "Paula, honey!"

Sara's eyes glistened and her head dropped.

"Yes, we're fine. I stopped by for another dose of Christmas. We were just getting ready to light the tree and wait to hear from you. I'll bet you had one hell of a trip, huh?"

Listening, he looked at Sara with a grin on his face. He held out his arm and she nestled against him. "Were we worried? I was a little nervous, but your mom made me settle down. She said she knew everything was all right. Here she is now. Tell Dan hi for me."

He handed the phone to Sara and hurried to the bathroom. Leaning heavily on the sink counter he took deep breaths. His ashen face reflected in the mirror and trembling fingers that raked through his hair proved his fear had been real. Fate would have seen it as a grand joke to give him a daughter, then take her away.

Sara was making noise in the kitchen, indicating she was off the phone. He splashed water on his face, and when he looked into the mirror, he saw a man in control.

He found Sara in the living room, turning on lights. "What's the story?"

"Mostly traffic and weather. Dan barely kept them out of a five car pile-up, but there was a horrible accident about seventy miles out of Atlanta. After sitting for almost an hour, traffic was rerouted. Dan's cell phone went dead and the charger was packed, and when they stopped to call his home no one answered."

"I'll bet the phone company had trouble with the lines."

"That was it. Evidently Alice was lucky to get through to me. It was all a series of mishaps and no one big thing. They're tired but safe." She closed her eyes. "Thank God!"

"That's for sure." He jammed his hands in his pockets and shifted his weight from foot to foot, uncertain what to do now that his heartbeat had normalized and his reason for being there had vanished. "Well, I guess I'll go on home. Even though the kids were safe all along, I'm glad you called me."

Sara seemed equally unsure about their positions now that she knew Paula was okay. "Thanks for coming. I know I overreacted."

He wrinkled his brow. "No. It was natural to worry. To tell the truth, I was kind of nervous, too."

She smiled. "You were? You didn't act it."

He smiled back. "Isn't that why you called me?" She gave a half shrug.

The last time they'd talked, he'd insisted he wanted nothing from her, yet now he did. He wanted her to ask him to hang around a while longer. He wanted her forgiveness for all the times he'd let her down. He wanted another chance.

All he'd thought about since Sunday night when she shut the door was how tired he was of living like this. He'd let the past, his pride and insecurities rule him. Seeing her today needing him in her fear—*him*, not just anyone—slammed home the truth. He could continue letting old hurts obsess him, or let her know he loved her, and the past be damned.

Sara had had a reason to ask him here. What he needed now was a reason not to go. If he could find the right words, maybe she'd believe this time would be different.

He stalled. "There's lots of flooding around town, so don't go out if you don't have to. Do you have everything you need for tonight? Is there anything I can do while I'm here?"

"I'm fine. Thanks again for coming. I couldn't have stood being here alone waiting for news or hearing they'd…" She turned her face away and took a deep breath. Before he could comfort her, she scooted around him and held out his coat.

Couldn't be any plainer than that. He slipped into it and fitted his hat to his head.

The phone rang again.

"Would you wait a minute and make sure that's not Paula calling back for some reason?"

"Sure."

She went into the kitchen where she'd left her cell phone. Her voice rose for a few words then she hung up. She rushed back into the hall and grabbed her coat off the peg.

"What's wrong?" He didn't have to hear her voice to know something was up. The look on her face said it all. He took her coat and held it for her.

"That was Nicole. I have to get down to the firehouse." She reached for her purse.

"Should I drive you or meet you there?"

She looked at him in surprise. "Neither. My worst fear was over Paula, but I can handle this alone. Thanks again."

She literally pushed him out the door and closed it behind them. Her car was parked next to his truck. She didn't wait for him to back out before she took off.

What the hell? Okay, he'd said some harsh things the other night, but damn. This was obviously an emergency and he couldn't let her face whatever it was alone.

He backed out and turned after her.

* * * *

The rain let up marginally. That was the only good thing Sara could say about the trip to the firehouse. She arrived to find a city fire truck, the fire chief, and Nicole and John on the scene.

"What happened?"

Nicole looked too upset to talk. John said, "A short in the wiring under the ramp set off the alarm. The heat funneled upstairs, where the sprinklers went off."

"Sara, they say the upstairs is a mess. Water came in around at least one of the skylights, and we've had all this rain." Nicole clutched John's hand.

"The leak might even be the cause of the short," John added. "They won't know until they can make a more thorough investigation."

"Oh, Nicole!" The two women hugged. Sara had known Nicole only a short time, but she'd always been upbeat and sassy. The damage must be very bad for her to be this upset.

"Can we get in and look around?" Sara asked the chief.

"There's not much in there, so it should be okay. Still, watch yourselves. Some of the ceiling tiles are falling downstairs and the power's out. Gotta flashlight?"

John held up a large one. "I'll go in and check things out," he said.

Sara shook her head. "I want to go with you. I won't be able to sleep at all tonight if I don't know what we're facing."

His eyes narrowed in concern. "Are you sure?"

"It's our business. Do you want to come, Nicole?"

"I guess." She looked up at John wistfully. He wrapped his arm around her shoulders. They kissed and smiled with such tenderness Sara's chest tightened.

This was love. Holding tight in bad times as well as good, trusting that the other will be there no matter what.

Burning Bridges

No question, she and Paul were poster children for the worst way to have a relationship. She'd seen Matthew's qualities and faults right from the beginning, since they'd met as adults. There was no guile or games; she'd always known what she was getting. That's the way it might have been with Paul if they'd met last week instead of a lifetime ago.

For the sake of their daughter, she'd been willing to work at some kind of relationship since the day she'd taken off her false rings. Paul had been the one to call a halt, making it perfectly clear he wasn't interested in nurturing a love like Nicole and John had. Not with her, anyway. When it came to Paul, she was doomed. Someday she'd convince her heart.

A couple of firefighters exited the building, dragging hoses and equipment with them. Standing apart from John and Nicole, she hugged herself against the damp, cold air, and the starkness of her near future. Questions bombarded her. What would the insurance pay? Assuming the problem was workmanship, would they have to sue the contractor? How long before they could open and what would she do with her inventory until then?

Thank God she'd received the line of credit. Risking the house, chancing her last pillar of financial support, was worth it if she could keep the business and succeed on her own.

Someone touched her shoulder. She turned saying, "We'll make it, Nicole," then stopped when she saw Paul, not Nicole, standing beside her.

His eyes focused on her face with concern. "I'm so sorry about this, Sara. What can I do?"

She shivered at his closeness. She wanted to lean into his warmth and borrow his strength. "Be here for me?"

As if reading her mind, he wrapped her in his arms and held her close. "I will. I'm not going anywhere." He spoke into her ear, his breath puffing against her hair.

I wish I could believe that.

Doomed she might be, but no one sent heat through her like Paul. *This* Paul, not the ideal of her memory. He'd said he would soon be leaving town. That's the only way she'd move on with her life because as long as she saw him, heard his voice or his laugh, she'd want him.

With one arm tight around her, he introduced himself to John Brown, then the four walked through the building.

There was no stopping her tears when she saw the extent of the damage. The fire itself hadn't harmed much, although the ramp would need repairs after the wiring was examined. The biggest problems were smoke and water damage.

The day's downpour found entrance through the skylights, soaking the floors and seeping through to the ground floor before the sprinklers added their insult. Smoke darkened the ceilings and walls, and the outside wall behind the ramp was scorched.

"Our beautiful floors," she cried to Nicole after they exited. The fire truck was about to pull away. The flashing lights and acrid odor gave the scene a surreal atmosphere. *Like my whole day.*

"And the walls. You did all that painting and stenciling." Nicole's tears flowed as freely as Sara's.

Sara wondered what Paul and John were saying a few feet away. She looked at Nicole. "What do you think our insurance will cover?"

"Most of it, I'd say, although I don't know how long it will take to settle. The contractor has a lot to answer for with those skylights." Nicole took a tissue from her jeans pocket and blew her nose. "At least we didn't have your artwork in yet, and none of the kitchen equipment appears to be damaged. But, Sara, we won't be opening on time, and…"

"Paula's reception!" they said in unison.

The men joined them. Paul spoke first. "Sara, John and Nicole haven't eaten and neither have we—"

When did he start thinking of us as "we"?

"So, let's get out of the rain and away from here. We'll have some dinner and then talk about what to do first." He waited for her reply.

"I can meet you and John," she said, addressing Nicole. She shifted her gaze to Paul. "But I'm sure you have work or something to do."

"Nothing's more important than you," he replied. Turning to Nicole he said, "Are you all right with that?"

"Come on, honey. You'll feel a little better after eating," John told his wife.

Nicole cast a glance at the ruined building. "Okay," she said. "I suppose you're right."

"We'll meet you at the hotel restaurant?" John took Nicole's hand and they started for their car.

"Right. We'll drop one of the vehicles at Sara's and be right down." Paul faced Sara. "Let's sit in the truck a minute, okay?"

Cupping her elbow, he spoke as they walked. "Just so you know, I'm going to help however I can unless you tell me not to, straight out. Just like waiting to hear from the kids, this isn't something you should have to deal with alone." He opened the door and helped her in.

What could she say? That she was touched he cared enough to be there for her? His statement made it clear he was here for the emergency, but what about the dull ache of need she felt for him all the time? She was tired of riding the roller coaster.

"Unless," he continued, when he climbed behind the wheel, "you have someone else you'd rather call." His clenched jaw told her he meant Matthew.

Damn it! She hated that he'd asked her yet again.

He closed his eyes for the space of two heartbeats. When he looked at her, his gaze was calm and confident.

"Let me rephrase that. I don't care if you have someone else you'd rather call. I'm here and I'm staying. If you tell me to go away tonight, I'll be back tomorrow. And if you tell me to leave then, I'll be back the next day. I'm not leaving."

251

His big hand cradled her cheek. "All of that crap I said on Sunday? I've wished every second of every day since then I could take it back and not look foolish or weak."

She was afraid to breathe, afraid to speak. What if she'd only imagined his words?

"Why?" Her hand reached out for his. He held on as though his life depended on her.

"You need me. God knows, I need you, and I love you, Sara. I hope someday you can love me again."

She tilted her chin in challenge. "What about the money I have? What if I said it is from Matthew?"

"I'd say I wish you'd give it back. If you didn't want to, then I'd have to find a way to live with that because I'm not leaving. Do you hear? I'm a pretty good investor, and I've saved most everything I've made. You don't need to turn to anyone else."

"I'm afraid to trust you."

"Just give me a chance. Can you do that? I know it's asking a lot, but I promise, things will be different."

She looked into his eyes and saw into his soul. He wanted her. He needed her. They could make each other whole again.

Since Paul left her behind, a naïve girl of seventeen, she'd regretted so much. Allowing desire to dictate her actions, doubting herself in ways that kept her from fully living, and letting her insecurities seep into Paula's life experiences. But she needn't regret loving Paul. The timing had been wrong, and her parents and the war—all of that had been wrong, but not their feelings.

"I'm used to secrets, Paul. I used them as protection until I got so used to them they became part of my life."

He lifted her hand and kissed each finger. "I haven't made it easy for you to share with me."

Burning Bridges

The sincerity in his voice and the hope in his eyes made up her mind. "I have a loan, using the house Aunt Barbara left me as collateral. I didn't want Mother and Paula to know because they'd worry. The house is my only real asset."

Sara sat back from him, against the door. "You had no way of knowing, but Matthew showed up at the house Sunday morning. He'd been out drinking all night and looked awful, poor man. Before he left, he swore you'd make me so unhappy my heart would break. He said you hadn't been there for me from the beginning and that you wouldn't change. I don't know if I can chance that he's right."

Paul's jaw tightened. "I am a damn fool." His voice quavered with emotion. "But I'm a fool who loves you. Let me prove it."

* * * *

Hours later, Paul closed Sara's front door behind them and turned the lock. The crisis wasn't solved, but some of the day's tension drained out of him. Safe and comfortable, the door was barred against the wolf, and the woman he loved was protected inside.

He hung his jacket on the peg beside Sara's coat. "Do you think Paula will mind having her reception in the old gallery?

"You know," Sara hesitated, staring into space as though seeking an answer, "I think she might like it better. The new space would have been prettier and more sophisticated, but the old place is what she grew up knowing." She sighed. "It'll take some work. I haven't been paying much attention to keeping things neat."

"I'll help." He followed her into the living room and watched while she turned on a lamp. "After meeting with the insurance agent tomorrow, I'll show you the storage space I have. It's dry and there's plenty of room. I think your inventory will be fine until the new place is restored."

She faced him. "Paul," she said in a low voice. "This whole evening would have been awful without you. I can't thank you enough."

He loosely wrapped his arms around her so he could see her face when he spoke. "I always want to be there for you. And I know you'll be there for me. It's the kind of couple we'll be. People will point to us and say, 'There're the Steinerts. That's what marriage is all about.'"

253

"Marriage?" She quirked her brows. "Aren't you confused? Just the other day you said you didn't want to see me after Paula and Dan leave."

"Let's sit down and talk for a few minutes."

She sat on the sofa. Squared immediately filled her lap. Paul lit the tree and then joined her, draping his arm across her shoulders and tucking her against his side. For a while they sat quietly, watching the play of lights on tinsel and shiny glass bulbs.

"I have a proposal," he began, then laughed when she started. "Not that kind. Not yet. I'd like to stay here until after Christmas. We'll be alone, with nothing to do but get to know each other. What do you think?"

"When you say get to know each other, do you mean…?" She licked her lips and started again. "Are you asking me to sleep with you?" Her voice held no inflection, and he wondered if she hoped to be with him, or not.

"I'd love having sex with you but that's not what I have in mind. It's taken me a while, but I know now how stupid I was to think we could pick up where we left off. Frankly, I was stupid to want to. Sara Richards isn't a complete stranger to me. She's the girl I fell in love with, but with depth and mystery and beauty added."

He kissed her temple, keeping it a gentle touch. "I want you to tell me about yourself, about all of the things that have happened over the years. We won't rush. When we finish, I want to know you. I want to be your best friend. Then I'll be your lover, if you'll have me."

Sara stroked Squared's back but said nothing.

A twinge of panic crawled up Paul's back. "We made a mess of things, there's no question about that. Is it too late? Because it's always going to be you for me. Even when I hated you, I knew I'd never love anyone else." He snorted. "Does that even make sense?"

"It does to me."

They were quiet for a while then, "You hated me?" Her voice was low and full of feeling, but she turned and gazed directly into his eyes.

"I'm ashamed to say, if I'd come to find you after I got home from Nam, you wouldn't have wanted me. All those months of no letters and then finding out you were married with a child... My mind was poisoned, and I don't know that I would have listened, no matter what you said."

"I hated you, too, when I found out I was pregnant and had to go to my parents alone."

He rested his cheek on her hair. "I'm so sorry."

She slowly shook her head. "Let's not say we're sorry anymore. I want to move forward."

"I do, too. I want to share everything I know and am, and I hope you'll do the same." He smiled though she faced away. "For instance, I like Chinese food, so if you want to order from your favorite restaurant, it's fine with me. Any night except tree-trimming night, of course."

When she turned to him, her smile was full of mischief. "Liking Chinese is a real plus, but you don't know what you're asking. I can really *talk*."

"You don't know farmers. For years I worked alone in the fields. I've stored up conversation most of my life, just waiting for someone to listen."

"I love you, Paul."

Her unwavering gaze, the emotion in her voice left no room for doubt. Sara was his.

Emotion welled up within him. In his heart, he finally came home. From the war, from years turned in on himself, from the doubts he'd harbored. Waiting for him was the love he'd always needed, in Sara's arms and their daughter's eyes.

The final bridge linking him to a life without Sara, burned.

Epilogue

Paul crossed the church vestibule and held out his arm to his daughter. For a brief time, he felt they were the only two people in the world, and he wished he had a little longer before having to share her with the church full of people. There was so much he still wanted to say.

"You look beautiful, Paula."

"Thanks." She blushed at his words. "I'm very nervous. Are you?"

"Nah," he lied. "What's to be nervous about? You're marrying a great guy and you have a wonderful life ahead of you. I can't wish you enough happiness, sweetheart." He took a ragged breath, afraid he would embarrass himself by tearing up.

She smiled and squeezed his arm.

He leaned over and peeked into the church. The maid of honor was almost down the aisle. Soon it would be their turn.

"I want to thank you again for the check and the car. You've relieved a lot of pressure."

"Your mom and I are happy to do it, and more, so if you need anything..."

She chuckled. "Don't worry. We've planned this pretty well, so I think we'll be all right." She looked toward the door and took a deep breath. "Mom told me about your Christmas gift. A list of towns named Beaufort in France, where she can contact artists? Very romantic."

He winked. "I have my moments. I'm hoping it will be a honeymoon."

"I knew you two were right for each other all along. I can't wait to tell my new Chicago friends that I have to go home for my parents' wedding," she said with a smile.

The music started again, louder, the opening chords insistent. He started to move but Paula stopped him. "I want to tell you something."

Panicking, Paul saw she was ready to cry. If she did, there'd be no hope for him.

"Remember Abigail Horton, the girl with glue in her hair?"

He nodded. Paula stood on tiptoe to whisper in his ear. "She said my mom wasn't married and the reason I didn't have a father was that he didn't want me. She said I was an accident."

Tears burned his eyes. "Never believe that. Having you for a daughter is the most precious gift I've ever received, along with your mom's love. I'm your father forever, and I love you."

Her eyes were like shimmering sapphires when the wedding march began.

"I wish Abigail Horton could see us now," Paula said, and they stepped off.

In a daze, Paul led her down the aisle, keeping a steady, slow pace. His breathing was regular and his hands were calm, but he was only walking the straight path from the back of the church to the front. He didn't see Mark, or Becca. Mitch, in another pew, was missed altogether. He didn't notice Matthew or even Dan. He saw only Sara, waiting for him.

When they stopped at last, he took Paula's hand.

"Who gives this woman?" The minister's voice boomed.

Paul stood silently for seconds. He felt Paula look at him, but he turned to gaze at Sara. He held out his free hand and she took it, moving from the pew to stand beside him.

"We do," he said in a clear, strong voice that filled the hush of the church. "Her mother and her father."

ABOUT THE AUTHOR

As you probably know, many people look at reviews on Amazon and/or Goodreads before they decide to purchase a book. If you liked this book could you please take a minute to leave a review and give your feedback?

Burning Bridges is Anne Krist's first novel, but it's only the latest book for her counterparts, Dee S. Knight and Jenna Stewart. As Dee, she's spent the last few years happily arranging new and exciting ways for her heroes and heroines to uh...get together while they fall in love. Jenna enjoys shapeshifting wolves and ménage—oh my! Anne's characters will have just as much fun falling head over heels, though they might use a bit more discretion. Dee's mother and aunt hope so, anyway.

As Anne, Jenna or Dee, she resides with her own hero, living the adventure they call life.

Dee shares a newsletter (Aussie to Yank) with Aussie author, Jan Selbourne. Sign up here (https://landing.mailerlite.com/webforms/landing/h8t2y6) and have access to our secret free stuff folder!

Find all three ladies at https://nomadauthors.com. They have lots of books to share.

Printed in Great Britain
by Amazon